A Siren Sings Her Heart Out

The Misadventures of a Paranormal Post-Relationship Personal Effects Repossession Specialist, Book Three

Scott Burtness

FREE Short Story

Get *Five Stars,* a FREE demonic horror comedy short story, when you sign up for **The Paranomedy Pint**, Scott's once-a-month email featuring a great book to read, a fun show to watch, something terrific to drink, and a little paranormal weirdness to enjoy!!

For Liz.
This song's for you.

CONTENTS

SOMEWHERE IN MINNESOTA...

How does the siren like her whiskey?

On the rocks.

CHAPTER 1

The May Flower
June 2nd, 1891
Capsized in heavy seas four miles from the Duluth, MN harbor.
Three survivors. The Captain was lost.

LESSON LEARNED. NEVER DRINK with a KJ.

The evening had started out well enough. I'd needed a drink, and I'd found a bar. The Thirsty Gull was a squat box with a pitched roof and windows that struggled to serve their purpose. Inside, everything was sticky, and it smelled like old fish. None of that mattered. There'd been an open stool when I'd arrived, and a bearded, bear-sized bartender had served me a beer when I ordered one. In my book, that made it as good of a place to drink as any other. My drive north from Minneapolis to the tiny town of Knife River only took a few hours, but those hours had been on my old and poorly maintained Moto Guzzi. If you'd been in the saddle, you'd have wanted a drink, too.

The town of Knife River sat at the mouth of the Knife River. Say what you want about Minnesotans. We're nothing if not creative when it comes to naming stuff. That river opened into the southwestern spur of Lake Superior. From the shore, you could look to the right and make out a thin, dark line called Wisconsin. With a little imagination–or a fantastic telescope–you could gaze across the silver-blue water and spot Michigan's Upper Peninsula. Mostly, though, you could look anywhere in Knife River and see a whole lot of nothing. The town itself was a town in name only. There were a bunch of trees on one side, a bunch of water on the other, and a few houses in between. After the misadventures

I had recently survived, I'd needed to get away, keep my head down, and maybe even clear that head a bit. A few weeks on the northern edge of nothing seemed like a good place for that. A little peace and quiet, a little anonymity, and a lot of alcohol were exactly what I'd wanted. I'd found a small lakeside cabin to rent–its obvious disrepair fitting it nicely into my budget–and had found the bar shortly after. My first round was still half full when I met the fellow that would show my liver a thing or three.

"Evening, Mister Hanks. Whiskey, please," the man said after washing up against the bar rail.

With a practiced nonchalance, I studied him. It wasn't that I had been interested in who he was or what he was about. I just liked to flex my nonchalant observation skills now and then. One never knew when you'd need to quietly observe someone from a few stools over. It was a helpful skill to have, and it required practice like any other. I made a small show of flicking invisible fuzz off of my jacket sleeve and stole a glance. Turned my head to and fro to stretch my neck, let my eyes flick toward him for a split second, then gave my shoulders a roll for good measure. Took a drink of beer and peeked over the pint's rim. In dribs and drabs, a picture of the man had come together.

He was more than a few years my senior, maybe even early fifties. That, or the creases on his face were from long days under a bright sun instead of age, and that jawline beard's salt and pepper was a bit premature. I pegged him for a fisherman, but wouldn't expect anyone to give me a prize for that deductive reasoning. It was a bar on the shore of Lake Superior, after all. There were other clues as well. A bucket hat that sat atop his unruly hair with the ease of long familiarity. Painted lures dangled from fishhooks along its brim. A Nylon vest covered with mesh pockets and a multitude of zippers draped his torso. His once-white shirt was grayed with use and patterned with stubborn stains. Lightweight trousers that would dry quickly in a light breeze covered sturdy legs, and boat shoes that had definitely seen their fair share of boat decks enveloped his feet. Attire aside, a few other details had cinched it for me. His rolled-up sleeves showed one corded forearm with a faded marlin tattoo. The other had a freshly inked silhouette of a buxom and winged woman emerging from stylized waves. Sometimes, two and two really does equal four, so yeah. I pegged him as a fisherman. A fisherman moonlighting as a karaoke jockey, though? Didn't see that coming.

"Actually, make it two, Tom," the man said, amending his order, "and be generous with our curious new stranger."

Whoops. Guess my nonchalant observation skills need some work, I thought.

While I made an awkward show of studying the bar's lacquered wood, he raised an eyebrow and gave me a side-eye.

"Unless you don't like whiskey," he added, "in which case you're welcome to find some other spot that caters to brutes and heathens."

That last bit came with a broad smile. When I didn't see any malice in it, I met his eyes and shrugged.

"Even if I didn't like whiskey," I replied, "I'd be a damned fool to pass up a free drink."

"Oliver Corbyn," he said after sliding down the bar and extending a hand, "but most folks call me Ollie."

"Your name is really Tom Hanks?" I asked the bartender.

He might've blushed but the bramble patch covering his face made it hard to tell. He definitely nodded, though.

"Nice to meet you, Tom and Ollie. I'm August," I replied, "but most folks call me August."

Oliver chuckled. "Welcome to Knife River. We're plenty used to strangers up here. Not this late in the season, though. What brings you up this way?"

I might not have spent much time on the lake, but I could still tell when waters were being tested. Experience had taught me that the right truth was easier to tell than a flat-out lie.

"Up from the Twin Cities," I said. "Had a crazy few months. Thought it would be nice to get away."

"To Knife River, eh? That's a choice. Most folks stop in Duluth, or maybe keep going. Two Harbors. Even Grand Marais. But you're here."

"Yep."

We held each other's stare for a few beats. I hadn't picked up on any mean vibes. Just an open assessment. Who knows what he saw in me, but it apparently passed inspection.

"Here's to you being here," he finally said with a tip of his rocks glass. "Hope it meets your expectations."

I let a sip of the whiskey pass my lips, and Ollie grinned when my eyes widened.

"It's off to a good start," I exclaimed with a surprised look at the glass. I wasn't one to judge, but had judged The Thirsty Gull regardless. After that sip, I decided I'd underestimated the place. "A damned good start, indeed."

Me and Ollie traded rounds while locals found their way in. Most appeared to be human, but that didn't mean much. Plenty of paranormals–PNs for short–could pass for regular people. I tried to glimpse the faint glow in their eyes that might signal a vampire, the brutish posture that could give away a werewolf, or the awkward gait that always seemed a sure tell for merfolk. Despite my surreptitious inspection, though, I didn't spot anything obvious. Well, except for a gnome couple that waddled in like round stones with feet. While none were easily pegged as PNs, everyone gave the impression of being regulars. That was a certainty. Everyone knew Tom the bartender by name, which was expected. More surprising was the fact that they all knew Oliver Corbyn and were even more excited to see him than the guy filling their glasses.

"You famous or something?" I asked my newfound drinking buddy, then silently congratulated myself on not slurring. The whiskey and beers had been working their magic, but I hadn't fully succumbed to their spells.

"Sure, I am," he replied with a self-deprecating wink. "Doesn't take much in these parts, though. There's only a couple hundred folks that call Knife River home. Hell. A town this small, we can all take turns. I get to be famous on Thursday nights."

I twirled my finger, and Tom poured a fresh pair of pints.

"What are you famous for?" I asked. "Caught the biggest fish or something?"

"That, too," Ollie remarked, "but the real reason? Well, I imagine you'll see soon enough."

With that cryptic statement, he took his drink and walked across the barroom to a small platform in the corner. I'd noticed it but hadn't really paid it any mind. Plenty of bars had live music of one variety or another. As the fisherman mounted its steps and futzed with a mic stand, I idly wondered what he played.

Fiddle, I decided. *Lots of fishermen play the fiddle.*

He powered up what looked like a portable speaker, and a variety of blue and red lights winked. The thing was the size of a small suitcase with two wheels on the bottom and a handle on top. Two cords snaked out from its front. One to a microphone on a stand center stage and the other to a small monitor on the floor. I hadn't noticed the monitor until Oliver flipped it on and tilted its screen. Lit from below, his craggy features took on a different cast. Gone was the friendly local fisherman. In his place, a showman appeared like the ring master from an old-timey circus.

"Is this thing on?" he asked into the hot mic.

"Unfortunately," someone in the gathered crowd replied, eliciting a laugh from the rest.

Oliver laughed as well and turned to drag a small table from the platform's corner. After positioning it at the edge of the stage, he turned back and produced a plastic fishbowl, a three-ring binder, a stack of small paper slips, and a little box of golf pencils. As he placed each item on the table's top, a dark suspicion formed deep in the corners of my mind. A slow-dawning and horrible realization. Oliver Corbyn wasn't going to play the fiddle. Oliver Corbyn wasn't going to play anything. Oliver Corbyn was going to sing karaoke.

"Crap…" I groaned, not realizing I'd said it aloud until a woman a few barstools down cast me a dark look.

Ignoring her, I looked at my mostly full beer, then looked up at Ollie, then looked at my beer, then looked again at Ollie. There wasn't time. There just wasn't enough time. Even if I slammed the pint, I wouldn't be able to finish it, pay, and bolt from the bar before the guy started to sing.

It's worth a try, though, I decided.

With grim determination, I chugged and managed to get half the pint down before Ollie pressed a big blue triangle on the wheeled speaker, and the first bar of music filled the Gull. It disgusted me to realize that my remaining gulps were in time to Billy Joel's *Piano Man.* With a glower for the ages, I slammed my empty pint down right as Oliver belted out the first few words.

"Crap…" I groaned again.

With growing desperation, I tried to get Tom's attention, but the easy-going bear ignored me. Every eyeball in the place was glued to the guy on the stage as he did his best Billy Joel. Stricken, I watched, too. It was terrible. It was tortuous.

It's actually not that bad, a traitorous part of my brain opined.

It's karaoke. By definition, that means it's bad, the rest of my brain replied, deeply offended.

Sure, karaoke is bad, but Ollie isn't that bad, that rotten part of my brain persisted.

Shut the hell up.

I tried to deny it, but that little corner of my brain had a point. Oliver wasn't just not bad. Oliver was pretty good. The guy had a surprising baritone that would've filled the space without the mic and amp. He was a gifted performer, too. There was no awkward hunch over the mic with face down and hands shoved in his pockets. The platform stage was small, but he used every inch. Swaying dramatically for the verses. Leaning into the refrains with unfettered passion. Eyes touching every single person in the place, including mine.

If Ollie had been telling the truth about the town's population, easily a quarter or more of the residents were in the room. Their combined voices joined in the refrain. I dug in my heels and fought the urge to join in. Finally–finally!–Oliver Corbyn's performance ended. Everyone clapped and damned if my hands didn't twitch. I covered the embarrassing impulse by waving at Tom.

"Coming up," he announced while sliding a pint under the tap.

"No. Hell no. Check, please, and step on it."

"Seriously?" he asked with a raised eyebrow. "You're leaving?"

The guy had terrible timing. His booming voice filled the quiet that had followed the applause. Suddenly, everyone in the place was looking at me, some with surprise, others with thinly veiled judgment.

"...No," I managed while shoving my head far down into my shoulders. "Dammit. Fine. Whiskey, double."

"Make it two, Mister Hanks!" Oliver Corbyn announced from the stage. A patron delivered the amber liquid to the KJ, and he lifted it high. "To our new visitor, August. May you find what you're looking for. And if not, may you find what you were meant to."

The crowd's glassware glinted in the track lighting. A room full of lips parted, and a room full of whistles were wetted, including mine. The crucial difference was their drinks made them happy. Mine was more functional than fun. An effort to build a high-proof wall between me and what I was about to endure.

"Crap," I muttered again but much more quietly, then watched in trepidation as a woman took the stage and accepted the mic.

She didn't look like a singer, and proved that looks aren't deceiving. When she started in on Bananarama's *Walk Like an Egyptian,* it was all I could do to not walk out. She was terrible. My disposition gave a self-satisfied *hmph* and a snotty, 'Told you so,' but my thumb tapped the side of my pint in time, regardless.

After too many rounds to think clearly, I found myself thinking too much. It was especially frustrating when I considered why I'd headed north in the first place. I'd left Minneapolis on my old Moto Guzzi to clear my head. Instead, it seemed like every song the karaoke crowd chose was determined to drag my thoughts right back to all the things I wanted to avoid.

A guy in dingy jeans and a mechanic shirt sang Billy Joel's *Tell Her About It*, and I couldn't decide who to tell. The centuries old demon I'd had a hell of a one-night stand with? The sultry succubus bartender that still haunted my dreams? The oracle who'd dazzled me with more than her penchant for prophetic horoscopes, then abandoned me while I slept?

A woman in her seventies, hair pulled into a bun so tight it gave her face a comically surprised expression, sang Tears for Fears' *Everybody Wants to Rule the World*, and my mind spiraled down the rabbit hole of reptilians messing with our DNA.

One half of the gnome couple–it was impossible to tell which half–sang Elvis Presley's *Suspicious Minds* after Oliver kindly shortened the mic stand. The little fellow–or lady–had a voice rough as rocky soil, but hit all the notes with ease. Each verse sent Jay's conspiracy theories romping around my skull.

A middle-aged lady in a pink polo and crisp white apron belted out Hall and Oates' *Private Eyes*, and a leprechaun's revelation that a powerful group of paranormals had taken an interest in me loomed large in my mind.

A woman in a knee-length sweater dress made a go of Kenny Loggins' *Highway to the Danger Zone*, and Jay's headlong plunge into elemental magic and necromancy screamed in my ears like a klaxon.

"Wishallayou woul'shutup," I complained to the coaster beneath my current beer, or maybe to the worn and sticky bar it was sitting on, or possibly to my boots far below as they tried not to slip off my stool's footrest.

Accosting my boots just made me angrier. I didn't want them to shut up. They weren't the ones struggling to find the right notes. Surprisingly, the damned boots laughed at my admonishment. My eyes narrowed, deeply dubious, before I realized the laugh had come from a guy beside me.

"You know what they say," Oliver Corbyn remarked with the waggle of a finger. "You may not be able to carry a tune, but you can karaoke!"

"No, y'can't," I protested, then blinked. "Oh. Ollie. Hey, there. You can. These'shother assholesh. No. Nope."

The fisherman laughed again and patted my shoulder in sympathy.

"Well, how about you show them how it's done? You strike me as a grunge fan. C'mon up, August. Give these fine folks a song to remember. Hmmm. Stone Temple Pilots, perhaps?"

Before I could understand what was happening, he'd gripped my forearm and hoisted me off my bar stool. He drew me up to the stage like I was a bit of flotsam in his wake. A microphone appeared in my hand, and a monitor lit me from beneath.

"I hope you don't mind the song *Plush* by STP," Ollie said, "because you're about to sing it."

The opening riffs to what was one of my favorite songs punched through the speakers. A sea of eager eyes stared up at me. Dumbstruck, I looked back and tried to figure out when I'd fallen asleep. I must've been asleep, because I was fully in the grip of a goddamned nightmare. Terror washed through me and sobered me up faster than a plunge into Lake Superior's icy waters. All rational thought came undone, leaving nothing but a primal will to survive. As my rotten luck would have it, that instinct decided the best way out of that mess was to forge ahead.

"And I feel...," I heard my voice sing. Actually fucking sing.

That opening line was brutal. A startled cow's exclamation would've been easier on the ears. The next line wasn't as painful, but still made me cringe. When I reached the third, it almost sounded like maybe I could possibly carry a tune. Almost. Even more shocking, the entire crowd sang along with me.

Words floated across the monitor at my feet. Somehow, some way, my voice turned them into a song. When I got to the end of the song, a sensation I hadn't known existed washed over me. Even if I had been sober, which I definitely was not, I wouldn't have had known how to describe it. As I stumbled down the steps and endured the high-fives and hearty pats on my back, an awkward smile lurched onto my face. It wasn't until much later, after I'd wobbled through the night to my rented cabin, fumbled at fitting a key in the lock, and fallen onto the bed's old mattress, did I realize what I'd done.

I'd actually sung a goddamned song at a goddamned karaoke bar.

"Lesson learned, August," I complained somewhere between pulling off my clothes and falling across the bed. "Never drink with a KJ."

Chapter 2

SS Western Reserve
August 30th, 1892
Broke in two en route to Two Harbors, MN.
Twenty-six hands lost. One survivor.

DAWN BROKE, AND I learned the hard way that my cabin's only window faced east. I opened my eyes and that morning sun lanced into my brain, so I squeezed them shut again with a groan. The hangover was one for the record books. Long experience had taught me that the only remedy for my ailment was a greasy breakfast and a hot mug of shitty coffee. With a grimace, I pulled on the previous day's clothes and squinted my way outside. It wasn't until after I'd made a frantic circle around the grounds that I remembered my Guzzi was at the bar.

"The bar I sang karaoke at," I admitted with a grimace.

After pointing my boots toward the pub, I set off on a determined march. An angry recrimination accompanied each step.

Stu. Pid. Stu. Pid. Kar. E. Oke. Sucks. Stu. Pid. Stu. Pid.

My bike was sitting forlornly on the crushed gravel of the lot. I muttered an apology, swung a leg over the saddle, then kicked it to life. I remembered passing a diner on the way into town and figured it was a decent place to try.

"As long as no one's singing," I amended.

I'd been right about the diner. It was open, had some solid options that were decently priced, and the coffee passed muster, albeit barely. I didn't care, though. It wasn't like

I was there to enjoy myself. Breakfast after a night of drinking was simply a thing to be done. I hunched on my stool at the diner's counter and methodically forked dry eggs, burnt bacon, and soggy toast into my mouth. After I ate about half the plate, the queasiness in my stomach subsided, and the hammers behind my eyeballs stopped pounding. Something like contentment swelled in my chest. And then...

"Hey, rockstar," the waitress said with a wink while refilling my coffee. "You did good last night, especially if what Tom said was true."

That fleeting moment of satisfaction shattered as recollections of the past night resurfaced. My forehead wrinkled as I tried to place her. I hated it when someone knew me and I didn't have a clue who they were.

"That you and Ollie nearly cleared out his whiskey,' she explained, "and damn near tapped the beer keg."

She finished topping off my coffee, and I took a welcome sip.

"Yeah, well," I managed, while suffering through an embarrassed blush. "I was thirsty."

"That'll happen," she agreed. "So? How was breakfast?"

I poked at the remaining eggs.

"Fine."

"Liar," she replied with a knowing grin. "Skeet is a terrible cook, but our regular cook... is gone."

I glanced up at the serve-through window and saw a blocky head on wide shoulders amble past. I wasn't one to judge, but having an orc as a cook probably violated ten different health and safety regulations.

"Maybe the regular cook was thirsty last night, too?" I suggested.

I'd expected a good-natured eye-roll or even a scowl. What I got was a flat and stoic, "No. Larry always took a few nights off around the full moon, but this time he never came back."

Her shoulders had tensed. When she dropped a check on the counter, it felt more like an act of defiance than anything else.

"See you at the Gull next week, right?" she asked with a smile that couldn't have been more forced.

I managed a noncommittal shrug, which she answered with a knowing wink.

"Sure, we will. 'Til then, August."

She turned away, humming a few bars of Hall and Oates' *Private Eyes,* and I suddenly recognized her. The polo and the apron should've given me a hint, but to be fair, I was hungover as hell. Belatedly, I realized that everyone in the whole damn town likely knew who I was, or at least knew my first name and love of nineties grunge.

As if reading my thoughts, the orc in the kitchen looked at me. Our eyes met, and it raised its hand to its mouth, fingers curled in a fist. While I watched, confused, those fingers uncurled. The orc splayed them wide and pushed its open palm out from its lips. Odd gesture completed, its hand fell to its side.

The hell? I wondered. *Does it think I'm going to projectile vomit or something? The food wasn't that bad.*

After an awkward moment that lasted too long, I said the breakfast really was great. When that didn't get a response, I added another compliment. Something about feeling ready to take on the world after such a hearty meal. The orc's eyes widened, but whether he believed my lies or not was impossible to tell. Another awkward moment stretched.

Suddenly churlish, I broke eye contact with the thing, dropped a few bills on the counter, and headed for my bike. I'd tamed the hangover, but knew it would take a little hair of the dog to put it to rest. Fortunately, I had a case of pilsner waiting in my fridge. With a little luck, the dinged up appliance had kept it cold. If my luck didn't hold, I wasn't above drinking warm beer.

A few minutes later, I relaxed into an old Adirondack chair with cracked boards and chipped paint. My cabin was behind me and a low bluff overlooking the big lake was in front. The beer wasn't exactly cold, but a smidge below room temperature was still better than warm. While I sat and drank, drank and sat, I ruminated on the past few days.

It seemed hard to fathom, but less than a week ago, my best friend had freed a ghost. Nothing wrong there. It was a good thing to do. A woman's spirit had been bound to a baby spoon for nearly a hundred and fifty years. Setting her free was a kindness. It was the next part that had rattled me. Jay wanted to shove the ghost into a living hag's body. Doing so would have effectively killed the hag and cursed a lady from the late 1800s to a horrible existence. Bad enough to be reincarnated in the modern world with all of its confusion and clamor. Worse to experience that new and terrifying world in a hag's skin. The facts that Jay could do that and, worse, that he'd been willing to do that had scared the crap out of me. To top it off, some jackass of a nix splashed my name and face all over the internet. Plenty of folks would love the celebrity. For me, all it accomplished was to awaken the old fear of my past finding me. I'd also met my Fetch, a personification of my impending death. I would've met my literal death as well, had a mysterious leprechaun not intervened. To cap it off, I'd learned that maybe–just maybe–a race of humanoid reptilians from deep under the planet's crust might have infiltrated the government. It was a lot to process, and so, me being me, I'd fled. Why I'd chosen the north shore, where Minnesota's arrowhead plunged into Lake Superior, I couldn't say. Perhaps my tortured soul was seeking kinship with the lake's constant turmoil, with its tides and waves and endless storms above, and the bones of unfortunate ships below. I certainly felt shipwrecked inside. My last few misadventures had left me in tatters. When I looked out across the uneasy waters, I saw more than a reflection of my emotions. I saw acceptance. Reassurance. A promise that the world had always been and would always be a place of unbridled chaos, and there wasn't a damned thing I could do about it.

"Nice, August. Real nice," I complained to myself. "Extra points for your boundless optimism."

Disgruntled, I lifted myself out of my chair and headed inside. The blinds were closed, which meant a much more bearable gloom suffused the room. A threadbare armchair offered itself up as a reasonable replacement for the Adirondack, and I bought what it was selling. The chair took my weight, and its fabric coughed up small clouds of dust. My free hand waved absently at the specs in the room's half light, and my other hand brought more beer to my lips. By the time I'd emptied the can, I was restless. There wasn't any place I had to be, which meant I could go anywhere. On a whim, I decided to take a toodle along the lakeshore. If nothing else, the rugged shoreline offered some stunning views. After seeing all the pretty stuff, I could grab some food, meander south again, and be back in time to find an open barstool at The Thirsty Gull. It was as good of a plan as any, so I set it in motion.

About a half hour later, I stood at the base of Split Rock Lighthouse and peered up. The lighthouse wasn't as cool as you might think. People traveled hundreds of miles to see it, but hell if I knew why. Some likely claimed an interest in the history. Others, an appreciation for the hardiness for the solitary nutsos that had manned the light hour after hour, day after day for years of their lives. Some might've even just liked the unique architecture. The world was full of lighthouses, and no two were the same. More than all of that, I suspected that people only enjoyed looking at lighthouses because travel guides told them to. Since travel guides weren't something I read, I was under no obligation to feel anything. For me, it was simply a place to be.

"Impressive, eh?" I heard someone say. A moment later, I realized they were talking to me.

"Sure," I lied.

My response had been a mistake. Even though I'd done my best to make that single syllable as unwelcoming as possible, the guy took it as an invitation. He stepped closer, and upon quick inspection, I knew I was in for it. He had that quintessential tourist look. Past retirement age, with pleated khakis and a polar fleece pullover and—wait for it—a book whose glossy cover proclaimed it to be the definitive guide to America's lighthouses.

"There was a storm back in 1905 that wrecked nearly thirty ships," he started in a lecturing tone. "The U.S. Lighthouse Service recognized the problem, and this thousand-watt gem went into service in 1910. This used to be called Stony Point, you know."

"Huh," I said, again trying in my monosyllabic way to get the guy to bugger off. Spoiler: he didn't.

"Sure was. A regular death trap, especially for the big steel freighters."

I rolled my eyes. "Buddy, I can buy my own book if I ever decide to care enough about any of that."

"Oh, you should!" he responded, oblivious. "Have you been to the gift shop yet? It's right there on the counter. You can't miss it."

"Oh, I bet I can."

Tourist McNuissance accepted the challenge, licked a finger, and started flipping through pages.

"Here. Here's a bit those other landmark guides won't tell you. Everyone knows that lighthouses warn ships about rocks and shallow berths. Some, though... Well, some warn those ships about much worse things than rocks. I told you this used to be called Stony Point, but they changed it to Split Rock. Most guidebooks will say it's because the lobbyists petitioning for lighthouse called it that. What those other guidebooks don't say is why they called it that."

He paused, waiting for me to take the bait. I didn't, but that didn't stop him.

"Split Rock wasn't a geological feature," he prattled on. "It was a name. The name of a troll up in these parts that caused all sorts of trouble. The darned thing liked to splash around and muck about near here. Unfortunately, some of that mucking about included punching holes in ships that got too close to its self-proclaimed bathtub."

I found myself thinking of Canute, the old troll in Northeast Minneapolis I'd helped a few months prior. It was easy to picture him knocking over the occasional tugboat for no other reason than it was something to do.

"Yeah, trolls are the pits," I agreed.

The guy chortled. "Oh, they aren't even the worst of what some lighthouses warn against. Lake monsters, harpies, you name it. Back in the day, back when folks had their heads on straight, we'd build lighthouses to warn ships of their territories. Keep the humans safe."

The emphasis he put on the word 'human' made my lip curl. In my albeit limited experience, humans and paranormals got along fine. I had to remind myself that not everyone was as enlightened as I was, a thought which made me laugh.

"Nothing funny about it," he replied in a tone suddenly gone sullen.

"Oh, no. Not at all. Except you've got it all wrong. It isn't the paranormals trying to take out the humans. It's the reptilians. You know, from down there."

I pointed pointedly at the ground and widened my eyes in my best impersonation of Jay. Finally–finally–the guy took a step back.

"Uh, sure," he said with another step. "Okay. Well, gee whiz. Look at the time, would ya? Lots to see. Gotta keep moving."

"Walking reptiles!" I shouted at his retreating back. "Messing with your food! Don't eat the corn flakes!"

Watching the douchebag hoof it to the nearby parking lot made my day. With a last look at the lighthouse and its small crowd of admirers, I meandered back to my bike, strapped on my half shell, rolled my shoulders to work out the kinks, and hit the road. My encounter with the tourist cleared most of my hangover. Sometimes, you need a little hair of the dog. Other times, you just need to be the dog and nip some annoying jackass to feel better.

The drive back to Knife River took a bit longer than expected. There was a decent amount of late-season traffic, likely folks looking to catch the tail end of the changing leaves. I suffered through being stuck behind the slowpokes and did my best to not let it bug me too much. With maybe fifteen minutes or so left to reach my cabin, I spotted something truly rare in this modern age: a payphone. Impulse made me squeeze the handbrake and turn into the gas station lot. I shoved a hand into my jacket pocket and found a quarter. Before I could stop myself, I punched in some numbers, pushed the handset's cold plastic up against my ear, and listened to the ringing. After each one, my arm twitched with indecision.

Calm down, you big baby, I reprimanded myself. *He's your friend. He's still your friend.*

When the line connected, there was nothing but soft static for a long moment.

"Hello?" I finally asked. "Jay? That you?"

The response was immediate.

"August! Holy crap. Where are you calling from? I didn't recognize the number. Figured it was, you know. Them. I only picked up because if it was, well, I got some new gear. Hang on a sec..."

My mouth had been hanging open, a word waiting to see if it might get in edge-wise. When Jay put me on hold, that waiting word decided it wasn't worth the effort, and my jaw clenched shut.

"I found this tracing software," Jay said a moment later. "It cracks encryptions and wild card shortcuts. It can pinpoint where someone is calling from or logged in at in like seven seconds. You're in Lake County, huh? Larsmont? Geez. Is that even a place? Lemme see... No, not really. Unincorporated. Barely more than a hundred people living there. Smart. Very smart. You wanted to be off the grid. Looks like you've nailed it."

"Uh," I finally uttered. "I'm at a gas station. Rented a cabin in Knife River, not far from here."

"A cabin? You? Wow, August. A cabin. It's like I barely even know you anymore."

He said it with a laugh, but to me, there was nothing funny about it.

"Yeah, well. Anyway," I diverted. "Thought I'd let you know I'm fine. How are you? I mean, how are things? With you?"

A full three minutes later, I was still wishing I hadn't asked. Jay wasn't just doing fine. He was doing better than fine. Incredible, actually. He'd found some YouTube videos on water magic and was literally soaking in every lesson and doing some pretty wild shit. My head gave a perfunctory nod. When I realized he couldn't see that, I made myself say things like, 'Wow,' and, 'That sounds cool,' and, 'Huh. Damn.' The whole time, my insides were twisting into tighter and tighter knots.

"We should really be talking about this over a couple of beers," he chided after the string in his back finally ran out. "How long do you think you'll be gone for?"

I didn't know, and said as much. A sudden guilt twinged, so I added, "I guess I'll have to keep an eye on the weather. Driving back down to Minneapolis in a snowstorm would suck on my bike."

"So, not too long, then?" he asked. "I mean, it's early October. Honestly, I'm surprised you didn't have to shovel a path to the phone."

"Yeah. Gotta love Minnesota," I acknowledged with a slight uncoiling of the tension in my chest. Talking about the weather was safer ground as opposed to talking about how Jay could practically control the weather.

"Well, you be safe up there, August. Try not to get caught up in any end-of-the-world calamities or nefarious reptilian plots, okay?"

That belt around my ribcage tightened right back up again.

"Yeah, will do," I said, pushing the words through my clenched teeth. "Anyway, you take care, alright? Make some art or something."

Jay promised he would and ended the call. I stood holding the receiver for a long moment before returning it to its cradle. The solitude I'd sought now felt like loneliness. For better or worse, the only cure I knew for loneliness was another drink.

The Gull was slow, which made sense given the early hour. Tom dropped a pint on a coaster and made an attempt at small talk. I tried as well, but within a couple of exchanges, we realized small talk wouldn't be our thing.

"Sorry," he muttered, blushing through his epically bristly beard. "Guess I'm only half-here. Got a lot on my mind."

That little voice of intuition that I could never quite silence piped up.

He got dumped.

Shut up, I replied. *This isn't a work trip.*

Yeah, but what else are you going to do?

I had a point. What else was I planning to do? Drink all day, every day, until I was out of cash?

Yup. That would be a fine plan.

I wasn't entirely persuaded. A sudden claustrophobia squeezed. The idea of weeks of nothing had its appeal, but the reality would be another thing altogether. Spots like Knife River were plenty busy during the summer months. Folks that wanted to fish or take scenic tours of the lakeshore would keep its variety of rental options occupied and its small marina hopping. Come fall, some folks would stop by to look at the changing leaves. Winter, though, would be something else altogether. The cabins would empty, and the boats in the harbor would go into dry dock. The Thirsty Gull wasn't exactly a destination, and the nearby diner was only fit for those with no other options. Knife River was already showing signs of the impending slowdown. I'd spotted a handful of touristy gift shops with 'closed for the season' in the windows. Even my current digs had been a fluke. Only the prospect of getting a few more bucks out of the decrepit building had convinced the owner to let me stay.

It was a long way round to a short conclusion. If I didn't find some way to occupy my time, I was going to be bored to tears.

"Folks often do," I said, doing my best to sound commiserating. I slid a hand into my jacket's inner pocket. "Maybe something I can help with?"

Tom frowned and took the offered card. A moment later, the wooly caterpillars above his eyes rose up with understanding.

"This is what you do?" he asked. "Seriously? You do this?"

"Someone has to," I replied. "Might as well be me. All I need is a little info and a little cash, and that favorite whatever that you can't live without will be returned to its rightful owner."

"Wow. Damn. I mean, I don't know."

I nodded, sipped my beer, and waited as the wheels in Tom's gearbox turned.

"How much?" he finally asked.

The past few jobs had instilled me with a bit more caution, so I went with an obvious question.

"What's your ex?"

"What do you mean?"

"Is she human? Vampire? Wereotter? Insane warlock bent on destroying the world? What would I be dealing with?"

Tom blushed. "Oh. That. She's human. Just human. I mean, not 'just' human. That didn't come out right. Just, you know. She won't try to eat you or whatever."

"That helps. How about fifty bucks?"

"That's it?" he asked, clearly surprised.

A particularly tough job earlier that summer had left me flush with cash. I didn't figure pouring drinks at a small town's dive bar was especially lucrative, so going easy on Tom's wallet seemed like the right thing to do. Plus, it never hurt to be on the local bartender's good side.

"It's usually a hundred," I informed him, "but I'll throw in the friends and family discount. Fifty bucks, and you'll have your special whatever back."

Tom looked puzzled, but didn't haggle the price higher. Instead, he put a collection of fives and tens on the bar with a grateful grin.

"So? What do you want me to repo?" I asked.

I'd never have thought a guy the size of Tom could've looked embarrassed, but wonders never ceased.

"Wilson."

I leaned back on my stool and held up my hands. "Whoah, whoah. Read the card, buddy. No kids."

"I did! Card says 'some pets.' I had a pet fish. Wilson."

"Your name is Tom Hanks, and you had a fish named Wilson?"

Tom blushed. "Well. We had each other, no matter what. So... Yeah."

I blinked, then blinked again, then set that aside. Repo'ing a fish, even one with a stupid name, wouldn't be so bad. I asked for the pertinent details–mainly where his ex lived, if I should knock when she was around or break in when she wasn't, and if the fish needed salt water or fresh–and then ordered another round. Having a job felt good. Normal. Like the universe was tilting back into a more acceptable alignment. I'd find a store to pick up a Tupperware in the morning, swing by Tom's ex the next day, knock–which he said would be fine–and ask for Wilson. Easy peasy.

Christ, was I in for a surprise.

CHAPTER 3

Samuel P. Ely
October 29th, 1896
Caught in a violent gale and broke from a tug at Two Harbors, MN.
All hands survived.

O NE PERK OF SMALL towns: finding your way around doesn't take much effort. I'd actively eschewed modern technology, a fact that drove Jay to distraction on more than one occasion. It wasn't that I didn't want the convenience of a supercomputer in my pocket. I just preferred not to have a digital tracker telling everyone in the flippin' world my whereabouts. On the upside, I fancied myself to be a bit of a rarity in this modern world. I could navigate a new town with only my eyes and a few smarts. Tom Hanks had told me what streets to follow, where to turn, and what his ex's house looked like. It was all I had needed.

I studied the modest house from the saddle of my bike. It exuded functional simplicity, and I could see why Tom had liked it. The old Tudor's beige stucco showed signs of wear, but its cracks had been diligently repaired. Its windows had simple shutters to weather the lake's storms, and the yard was sparse but tidy. With a nod of approval at Tom's pragmatism, I lifted my Tupperware from the bike's sidecar and sloshed the lake water a few times. The plan was simple. Knock, explain that Tom wanted Wilson back, ignore whatever his ex's response would be–tears, cursing, maybe an angry, 'Fine! Just take the damned thing and tell him to get lost!'–and then swing back to the bar. I'd been there twice and Tom had been working both times, so odds were good he'd be there again. If not, I'd just drink until he rolled in, then use his money to pay my bar tab.

As it turned out, the doorbell worked, so I didn't have to knock. The woman who answered was Tom-sized, and I impulsively took a step back. On the upside, I wasn't inside the house. That meant I wasn't at risk of getting thrown through a window. Another perk? I could see both her hands. That meant I wasn't about to get brained with a frying pan. Considering some of the jobs I'd had, things were off to a great start.

"Can I help you?" she asked in a voice almost as deep as her bartending ex's.

After a steadying breath—because frying pan or not, the lady was intimidating—I pulled on my game face.

"August Shade," I proclaimed as officially as I could. Experience had taught me that sounding important was almost as good as being important. "Post-relationship personal effects repossession specialist. Your ex, Tom Hanks, hired me to reclaim his personal effects."

Her eyes narrowed, which I expected. Her explanation that Tom had already taken all of his stuff was also expected. When I said, sure, but he also wanted Wilson back, those narrowed eyes widened. I held up the Tupperware and sloshed the water a bit. It was then that she smiled. Really, really smiled.

"Ah. You bet'cha. Wilson. Sure, mister. Come on in."

She led me through a small living room and a smaller kitchen, my eyes searching for an aquarium. When I veered toward a hallway that likely led to a bedroom, thinking maybe the fish was on a dresser or something, she shook her head and opened a door to the backyard. Confused, I followed.

The back of the house was as mundane as the front, with the exception of an above-ground pool. Its white tube frame leaned tiredly as it tried to keep the blue plastic liner upright. Why someone would have a full pool when temperatures were flirting with freezing was beyond me. I took a few steps closer as my brain chugged away. Then there was the tiniest of thoughts, the smallest of realizations. I had just enough time to say, "Wait a second..." before a tentacle exploded out of the water and wrapped around my waist. That Tupperware I'd spent almost three dollars on sailed across the sky and a scream erupted from my throat.

"He knows Tom," the woman called out, "so don't be too rough, Wilson."

It was the last thing I heard before my feet lifted from the ground. More tentacles grabbed my arms and legs, and an eye as big as a watermelon peered at me from the side of a bulbous head. I kept screaming as I went down, my last breath coming out as a series of vulgar bubbles, and a rush of thoughts raced through my brain.

Tom did not know what a fish was.

Wilson was not a fish.

And a final thought before I impulsively shifted...

Some days, my job really sucked.

Shifting is a funny thing. As the only shifter I knew, I didn't have the benefit of comparing notes with my peers. My only point of reference was my own weird experience.

I considered what I could shift into. My repertoire, as I thought of it, was eclectic. On the bigger side, I had a gorilla, an elephant, and a big old bull. More modest options included my coyote, hound dog, and a Maine Coon cat. The wolverine was a particular favorite. Then there was the turkey. I hated being the turkey. Hated it. How I ended up with my particular menagerie was a series of memories I didn't like to revisit. Suffice it to say that I could only shift into a specific—albeit strange—array of animals, at least as a genuine shift. The other option was masking. For a minute or two, I could make myself almost look like someone or something, but not really. It was more like wearing a cheap mask of the person or animal. An actual shift wasn't becoming like an animal, or even becoming an animal. It was becoming the animal. An exact copy of one that had existed, had lived its own life. When I shifted into a gorilla, I wasn't just a gorilla. I was the gorilla that I'd bonded with. A tiny sliver of my humanness remained, but not much. Just enough to persuade the animal to do what I wanted, and enough to shift back after smashing things and scratching my butt.

Shifting was easiest with the primate, since our brains were so similar. The elephant's was bigger but still wired a lot like a human's. The coyote, hound dog, and even the wolverine weren't bad, either. That Maine Coon cat is where things got strange. I'm not a vain person by nature, so becoming the embodiment of vanity always left me feeling gross. And then there was my turkey. The other things were at least all mammals. Turkeys? Not mammals. There's no way to describe it. Not really. The best I've come up with is to imagine being a bird. Yeah. I'm terrible at describing things. Suffice it to say that putting my human awareness into a bird brain sucked. Even that surreal experience, though, had some key things in common with the rest. I breathed air and lived out of the water. I saw and heard and smelled and tasted things with senses designed for that reality. Another important similarity was my overall intelligence. There is a surprisingly small gap between a human and a turkey's smarts. Noticeable, sure, but honestly, humans really aren't that smart. Arrogant, sure, but that arrogance isn't exactly justified. Which brings me to the other animal in my repertoire. The one whose foreignness bent my brain into shapes so bizarre they didn't qualify as geometric. One whose way of thinking and perceiving the world was unbelievably wonky.

I prayed that strangest of strange shifts would help me survive meeting Wilson.

> *danger a predator larger by a factor of approximately two-thousand percent*
> *is attempting to grab a hold*
> *given the size differential it would likely have a gripping tensile strength of*
> *hold next thought primary importance*
> *water salinity well below thirty-six grams per liter*
> *sub-optimal salinity cannot separate oxygen effectively*
> *respiratory capacity reduced*
> *wait what the hell I can't breathe?*
> *evade squirt use melanin cloud hide twist thirteen percent*
> *change trajectory seeking cracks crevices hiding spots*
> *cannot breathe cannot evade without sufficient oxygen*
> *situation critical survival imperiled*

Where a very confused, very scared, very wet, and very oxygen-deprived human had been, there was now only a leather jacket, tee-shirt, and jeans clutched in a leviathan's tentacles. Beneath, beside, and below those empty garments, a small octopus ducked and darted. I babbled as I tried to find a rock to squeeze beneath or a crack to squish into. Breathing was beyond hard. Saltwater cephalopods weren't designed for freshwater, especially not the nasty water in Tom the bartender's shitty backyard aquarium. With mounting panic, my thoughts turned more human and significantly more imploring. Not that it would do much good. Octopi can't talk.

> *please Wilson please don't hurt me*
> *i can't believe Tom called you a fish*
> *holy crap stop trying to grab me you asshole*

The thoughts poured though my donut-shaped brain while I darted and dashed around Wilson's gigantic tentacles. If one got a hold of me, I'd be up inside that extra large beak attached to his extra large body in no time at all. Another squirt of ink erupted from my siphon and I used the cover to avoid another swipe by the fish I was supposed to repossess. I kept up a stream-of-consciousness prattle fueled by frustration and fear, and then, unexpectedly...

LITTLE TOM FRIEND STOP
EXERTION IN SUB-OPTIMAL LIQUID MEDIUM WILL EXHAUST YOU
SLOW FOCUS ON IN OUT SLOW BREATHS
I WILL HELP YOU

I wouldn't exactly say octopi were psychic, but after hearing–if you could call it that–Wilson talk back, I wouldn't not say that either. I slowed my mad dashes around the pool, thankful for the opportunity to catch what little breath I could in the inhospitable water. When the panic subsided, I floated up by the lake monster's eye.

thank you

thank you

thank you

I uncurled one tentacle and let it float in front of me while the other seven waited nervously to propel me away. Wilson coiled one of his arms in until it was a sucker-lined spiral. The very tip floated near mine, and then I felt the tiniest of touches.

HELLO TOM FRIEND HELLO

hey cool I'm August

Tom Hanks friend

Tom misses you wants me to bring you to him

...don't eat me

NO FEAR I WILL NOT EAT LITTLE COUSIN
TOM BRINGS FISH HAHA

Tom called you a fish

TOM DUMB
ALSO NICE THOUGH

The massive tentacle rippled, a gesture my octopus brain understood as laughter.

cannot breath well here no salt

I am going to shift again okay?

SHIFT? AH LITTLE COUSIN IS DIFFERENT
VERY DIFFERENT
CONSERVATION OF MASS NOT RELEVANT?
INTERESTING YES SHIFT

The lake monster pulled and coiled its tentacles beneath it, signaling a complete lack of hostility. With a grateful *thank you, Wilson*, I shifted. Once human again, I could stand on the bottom of the pool and break the water's surface. I spat out water tinged with the oily taste of my ink and turned, naked and shivering, to glare at Tom's ex. I didn't get the chance to berate her, though. She was too busy heaving out great big guffaws. She did spare me a look when I bent and flopped my naked ass over the pool's flimsy side, but that just sent her into even greater fits of laughter. When Wilson helpfully lifted three tentacles out of the pool, one holding my jacket, one holding my tee-shirt, and the last, my jeans, she fell on her back and rolled on the ground. The final disgrace was when Wilson tossed my socks and boots out and one sock landed on my face.

"Ha," I grumbled as I pulled on the soaked clothes.

"You're a shifter?" she gasped between belly laughs.

I grunted an affirmative, which sent her into even more violent fits of laughter. When she could breathe again, she blurted out, "Hey shifter, you dropped your Tupperware!"

Too cheap to let it go, I stomped over to where the plastic container had fallen. Each step sent water squirting up out of my boots. When I leaned down to pick it up, a veritable geyser shot up from the back of my jeans. An abundance of laughs accompanied the unfortunate occurrence.

"You tell Tom he can have Wilson," she finally managed as she found her feet, "but you'll need a bigger Tupperware. Hell, he shouldn't even be in the pool. Poor little guy should be in the lake, especially with winter coming."

I clenched my fists at my sides.

"Tom said Wilson was a fish."

"Tom is kinda dumb," she replied.

With a last glare, I promised I'd be back. Manners made me add a quick, "Thanks for not eating me, Wilson," and a tentacle waved happily in response.

The drive to my cabin was a miserable one, but I tried to find the silver lining. At least Tom's ex had a sense of humor. More often than not, people were anything but amused when I showed up. After tossing my soaked clothes in the shower and hanging my jacket on a towel hook, I pulled on a dry pair of jeans and a flannel from my duffel bag and readied myself to give Tom a serious piece of my mind.

"Fish come in lots of shapes and sizes," the bartender protested after I'd given him the curse-laden recap of meeting his pet 'fish,' Wilson.

It wasn't an argument worth pursuing, so I waved it aside and asked how he thought I'd be able to get a flipping lake monster back for him.

"I'd been kinda wondering that myself," Tom admitted, "but figured, you know, this is what you do."

"Wilson is not what I normally do," I growled, but there wasn't much ferocity behind it. They say time plus tragedy equals comedy. Apparently, enough time had passed because I grinned. That, or I'd had enough to drink. My first couple of rounds had been on the house, which was Tom's way of apologizing.

"Do you even have a place to put Wilson?" I asked. "Another pool? One that won't freeze next month? He's a little big for a bathtub."

The bartender had set his elbow on the bar and was resting his chin on his fist. He absently scratched at the bar top's old wood with a fingernail while thinking that one through.

"No, not really," he admitted. When my eyes narrowed, he stammered that everything had happened so fast. I'd said what I did, and he'd thought how great it would be to have Wilson back, and then I was on my way.

"Honestly," he said, looking forlorn, "he should be back in the lake. A cheap pool's no place for someone like Wilson. He deserves better. And feeding him is a full-time job. I practically have to buy half of Ollie's catch to keep that little rascal fed."

I nodded with relief. With my luck, I'd been worried Tom would've said that yes, the bathtub is exactly where he wanted his eight-tentacled fish, and that his apartment was on the top floor of a three-story walk-up.

"Well, I can't get him there on my bike. Wilson's huge, in case you hadn't noticed."

The bartender's brow furrowed in thought, and I could plainly see how the effort cost him.

"You got a sidecar on your bike," he announced, like he'd just discovered buried treasure.

"Um. Yeah. So?"

"Wilson looks really big, but he can squish down pretty small. What if we got a big tub or cooler full of water? Just enough for him to breathe for a few minutes while you drive him back to the lake?"

I blinked at Tom, waiting for him to realize how incredibly stupid that plan was. After a minute or so, I realized I was waiting in vain.

"Guess it'll have to do," I muttered. "But Tom?"

"Yeah, August?"

"If anything bad happens to Wilson, well, I don't do refunds."

The bartender regarded me with a solemn look.

"I understand. Now, hang on a sec. I'm pretty sure I have a big cooler in the back."

The ride back to Tom's ex's place–whose name he finally told me was Becca–was a slow one. Carrying the cooler to the lake, submerging it, dragging it back to my bike, and struggling to lift it up and into the sidecar had been its own ordeal. I wasn't in the mood to do it again, so I navigated the road's cracks and potholes like I was transporting a holy relic. When I pulled up in front of the house, I gave the bike's horn a toot, then waved toward the back when Becca poked her head out of the front door. The only upside I could find was that the backyard didn't have a fence. I rolled the bike up alongside the pool and waved back at a tentacle after silencing the engine.

"Hey, Wilson," I said. "Tom says you can smoosh down pretty small when you have to. Think you could shove that colossal head of yours in here? It'll only be until we get to the lake."

The word 'lake' had just passed my lips when all eight tentacles erupted from the water and waved around in a manic tangle.

"He said that?" Becca asked, eyes wide. "He's really letting Wilson go back to the lake?"

"Yup," I replied.

The big woman rubbed a hand across suddenly damp eyes.

"Well, I'll be," she said. "Maybe he's not so dumb after all."

I flipped the lid back on the cooler and leaned over the pool's flimsy rail. Wilson damn near filled the whole bottom, and I kicked myself for being a fool.

Welp, you never know until you try, right? I asked myself.

"Wilson? You ready to give this a go?"

In response, the monster rose and broke the surface of the water. He turned from one side to the other, regarding me and my stupid cooler with one luminous eye, then the other. A tentacle slipped out of the water and reached over the pool's edge. It dipped its tip into the cooler's water, then explored the insides. My face must've shown my complete lack of faith that even a part of him would fit, because that same tentacle curled and the tip poked up from the coil. After giving me the oversized octopus equivalent of a thumbs-up, more tentacles squirmed over the railing and braced themselves on the ground between the pool and my bike. When underwater, octopi can walk on their tentacles. I had no idea if they could accomplish the same feat on dry land, but Wilson was about to put an end to that mystery. After four of his tentacles braced on the grass, one wrapped around the bike's handlebar and another suckered onto the back of the sidecar. He leaned his colossal noggin forward and used his remaining two tentacles to push experimentally.

"Best get ready," Becca suggested. "He won't last long in that little bucket."

I swung a leg over my saddle and tried not to think about the giant suckers inches my face. I gave the old bike a kick, and Wilson twisted the throttle. Teamwork made the dream work. The engine barked and settled into a growl. I gave a satisfied dip of my chin, and the lake monster nodded back. It was go time.

Wilson dipped his mouth into the water, blew out a bunch of bubbles, took a big, big breath, and pushed hard with his tentacles. For a moment, I had a terrifying view of the monster's huge beak heading right toward me, then it plunged down and into the open cooler. Those last couple of bendy, sucker-lined arms left the pool. One braced against the sidecar. The other wrapped tightly around my waist. I bit back a scream and nudged his grip on the throttle aside. Slowly, carefully—and also unbelievably—the Guzzi rolled forward. In its saddle, a grouchy and–if we're being honest–terrified shifter. In its sidecar, a collection of gray-green tentacles and a ginormous fleshy sack named Wilson.

"Bye, Wilson!" Becca called as we idled away. "Bye!"

The lake monster risked one tentacle to wave in reply, then quickly returned to keeping his balance. Together, we rolled around the house, onto the road, and down the winding hill that would eventually bring us to water. I only hoped we'd get there fast enough.

Our route took us past a handful of houses and shops that made up Knife River's attempt at a downtown. Word must've gotten out about my ridiculous undertaking because people were lined up like we were a parade. It had to have been a spectacle. Me hunched over my bike's handlebars with a thick tentacle wrapped around my waist. Wilson with his big, fleshy head half-stuffed into a bright red cooler, eyes wide and arms waving happily in the wind. I ignored the gathered onlookers, except for a few of the PNs. We passed a diminutive nisse and a house-elf that looked like someone put Santa Claus in the wash and shrank him. I saw what might've been a nix–hard to tell given the distracting nature of my circumstances–emerging from a seafood market. A white horse had just shifted into a handsome young man, revealing himself for a Nokken. As we passed by, each raised a fist to the side of their mouth, then splayed their fingers and pushed their hand out. I replied to the strange local greeting with a thumbs up once or twice, but gave up being polite when the bike swerved dangerously.

"Doing okay, buddy?" I called out.

A tentacle patted me reassuringly on the helmet. I navigated a gentle bend, and Lake Superior opened up before us. A light breeze was pushing the water into small white-capped waves and tugging at my shirt. Standing near the boat launch, arms raised in a joyous and triumphant Y above his head, was Tom Hanks.

"Wilson!" he yelled. "Hi, Wilson! Who's a good boy? Who's the best boy?"

The lake monster wriggled like a gigantic octopus-shaped puppy and damn near caused me to swerve off the road.

"Settle down, you idiot," I snapped as I kept us upright and coasted to the water's edge.

The bike hadn't even stopped rolling when Wilson erupted from the cooler. His tentacles swerved and snapped, propelling the rest of him down the beach's rough pebbles. Tom ran beside him, whooping and clapping. When Wilson finally reached the water, he made a gigantic splash. Tom's pet fish sucked in a huge breath and pushed twin geysers out of his spiracles, the jets propelling him further into the waves. At the last possible second, two tentacles snapped out and wrapped around the bartender's arms. The big man barely had time to whoop in surprise before Wilson pulled him under.

"Tom Hanks!" I cried out in terror.

The small crowd that had gathered at the water to witness the reunion gasped. I spotted Ollie in the crowd and ran to him.

"What just happened? We have to help him!" I cried as I grabbed the older man's shoulder.

"Who? Tom? Nonsense. They're just playing."

Playing? my brain echoed.

I turned toward the water, eyes searching and failing to find any evidence of the human and his pet monster. Then Tom's head burst from the water maybe ten or fifteen yards from where he'd gone under. Wilson had the big man wrapped in a couple of tentacles. While I watched, speechless, I saw Tom's barrel-sized torso zig and zag through the small waves.

"Weeee!" he cried. "Yeah! Faster, Wilson! Faster!"

The pair spiraled and swerved as the lake monster jetted back and forth under the water, and Tom waved his arms like a kid on a roller coaster. My stomach turned inside out, and

I gagged.

"Yeah," Ollie agreed. "Not my idea of a good time, either, but to each their own."

The crowd was laughing and clapping and whistling, enjoying the show immensely. More than a few gave me a quick look of approval before returning their attention to the pair's antics.

"Tom and Becca hadn't been happy in a while," the fisherman confided, "and he's been a mopey brute ever since he moved out. That guy missed his little buddy something fierce. You did a good thing today, August Shade."

I scratched at where Wilson's sucker had left a welt on my neck. Compared to some of the bumps and bruises that always accompany my jobs, it wasn't bad at all.

"Another happy customer," I replied, earning a hearty slap on the back from my companion.

After another minute or two, Tom Hanks and Wilson tired of their shenanigans. Wilson gently placed his bearded buddy on the dock stretching into the harbor. That big, fleshy head poked up from the waves and two darkly luminous eyes stared up at the big man. The bartender rubbed what might've been lake water—but were definitely tears—from his eyes with one hand. The other tenderly held the end of a tentacle.

"See ya, Wilson," I heard him say. "You come visit as much as you want, okay?"

That tentacle slipped from Tom's hand, twirled, and booped him on the nose. The lake monster's head dipped beneath the surface, and I saw a dark silhouette swerve and sway toward the horizon. Soon, it was lost beneath the whitecaps.

Show over, the crowd dispersed. Humans and PNs made their way back to whatever they'd been doing before. I recognized one gnome from when I'd done karaoke and gave the little guy–or maybe lady–a friendly nod. In response, I got that same fist by the mouth gesture, then the gnome trundled off.

"Any idea what that's about?" I asked as I turned to face Ollie.

I'd been expecting his ready smile. Instead, his face was blank.

"Not a clue," he finally said with a shake of his head that sent his hat's fishing lures rattling. "Now, c'mon. Once old Tom dries out, I'm sure he'd love to buy you a drink."

I followed in his wake, the satisfaction of a job well done warming me against the autumn's chill. There was one sliver of cold, though. A little spur of ice that refused to melt. As I considered it, I realized its source.

I couldn't say why, but I was pretty sure Ollie was lying.

CHAPTER 4

SS Hudson
September 16th, 1901
Last seen listing badly as she passed the Apostle Islands.
All hands lost.

T HE REST OF THE week was busy. After helping to reunite Wilson and Tom Hanks, word of my particular services spread quickly. Normally, that wouldn't have been a bad thing. I enjoyed being busy, and sometimes I even liked my job. The tricky bit was doing what I did in a very small town. Back in Minneapolis, the city's population was over four hundred thousand. Factor in Saint Paul and the surrounding suburbs, and you were talking about close to four million people. Knife River's year-round population was just over two hundred. In other words, everyone had basically dated everyone else at some point. Establishing the chain of custody for someone's favorite whatever was... challenging.

Case in point: Bob and Sue and a particular flannel. I was at Sue's place because Sue was in possession of a flannel that belonged to Bob. According to Sue, though, it wasn't that simple. Sure, Bob wore the shit out of that flannel, but had it actually been his? He'd gotten it from Rachel, after all, and that good-for-nothing Rachel stole it from Roger back when they'd had a real humdinger of a fight at the grocery store about whether hot dish needs those crispy onion strings on top or not. And everyone knew it wasn't even Roger's flannel in the first place. He took it from his dad's closet so he could dress up for Christmas dinner a good two-three years back after Amber spoiled the rest of his wardrobe. She'd

31

caught Roger messing around with some tourist behind the hardware store. That Amber, she took a big jar of pickle brine, dumped it in the bathtub, and proceeded to soak damned near every piece of Roger's clothing in it. If he'd worked his full shift, he'd have had a tough choice to face: smell like pickles or deal with being buck naked until wash day.

"Uh… huh," I managed after she finally shut up. "But, after all that, it was Bob's, and he wants his flannel back."

"Of course he does," Sue spat. "It's a nice flannel. Has great napping. Real cotton, too. Not some cheap blend. Of course he wants it back, the cheating bastard. I swear, if I see Mandy wearing it tomorrow, I'm going to break Bob's nose. Don't tell me I won't!"

"Okay," I promised.

She glared at me, unsure of whether or not I'd taken her side. I held her gaze, doing my best to convey a complete disinterest in the whole affair. If Switzerland had a face, I hoped it looked a lot like mine.

It's a freaking flannel, for Pete's sake, I thought.

As was sometimes the case, I won the impromptu staring contest and saw the fight go out of her. At least, that's what I'd thought. She turned on her heel and stomped down a hallway. I heard hangers being dragged back and forth and a low string of curses. Then there was more stomping and the sound of drawers being opened, rummaged through, and slammed shut. A loud 'ah ha!' sounded from what was likely the kitchen, and then I heard another noise. A not-good-at-all noise. A sort of metal-on-metal noise.

"Shit," I muttered.

When Sue returned, she had the flannel shirt. Or, more accurately, she held tatters of black and gray patterned flannel fabric. It no longer fit the description of a shirt. A pair of sharp scissors had turned it into a tangled collection of rags.

"Nice," I said. "Real nice, lady."

"You tell that Bob that Mandy's gonna look real pretty in this shirt of his."

"Okay, I will." And with that, I left.

Roger had been pissed, but thankfully hadn't killed the messenger. As it turned out, that wasn't even the worst experience I had that week. One of the locals had fallen for a tourist and wanted me to drive to Canada to get her ThighMaster back. Flippin' Canada! When I declined, I got an earful and almost a neckful. I'd thought that peculiar shine in her eyes had been the misty tears of a jilted lover. I didn't realize I'd been talking to one of the few vampires that called Knife River home. And then there were the really unpleasant moments when I had to repo something from a former customer. One day started with a guy giving me details about a certain fishing lure. I repo'd it from the guy's ex around lunch. While I was there, the woman's friend, who had stopped by to chat and play Yahtzee, hired me on the spot. That afternoon, I returned the guy's lure and asked for a Fleetwood Mac album back in the same breath. It was insane. The town's dating scene was basically a merry-go-round. I made some quick cash, which was nice, but the constant walking on eggshells and never knowing what tangled love triangle was around the next corner was exhausting. By the time karaoke night rolled around, I was actually looking forward to it. Nothing, not even karaoke, could be worse than the handful of days I'd just had.

I rolled into The Thirsty Gull early, like I'd done pretty much every day prior. I had zero intention of singing again, but wasn't opposed to watching the show from the back of the house. After situating myself on a stool at the end of the bar and accepting a full pint from Tom Hanks, I let my thoughts meander while waiting for more folks to arrive. When they did, I seriously started to question my decision.

More and more of my very recent customers filed in. That wasn't so bad, as most had been happy with my services. It was when more and more of their exes showed up that I started to worry. I hid my face behind my beer and cursed my stupidity. Easily half my customers and as many of their exes had been at the bar for karaoke the week before. Hell, that was how a lot of them knew me. Each new knock on my door over the past week had inevitably come with a, "Saw you sing that *Stone Temple Pilots* song." When I found their ex, they were as likely to recognize me from that fateful night as not, too. Everyone literally knew everyone–including me–and now they were all packing into the bar.

"You seem tense," Oliver noted as he took the stool next to mine.

My already-hunched shoulders hunched more as I tried to hide behind his frame.

"Yeah, well. It's been a busy week, and it's just now hitting me how incredibly stupid I've been. You don't shit where you eat, Ollie."

"Fish do. They do it all the time."

"It was a metaphor."

"Idiom, actually."

I glowered and circled a finger for Tom to bring a round. Oliver smiled in response.

"Excellent! You're staying!" he said. "Ah, this will be a grand night."

The drinks arrived, and I brought my fresh pint to my lips while Ollie sniffed his whiskey.

"Not singing," I declared.

"Of course you're not," he agreed with a knowing wink. "Well, don't trouble yourself about all these fine folks. I've only heard dribs and drabs, but I think you've lanced more than a few boils."

When I raised a skeptical eyebrow, he gestured at the swelling crowd.

"Look around, man. What do you see? Angry people? Jealous ex-lovers?"

I straightened my spine a smidge and peered over his shoulder. Grudgingly, I picked up on what he was getting at. People were mingling easily. I saw more than a few of my customers clicking glasses with their exes. Even Bob. The old scoundrel had Sue on one arm and who I assumed was Mandy on the other. Her hair was tied up with strips of gray and black flannel. When she twirled one with a finger, they all laughed.

"The hell?" I wondered out loud.

"Small town, August. If you don't learn to bury the hatchet, there will be so many lying around, you'll cut your feet to ribbons trying to cross the room."

It was strange, but then again, maybe it wasn't. I reflected on my recent attempts at dating. Betty, Clarissa, Dagmara. I didn't harbor any of them ill will, and they'd each been messy enough breakups in their own ways. Clarissa, in a sad sort of way. Dagmara, in a tragic ending fit for a Shakespeare play. The messy end of my romantic escapades with Betty had been much more literal. Even so, if any of them walked into the bar at that moment, would it have been so bad?

If they all walked in at once, maybe, I decided.

"Alright, my friend," Oliver said. "I can see I've set the old wheels turning. I'll leave you to it and go set up. And no need to remind me you are definitely not singing. Anything at all. Especially not *Even Flow* by Pearl Jam. Nope. Not that. I am quite certain I will not find a slip of paper with that song and your name in my fishbowl."

Before I could sputter an objection, he'd walked away, whistling the grunge favorite and waving to the many patrons.

Tom scratched his beard. "I saw them in concert, you know. That was back in... Gosh. When was it? Smashing Pumpkins and the Red Hot Chili Peppers were there, too. Pearl Jam got booed off the stage."

"Great pep talk, Tom."

"No! That's not what I'm saying. Those people were crazy. It's a good song."

He wasn't wrong on either count. Most people were crazy, and it was a good song. Despite myself, I hummed it quietly to see if it was in my range.

"Oh, for Pete's sake, August," I snapped when I caught myself.

It was too late, though. Oliver Corbyn was a damned good fisherman and had just set his hook.

As was his custom, Ollie sang the first song. It warmed up the crowd and allowed him to sound check at the same time. After his rendition of The Bay City Rollers *Saturday Night*, he turned the mic over to the first singer he pulled from the fishbowl, and the night truly began.

Never in a million years would I have believed I'd willingly endure karaoke. There was something about the Gull, about Ollie, about the folks of Knife River, though, that made it strangely tolerable. Even enjoyable. I tipped back my pint, drank the last few drops, and waved to Tom for another. For weeks, I'd lived with a deep coiling in my chest. A pervasive worry. A constant fear that made breathing a chore. Now, it was loosening. I found myself thinking back to the prior spring. I'd been at my local watering hole getting drinks from Betty the bartender and wondering if I'd ever have a chance with the mercurial succubus. There'd been an all-woman grunge band pounding out covers of Nirvana to commemorate Kurt Cobain's death twenty-five years before. I'd been enjoying myself. Genuinely enjoying myself. Between the bartender, the beer, and the music, it had been a damned good night. Then a jealous warlock named Tony showed up, and every moment after had gone from bad to worse, and from worse to flippin' weird. I'd tumbled headlong into a spiral complete with that douchebag of a warlock, a spray-tanned vampire, heartbroken troll, one-eyed oracle, coblyn thugs, feuding hags, a centuries old demon, an ancient scarecrow, an honest-to-god ghost, and even supposed reptilians that had infiltrated the government. Doesn't matter who you are. A year like that will do a number on you. Now, though, all of that was finally fading in the rearview mirror.

The current singer belted out their last few notes, the crowd applauded, and then Ollie called my name.

"C'mon, August. You may not be able to carry a tune," he said, and then the whole crowd joined him for the punchline, "but you can karaoke!"

A sheepish grin wobbled across my face as I shuffled my feet toward the stage. People clapped and cheered, and my cheeks went red as a baboon's butt. I took the mic from

Ollie, glanced down at the monitor's screen, and readied myself to try some Pearl Jam. *Even Flow* was an iconic song, and I wanted to do it justice. My eyes glued to the monitor, my hands gripping the mic for dear life, I started to sing.

Near as I could tell, I was mostly on-key. I couldn't be sure, though, because damn near everybody else in the place was singing along. It was awesome. Intoxicating. Without realizing when or how it happend, I lost myself in the song. There was no 'me,' 'them,' and 'the music.' We were all one. Right up until I was halfway through the refrain and finally realized everyone else had gone silent.

I looked up from the monitor expecting to see faces. Instead, I saw the backs of heads. Inertia made me blurt out another lyric, then I stopped singing and peered beyond the mullets, braids, buzz cuts, and bald spots.

And damn near wet myself.

Why? Well, the short answer is, 'Because a siren.' If you aren't familiar with them, a more substantive explanation may be in order.

On a scale of 'one' to 'absolutely not,' sirens are a 'hell no, nope, no goddamned flipping way.' Even Canute, an old troll I'd helped a few months ago, wasn't that high up on the scale. Perhaps you're wondering why a siren of all things was top of my 'hell no' list. If that's the case, you obviously haven't met one. Maybe you know the basics: that a siren is some bird lady who hangs out at sea and sings, luring sailors to their demise. You're probably thinking, what's the big deal, right? Every now and then, we lose a sailor. Plenty more where they came from. There must be worse things to worry about than sirens.

I thought that exact same thing, right up until I saw one walking through the bar.

Let's start with what this particular siren looked like. I'll be kind and compare her lower half to an osprey's. Ospreys are birds of prey. They're called fish-hawks, and hawks of any variety are not to be messed with. They have evolved over eons to be masterful killers. If I were being less kind, I'd compare her lower half to an osprey from a toxic lake in the depths of the worst hell imaginable. So, I hope that by this point, you're picturing a flying murder machine from hell. And that's just describing her legs.

Somewhere around her lower torso, the human bits showed up. Like her flabby midriff and its network of wrinkles. Picture a long-haul trucker who spent their days drinking sugary sodas and eating double bacon cheeseburgers with potato chips. Uh huh. Just like that. The skin around the wrinkles was sallow and dimpled with oozing pustules and gaping pockmarks. So yeah. Fish-hawk-from-hell legs and long-haul-trucker belly. Plenty awful already, right? Now, let's talk about her breasts. I don't want to, but we really need to make sure we're on the same page here. Also, you can't not talk about something like that when they are on full display. Each one hung down like a deflated tire. Like a big glop of drab paint slowly oozing down the wall. Like a... Oh, hell. Nevermind. Suffice it to say, her dugs were extra duggy. Stretch marks creased the pale skin. Blue veins radiated out from each large and misshapen nipple and crawled up each boob like vines full of ill intent. Why those nipples existed, I couldn't say. My knowledge of sirens didn't include a chapter on their reproductive biology. Did they lay eggs or have babies? If the latter, the thought of something suckling on those breasts was enough to turn my stomach inside out.

Yeesh. Ugh. Just yuck. Moving on.

The siren had arms. Two in total, and being too long was the least of their offenses. Ropey muscles wrapped each one, and they ended with hands more akin to her raptor feet. There were wings, too. Dirty, dingy feathers covered their length, which reached almost to the floor. Anything capable of coordinating legs, arms, and wings was already something not worth trusting. On her? The feathered spans were chilling.

Last, but not least, the siren had a face. I use the term loosely, though. It had the requisite parts. Eyes and nose and mouth. Ears on either side. There was hair above and a chin below. You could look at that face and check all the boxes. The devil is in the details, though, and it was a devil's face, indeed. Those eyes were too far apart and black as pools of tar. The nose was a craggy mountain tipped on its side. Her mouth? Forget about it. Mouths should be for eating bites of food, not entire meals at once. Whoever came up with sirens hadn't gotten that particular memo, though. As she walked on those odd legs–knees bent in the wrong direction and talons clacking loudly in the now-silent bar–her mouth hung open in a wide and wicked smile. It reminded me of a useless bit of knowledge that had stuck in my brain for no good reason. Snakes have weird jaws. They don't unhinge per se, but the joints and ligaments allow for an astounding range of motion. Looking at the siren, it was clear her mouth would open a hell of a lot farther than it had any right to.

Added up, the damned thing was terrifying, so it didn't surprise me that everyone looked terrified. I had the best excuse, though. The winged monstrosity was stomping and scraping those taloned feet straight toward me. I held the mic near my chin, arms frozen and jaw slack, until the damned thing was standing directly beneath me. One of those ropey arms reached out, and a clawed finger hooked the cord. The siren tugged, and the mic slipped from my numb fingers with an amplified thud. With menacing slowness, she set to coiling its cord around her elbow. After she'd pulled in the slack, the siren hopped up to the platform, wings ruffling and refolding across her back. Still she coiled the mic's cord, each loop drawing her closer to the karaoke machine.

"No. Please…" I heard Oliver whimper.

The awful lines of the siren's face folded into something even worse. When she reached Oliver's prized possession, one finger slipped under its handle. The boxey speaker with the built-in CD player and microphone had to weigh thirty, maybe even forty, pounds. She lifted it easy as flipping on a light switch. Her other hand reached for the open CD binder. A claw flipped it shut with a snap, then she grabbed that as well. With those two simple gestures, all of Oliver Corbyn's KJ'ing accouterments were suddenly and irreversibly in the possession of a walking nightmare. Those wings stretched and ruffled again, and the entire room flinched. The siren sniffed, a sound that might have been haughty had it come from any other creature. Lips pursed, her eyes searched the fear-stricken faces, then settled on Oliver Corbyn.

"Bye bye baby. Baby, goodbye," she crooned.

I saw the effect the words had on Ollie, watched him crumble inside. A moment later, as the siren continued to sing, I recognized the song. The Four Seasons' *Bye Bye Baby* was a classic. Way better than its reimagining by The Bay City Rollers. The upbeat melody belied the heartache in the lyrics, a heartache that I saw in Oliver's eyes and–shockingly–reflected in the siren's.

"What the actual hell?" I breathed, realizing too late I'd said the words out loud.

I shouldn't have made a single solitary sound.

The siren was maybe halfway to the door when my stupid voice stopped her as surely as it stopped her song. She pivoted, the movement dragging one of her talons across the floor with a loud screech. Her eyes found mine, and her lips parted.

"No," Oliver whispered in a voice gone raw. "Don't. Please don't."

The siren's tar-black orbs looked from me to Oliver and back. Whatever it was he didn't want her to do, she apparently didn't care. Her lips parted. Those hanging dugs swayed with an indrawn breath, and everything went black.

~ee~

"Whaaa?" I sputtered in shock.

Reality came back in a mad cascade of disjointed pieces. I was on the floor. Ice cold water soaked my face. A myriad of hands held my shoulders, arms, and even my legs. My mind had gone good and truly blank. In that moment of shock, I didn't even know my name. The world held only unpleasant sensations. The cold wetness on my face, the painful squeezing of too many hands, the hard floor beneath me. Then a sudden realization eclipsed all of those discomforts. A dawning awareness whose cruel rays burned everything inside of me to ash.

My love, my one and only and truest love, had left me.

"No!" I cried, struggling against the hands that held me down. "Let me go. Let me go! I need her. I have to have her. Let me go!"

I saw a face, one I almost recognized. He looked at me with a great lake's worth of sadness in his eyes, then raised a fist and cocked his arm. I saw a tattoo on his forearm, the silhouette of a winged woman emerging from the waves, a moment before he swung. There was a flash of pain, then blackness.

⁓ℓℓℓ⁓

"Whaaaa?" I sputtered in shock.

My eyes opened. I sat up abruptly, then fell to the floor again as a wave of déjà vu washed over me. My face was cold and wet, the floor was hard beneath me, and a bunch of people were grabbing my shoulders, arms, and legs. A moment passed before I recognized a new sensation. One that hadn't accompanied my previous awakening. My jaw hurt like hell.

"We'll do this all night if we have to," a voice said, heavy with regret.

I blinked droplets from my eyelids and focused on a familiar face: Oliver Corbyn. He'd dragged a barstool over and was half-sitting, half-standing a short distance away.

"August?" he asked cautiously. "You here? All of you?"

It was a weird question. Weird enough to give me pause when I'd been about to unleash a torrent of curses.

"Of course, I'm here," I muttered. "How could I be anywhere else? The second I wake up, I've got half the town holding me down and you cold-cocking me for no damned reason."

I said the words but didn't quite believe them. Suddenly, what Ollie had asked made a certain amount of sense. I didn't feel like I was all there. Not entirely. There was a part of me that seemed missing. A dark ulcer where my heart should have been. My lips let a soft, pained sound slip through. It was almost a word, a single syllable that sounded suspiciously like, *Her.*

My soul followed that exhalation, and my body readied to follow. In response, Oliver scowled, stood, and pushed up a sleeve.

"No!" I protested. "I'm not. Dammit. I'm just..." I tried, then, "Geezus. Give me a minute. I'm not going anywhere."

The KJ tipped his chin. Someone behind me asked if he was sure, and he nodded again more firmly. Those restraining hands fell away, allowing me to sit up and fold myself into a more comfortable position. I poked experimentally at my sore jaw and decided nothing was broken. At least, not on my face.

"That was a siren," I said, voice flat as the dirty floor I sat on.

"That was," Ollie agreed as he settled back onto his barstool. "She's gone now. She left. Without you. How do you feel about that?"

It was another odd question, but one that was obviously important. I turned my head and saw everyone watching me in trepidation.

"I... Um. I guess..."

I miss her. I need her. I'm nothing without her.

"Not good," I admitted.

"What do you want to do about it?" he asked carefully.

I considered that. Some part of me wanted to follow her wherever she'd gone, but it felt like an amputee's phantom legs wanting to go for a run. The rest of me, though?

"Drink," I announced. "I want a damned drink."

Something like approval showed in Ollie's face. Before I knew what was happening, those hands that had held me down were lifting me up and half-carrying me to the bar. I was deposited on a barstool, and the wide face of Tom the bartender filled my view. Like Ollie, he looked sad, but that didn't stop him from dropping a rocks glass in front of me and pouring out four fingers of whiskey.

I stared at the amber liquid, struggling to comprehend what I was supposed to do next.

"You wanted a drink, August," a burly, bearded man said. "There you go, buddy. It's right there. You can do it."

My eyes narrowed, unsure if what he was saying was true. It seemed so pointless, so meaningless. I stared at the glass, flummoxed.

There was a creaking beside me as the next stool took some weight, then there was an arm around my shoulders. Another rocks glass appeared on the bar, and Tom Hanks tipped a bottle. A hand wrapped around the glass, lifted, and clinked its rim to mine.

"Here's to you being here," a voice said. "Hope it meets your expectations."

A shudder started at the crown of my head and raced down to the soles of my boots. I turned my head, and there was Oliver Corbyn, crooked bucket hat and nylon vest and all. I lifted my glass, took three long swallows, and slammed it down on the bar.

Tom refilled it with another heavy pour, and I downed it in a single throat-searing swig. The whiskey burned its way straight to the jagged hole where my heart had been. Like an iron poker taken from a fire, it cauterized the wound. The bloody torrent of loss dwindled to a trickle. I hoped that someday it would scab over. I knew it would never heal.

"If I'm being honest, Ollie," I said, voice roughened by the whiskey and by memories of my recent jobs, "given my thrice-damned luck, it does. It absolutely does."

Chapter 5

Thomas Wilson

June 7th, 1902

Struck by a wooden steamer near Duluth, MN.

Nine hands lost.

I N MY NOT-SO-DISTANT PAST, I'd been thrown through a window by a werewolf, walloped by a coblyn's contraption, squeezed half to death by a troll, nearly turned to stone by a Gorgon, damn near squished into roadkill by an enraged vampire, glamoured by an elf with a cow's tail, tossed through the night sky by a warlock's wind, chased by a goblin with a meat cleaver, shot by a reptilian, scared witless by an honest-to-god scarecrow, and damn near drowned by a lake monster named Wilson. As I mentally tallied up the abuse my stupid job had dumped on me over the years, I weighed each against what that siren had done. At the end of my careful consideration, I decided that the siren's song took the cake.

The mood in the The Thirsty Gull was somber. Most of the crowd had scurried out. Karaoke wasn't an option after the siren made off with the karaoke machine, and hanging around to feel bad about it wasn't as appealing as one might think. The handful of folks that remained had joined me and Ollie at the bar. At first, they'd been focused on me. How was I? What did I remember? Was the siren's song really that strong? What would I do if I saw the siren again? When my curt answers finally put an end to their questions, they started to question one another.

"How long we gonna let that thing terrorize us like that?"

"Someone ought to put an end to it. A harpoon, right through the heart."

"Snatching folks away is one thing. Taking Ollie's karaoke machine? That's criminal. Downright criminal."

Everyone shook their heads in commiseration. Everyone except Oliver Corbyn. He sat quietly and studied his whiskey.

"What are they talking about?" I asked him in a low voice. "Snatching folks away?"

The fisherman's exhalation could have sent a sailboat halfway across the lake.

"Sirens call out to sailors. Usually, those sailors don't make it home. It doesn't happen often. At least, it hadn't happened often for the last few decades," he said. "Over the past year or so, that changed. It wasn't just sailors going missing. It was folks from right here in town. Some humans, but more often, it's been the PNs that just up and vanish."

"No one thought much of it," one woman admitted. "Like Janulsha, that pretty nix that used to do hair at the Curl Up and Dye. She stopped showing up for work. We all sorta thought she'd just, you know, quit. Moved, or maybe went back to the lake for good."

"Then Arnold last year. He had to work the late shift at the boat works. When his wife woke up, he hadn't come home. They'd been having troubles, though, and he was an ogre, so..." another man added with a shrug to end his explanation for his disappearance.

One by one, they added more names to the list of those who'd gone missing. Given the mercurial nature of many paranormals, the townsfolk had decided it wasn't anything to get too worked up over.

"But with each new realization that someone was gone, someone who'd called Knife River home for years and years... Well, comes a point when you can't just explain it away. Something had to be going on." Oliver said, then added quietly, "And folks are pretty convinced it's been that siren."

There was an angry murmur of agreement.

"And now she's got your karaoke machine," the woman who'd told me about the nix said. "That's not right. It's a bridge too far. Taking people has been horrible. Taking our happiness? Our joy? It's too much, and that's a fact."

"Yeah," another piped up. "That there machine was more than just your personal effects. It was all of ours. You should get that back."

More voices raised in support, and suddenly the small group had packed in more closely around me.

"This is what you do, August," Tom said as he poured another round. "You gotta help

Ollie. Help all of us. You gotta get his KJ stuff back."

Incredulous, I started sputtering.

"Me? What? Why? No! No way. Absolutely not," I protested. "I only get stuff back from someone's ex. It's in the job description. Post-relationship. You were with someone. Now, you're not, and you want your whatever back from your ex. That's my lane. I don't go get shit from people you don't like, especially from murder bird ladies."

I watched everyone deflate like old balloons, and resented the ensuing guilt I felt. This wasn't my problem. If anything, this was a Northern Quorum problem. That shadowy paranormal cabal was much better equipped to deal with the siren. She was fearsome. Deadly. They could clip her wings. It didn't have to be me.

And then Oliver Corbyn whispered something.

"What's that?" I said.

"Hanelle is my ex," he said again louder.

The air rushed out of the room. Everyone looked at Oliver, and every look was one of disbelief.

"What are you saying, Ollie?" one of the guys asked.

"I think he's saying he was dating the siren," Tom Hanks supplied helpfully.

"That's what I thought he said, but that can't be what he said."

Oliver lifted his storm gray eyes and glared at the faces around him.

"It is what I said. And if someone wants to make a fuss about it," he continued while pushing up his shirt sleeves, "we can take that fuss outside."

Eyes blinked. Jaws dropped. Finally, Tom spoke again.

"Hey, c'mon. He was obviously caught by her song or whatever. He got away, but she's still got those wicked claws in his poor heart. That's all. Right Ollie?" he pleaded. "That's what you meant."

Oliver studied his whiskey again, lifted a shoulder, and let it drop.

"Yeah. Sure. That's what I meant."

Over the years, I'd met more than a few people who'd had their heart torn in two. Some were fine wearing the bloody half of their heart on their sleeve. Others tried to hide their true feelings, mask it with false bravado or cheer. After a while, you can tell when they're lying. Not only to you, but to themselves. I looked at Oliver Corbyn and realized the truth of things. What I saw shocked me. One might even say it disgusted me. The thought of someone falling in love with that nightmare bent my brain. And yet...

I lifted my glass, threw back the whiskey, and slammed the glass down with a gasp.

"To hell with it. Fine," I declared. "Ollie, I'll get your karaoke doodad back."

My proclamation pulled the group out of their collective stupor, and a cheer went up. Too many hands started pounding my back. I endured it and even let it boost my spirits a bit. The folks of Knife River were a decent bunch, and Oliver seemed like a standup guy through and through. It just seemed right to help him out in his time of need.

And that's why I'm doing this, I told myself. I'm doing this for him. For him. This is entirely for him.

Later, lying in my cabin's bed while the room spun around me, I kept telling myself that. I was going to find that monster to get Oliver Corbyn's karaoke machine back. It was definitely not because I wanted to see that siren again. Nope. It was most certainly not that.

Chapter 6

SS Robert Wallace
November 17th, 1902
Sank while hauling a cargo of iron ore out of Superior, WI.
All hands survived.

B EING A POST-RELATIONSHIP PERSONAL effects repossession specialist is a funny line of work. At first glance, it's not complicated. Someone has something that isn't really theirs. I show up, explain the reality of things, get the whatever back, and life goes on. It doesn't take a rocket scientist. Just a stubborn willingness to endure uncomfortable situations. Or get thrown through windows. Or teeter on the brink of the end of the world. Or worse, teeter on the brink of the flimsy veil that separates this world from the one beyond.

But I digress.

Most of the time, my work is straightforward enough. I am a neutral party. I don't have any skin in the game. All that messy emotional stuff has zilch to do with me. This particular job, however, was going to be different. Like it or not, I had more than skin in this game, and that worried me. After spending the day wondering how in the hell I'd pull this job off, I ended it pissed off and rudderless. It wasn't the tough job that had me so worked up. It was having no one to talk to about it.

For years, there'd been a constant thread in the volatility of my life: a guy named Jay to talk shit through with. It didn't matter how weird the job turned out to be. Jay was always a sounding board for me. Someone to help me think through the angles, curb my ill-advised impulses, and steer me toward a better way of doing things. Sure, Jay had his quirks, and some were definitely out there. Regardless, he'd always been the one person I could talk to about pretty much whatever. Suddenly, the desire to crack the tab on a can of Grain Belt Pilsner, settle into a beanbag on his studio floor, and share all the details of the past few days was overwhelming. I looked at the walls of my shitty room, grabbed my jacket from the back of a chair, and headed outside.

There was a chill in the air. A frigid reminder that winter came early to northeastern Minnesota. I could smell its telltale scent as I puttered down the highway. Calling Jay meant finding a payphone, and the only one I knew of was at the gas station I'd stopped at earlier in the week.

I killed the engine and blew on my cold hands. A sudden reluctance seized me and made me curse out loud. With a manufactured determination, I stomped over to the phone, shoved in a few coins, and grit my teeth while it rang.

"August," Jay said when he picked up. "Hey! What's up? How are things?"

"Hey," I replied. "Shit. Just realized I forgot something. Hang on."

I set the receiver on top of the boxy thing that used to be the very definition of a phone. After a quick trip back to my bike's sidecar, I returned to the phone and cradled the receiver between my ear and shoulder while I cracked open a can of beer.

"Okay, I'm back. Had to get a beer. You drinking?"

"Oh, crap. No. Um. One sec," he replied. A few moments passed, then, "Alright. I'm back. Good idea."

I smiled as I listed to him take a few swigs. "It's beer o'clock, isn't it? So. Now that we've got the required ingredients for a good, old-fashioned sit and visit, want to hear about my job?"

And just like that, the planet tilted back onto its axis. For a precious few minutes, things actually felt normal. I brought him up to speed on the past week's events. How me singing karaoke had set me up for a whirlwind of jobs in the small town. How the jobs had gone from easy peasy to fitting a giant octopus into a cooler in my bike's sidecar. And how I now had to find an honest-to-god siren and get a karaoke machine back from her.

"Wow, August. I've said it before, and I'll say it again. There are other jobs."

"Yeah, well. Yeah," I agreed sheepishly. "It's not that big of a deal. I mean, I'm sure it'll be fine. It's just..."

"It's just... what?" he prompted.

Saying the next part was harder than I'd imagined it would be. Or rather, it was exactly as hard as I thought it would be, but it surprised me regardless.

"I'm kind-of. Well, it's like... Dammit, Jay. I think I'm in love with the siren."

A long pause followed my friend's surprised laugh, then a single word.

"Seriously?"

"Yup. I mean, maybe? Or maybe not? Could be it's just her song and what that does. Feels like love, though."

I could picture Jay pursing his lips and worrying the tip of a long dreadlock.

"Siren, huh? So, like a mermaid?"

"No. Way worse. More like a harpy, I guess."

"And that's bad."

"Yup."

"Shit," he replied with an uncharacteristic curse.

"Yup."

I heard Jay swallow more of his beer. "So, what are you going to do?"

I barked out a harsh laugh. "My job, I guess. Just, you know. Wish me luck or something. I think I'm going to need it."

"I'll head up. You shouldn't do this alone, August. You said Knife River. I can be there tomorrow. I can be there tonight."

"No!" I protested. "I mean, no. It's not. You don't need to do that. This isn't so bad," I lied. "Just another job. Seriously. You've got other stuff to do."

I could practically hear the gears in Jay's brain turning.

"I am trying to get this new piece done. But that doesn't matter. Not if you're in danger. Say the word, August, and I'm there."

I didn't say the word. Instead, I said words intended to convince Jay things weren't so dire, that siren's reputations were way overblown, that this would be a simple job compared to others I'd survived. I promised I wasn't really in love with her. It was a little glamor. No biggie.

"Well, if you say so," Jay finally conceded. "Just try not almost getting killed this time. Mix things up a bit."

We shared a laugh–mine nervously relieved and his sounding a bit more genuine–and I promised I'd try my best not to die.

"So, the big question is," I said to redirect the conversation, "how do I find her?"

We pooled our collective knowledge about sirens. I had more to offer than Jay, given my very recent experience. Even so, it wasn't much. There are sirens, but also mermaids and harpies. Similar, maybe, but not the same. We tried to untangle the basics. Sirens were half-woman, half-bird. Mermaids were half-woman, half-fish. Sure, both trapped sailors with theirs songs, but that seemed to be the only thing they had in common. Mermaids were more inclined to play with their hapless boy toys. Sirens were prone to eating them if they didn't drown first, or eating them after they'd drowned. Either way, a siren's song was more of a dinner bell than anything else. Where sirens and harpies differed was that harpies couldn't sing. Or, if they could, Jay decided they'd probably sound even worse than me doing karaoke.

"I wasn't that bad," I grumbled.

"Oh, I'm sure you were great," he said with a lack of sincerity that made me grin.

After settling on what seemed to be the most helpful distinction, that sirens were more birdlike whereas mermaids were more fishlike, Jay suggested considering where other birds nested.

"I mean, if she's like a hawk or a falcon, would that help? Hang on one sec. I'll do a quick search."

I heard the clacking of fingers on a keyboard. Then Jay shared falcons liked to nest on cliff ledges or in broken trees.

"Not helpful," I complained. "This is the North Shore. There are hundreds of miles of cliffs and probably a million broken trees."

"Yeah," Jay agreed. "And we have no way of knowing how big their territories are. An eagle's can be up to fifteen square miles. If that siren is human-sized, that's like what, maybe ten times bigger than an eagle?"

Jay prattled on with his strange math and esoteric estimating. Meanwhile, something about the word 'territory' was scratching at a recent recollection.

"A lighthouse," I blurted. "I need to find a lighthouse."

The artist-turned-warlock asked why, so I shared a quick sketch of my trip to Split Rock. After mentioning the annoying tourist and his guidebook about lighthouses marking the territories of terrible PNs, Jay's fingers clacked in the background. Suddenly, he was peppering me with questions. What did it look like? Where did he get it? Did he mention the title?

I told him what I knew, which wasn't much. Then he whooped, the sound almost causing me to drop the phone.

"Found it. Yup. It's a guide to North American lighthouses by some guy named Henry. One sec. I'm grabbing the ebook version."

I added a few more coins to the payphone and blew on my stiff fingers.

"I'm fricking freezing here, Jay."

"Hang on! Just hang on. Okay. Minnesota. Minnesota... Hmmm. Not many here. Let's try Michigan. Whoah. Almost a hundred and thirty. Crap. One more sec."

More clacking filled my ear.

"Okay, much better," he proclaimed. "I pulled up a map so we can narrow the scope a bit. Maybe I should search a radius from Knife River?"

Despite myself, Jay's enthusiasm was infectious.

"Try islands," I said, inspired. "A siren wouldn't be on shore. She'd want to be out where the ships are a long way from home, right?"

"Good idea. Oh! Isle Royale. Rock of Ages lighthouse. Let me check that one."

I nodded approvingly, then remembered he couldn't see me.

"Good name. Sounds promising."

Jay sucked in a breath. "It's more than promising, August. I think this is it. Holy crap. I think this is it. Listen."

Jay prattled off some details about when the lighthouse was built, how it ended up being part of Michigan's territory instead of Minnesota, and other tidbits that meant exactly nothing to me. Then he got to the juicy part.

"As was common during the Westward Expansion, the lighthouse served a dual purpose. Isle Royale was the largest and highest island of an archipelago, with over four hundred and fifty smaller islands covering eight hundred and fifty square miles. The addition of a lighthouse to warn ships of the danger posed by the islands and shallow waters was necessary to mitigate the risk of ships bottoming out. What most accounts of its history neglect to mention, though, is that the Isle Royale was also believed to harbor a fearsome siren that preyed on sailors. Ship captains that saw the light knew that they not only needed to give a wide berth, but to also restrain members of their crew who were of weaker constitution, or to stopper their ears with bits of rags. Construction of the lighthouse was dangerous, but less so than trying to rid the isle of its evil."

"Well, that settles that," I commented.

"Teamwork makes the dream work," Jay replied with a laugh.

The lure of comradery was almost as strong as the siren's call. For a moment, it was like it had always been. Me and my best friend figuring shit out together. Then I made the mistake of exhaling. My breath made a wispy cloud in the cold air. Instantly, I pictured a spirit being drawn out of a haunted spoon, and the look in Jay's eyes when he nearly damned that poor woman's spirit to a horrible second life.

A shudder shook me out of my dark musing, and I heard Jay offering helpful tips, like seeing if I could fit a life preserver over a suit of armor. I forced out a laugh, then awkwardly said I was out of change. We made a quick farewell, and I hung up the phone.

Maybe everything's fine, I told myself. *He sounded fine. Completely normal. Maybe you were worried about nothing.*

Uh huh, I replied. *Nothing at all. Right.*

My worrying about Jay was teetering on obsessing about Jay, so I gave myself a mental shove. There were more immediate concerns than what Jay might or might not be doing while I was away. Top of the list was how to get to an island somewhere in the middle of a Great Lake. The Guzzi offered a lot of perks, but it didn't float.

Speaking of my old bike, it took a bit of convincing, then grudgingly agreed to run until I got back to my cabin. I pulled a beer from the fridge, settled into the cracked and weathered Adirondack chair by the fire pit, and stared out past where the gray water met the gray clouds. Somewhere out there, a siren squatted in her nest. My imagination filled in the details, like the nest being made of human bones. I was going to do something stupid. That had never stopped me before, though, and wasn't likely to this time. Especially when the lady at the other end of that decision had her talons sunk deep into my tattered heart.

A decent percentage of the fridge's beer was gone and the sun had long since set when I decided to call it a night. Despite knowing I'd need to be rested for the day ahead, it took a long time to fall asleep. Every time I tried, I imagined a softly singing voice, sat up eagerly, then flopped down, dejected. Finally, my blood's alcohol content drew me into a fitful slumber. A slumber full of nightmares dressed up like happy dreams.

⁓

The marina seemed like the best place to start. When the sun's first rays cracked the far-off horizon, me and my hangover were waiting by the docks.

"Rock of Ages?" I asked a couple that were clearly retirees. "Isle Royale? You heading anywhere near Rock of Ages or that Royal Island place?"

The pair gave me a wide berth, as did a group of corporate bros before they headed out on a small but expensive looking yacht. The working folk, ones that just wanted to sail out, catch their limit, and head home, all shook their heads. Only one sailor, a woman I recognized from the Gull, stopped. When she did, she put a weathered hand on my shoulder.

"We know you mean well, but you don't want to be going out there," she said.

"Damned right, I don't," I replied. "Someone has to, though. Might as well be me."

That earned me a look of grudging respect, but she followed it with, "Stupid landlubber," and went on her way.

My bravado from the night before wasn't enjoying the new day's dose of reality. I'd thrown down the gauntlet. Boldly proclaimed I was going to do a thing. A thing so audacious that only the clinically insane would consider doing it. And I'd done that without a single thought as to how I'd actually get to the place I needed to go.

"Fucking hell, August," I muttered.

I considered my options, of which there were few. I could wait, night after night, in the karaoke bar and see if the siren popped by again. It was an appealing option, mainly because I knew the odds were low that she would. Another would be to charter a boat. Totally feasible. People did it all the time. Of course, those people had money or at least credit cards. I'd only brought enough cash to keep a roof over my head and beer in the fridge for a few weeks. The other choice, backing out, was untenable. With a glower, I squared my shoulders, stuck up my thumb, and kept asking the departing boaters if I could hitch a ride. All said no until someone didn't.

"We're going past Rock of Ages," the man replied through lips that barely moved.

"But you can't come," the woman with him added sharply. "Sorry, not sorry."

They were an odd pair, and neither looked seaworthy. He was maybe in his early sixties and immaculate. My first thought was that he couldn't be real because no real thing could be so clean and tidy. That notion had just crossed my mind when he pulled a bottle of hand sanitizer from a satchel and scrubbed his hands. I scrutinized his artfully arranged silver hair and carefully trimmed white beard, the precise lines of a recently ironed shirt and creased khakis, the boat shoes–his only indication of the day's chosen activity–that seemed like they'd just been removed from the box. While I studied him, he slid a phone from his pocket, tapped its screen, swiped a few times, and put it away with a cryptic *hmph.*

The woman beside him, the one that had just told me I couldn't hitch a ride, looked to be barely a third his age. Where he projected order and discipline and–if we're being honest–more than a little OCD, she… didn't. I wondered if she'd ever combed her hair or if she always tied it up with whatever was in arm's reach. I wondered if she realized her sweatshirt was on inside-out. I wondered if her thick corduroy trousers would ever dry after some lake spray hit them. Her only concessions to going on a boat were her sandals, a style with nylon straps that wrapped around her feet and ankles. As long as she only encountered ankle-deep water, she'd only suffer frozen toes. Anything more, and the lady would be soggy for days. Not that I was in a position to judge. My boots, jeans, and biker jacket weren't exactly sailing attire. I did judge, though. I hadn't planned on a taking a boat ride when I'd headed north from Minneapolis, so my lack of boat clothes made sense. She had planned to go on a boat, which made her outfit look stupid.

"Perhaps he has some experience with boats," the older man suggested. "You and I would certainly benefit from that."

"Sh'yah," she scoffed. "I'll bet he doesn't even know which side goes in the water."

Like him, she had a bag over her shoulder. Unlike his satchel, which looked expensive and perfectly suited to its intended purpose, her backpack looked like it had fallen off a bus and been run over by a car, and then stuffed with reams of paper taken from a recycling bin. Most of that paper was about to fall out, seeing as how she'd neglected to zip the bag shut.

"At least I know how to use a zipper," I shot back. If we were going with insults, I hoped the kid had plenty of ice ready for the impending burns.

"Do you know anything about boats?" she challenged while shoving at the papers and yanking the zipper shut.

"I know I need one to get to Isle Royale. It's an island with a lighthouse over there," I said with a vague wave of my hand.

"We know what it is," the woman snapped. "We know where it is. We know how to get there. What we don't need is someone else coming with."

She'd pointed the last remark at her colleague. In response, he gave me another long appraisal.

"What's out there for you?" he asked.

My words came out in a flat monotone. "Visiting a friend. Just need to pop by and pick something up, then I'm out of your hair."

"You'll be on our boat. That means you'll be in our hair," the man said.

I wrangled my impatience into submission. "Sure, but after that, I'm out of your hair. Which is very nice, by the way. Yours?" I added with a skewed look at the girl, "Yeah. Not so much."

"Where are you from?" the man asked unexpectedly.

"Here," I lied.

The younger woman scoffed and tacked on a, "Liar." The way she said it was so salty, I worried about all the freshwater fish in the lake.

"A moment," the man said, "to confer with my colleague."

I muttered something about not having all day and walked a few paces down the dock. While they conferred or whatever, I ignored the part of my brain that was screaming at all my stupid choices.

Do NOT go to Rock of Ages. Dude, listen. Seriously. Don't go. If you do, you die. Hell, these two might die.

That last bit caught on a thread of guilt and tugged. I landed myself in plenty of messes. Dragging a couple of innocent bystanders into this one? Putting them in harm's way? I'm a jerk, not an asshole, and making those two go anywhere near that damned siren was textbook asshole.

It's daytime, though, so they should be safe, I decided.

Uh huh. Because your extensive research concluded beyond all doubt that sirens only hunt at night.

The risk was too great. I drew a breath and readied myself to send them on their way. Before I could, though, the man beckoned with his perfectly manicured fingers.

"Come aboard," he said. "We'll take you."

The first leg of the journey consisted of me learning things I didn't really care to learn. The first thing I learned was his name: Cedric Mulberry the Third. It was presented as something of great significance. Then I learned he was a theoretical physicist, astronomer, and mathematician. He had won a Nobel Prize in astrophysics and currently taught at an Ivy League school. He had more letters after his name than I had in my actual name. I knew this because he told me, even though I hadn't asked.

Lana Delridge was a graduate student at the same snobby university. She graduated from high school top of her class, was the undergrad valedictorian, and was now riding a full scholarship for a combined course of study in physics, thermal dynamics, and astronomy. Her thesis was on extraterrestrial metallic compounds. I knew this because Cedric told me, albeit with a surreptitious roll of his eyes. The charming Miss Delridge herself hadn't spoken a single word to me since I'd stepped onto their boat.

The trip was about as exciting as one might imagine, which is to say it wasn't exciting at all. A few boats of various sizes passed on either side, including a cargo ship that was big as a city block. Soon, though, it was just us. According to Cedric, it was around a hundred and twenty-five miles to Isle Royale. I had no way of knowing how fast we were going, but guessed it had to be fifty, maybe even sixty miles an hour. That meant a couple hours, give or take, before we reached the lighthouse. The weather was on our side and the water was smooth. I only wished the boat could go faster.

An hour or so into our journey, Lana retrieved a metal suitcase from a stowaway hatch. It looked like a serious piece of hardware. Like you could drop a nuke on it and count yourself lucky if you managed to scuff its shiny finish. Her thumbs worked at the combination dials, then she cast a wicked glance over her shoulder at me and shifted her body to block my view. A moment later, the case popped open to reveal a computer. A monitor filled one half, and a keyboard the other. Lana sat on the bench, industrial laptop settled appropriately on her lap, and started tapping at the keys.

"Test script running," she intoned. "Compiling. Results, ninety-seven percent. MBE is working. Spectrometer parameters are optimized. Organic and inorganic compounds accounted for with a twenty-three percent deviation to account for unknowns."

"Twenty-three?" Cedric asked, glancing over his shoulder. "That's generous."

"We don't know what's down there," she pushed back. "Isn't it better to get more data and analyze it?"

"It is, but we also don't need false-positives," he chided. "Perhaps someday, you'll understand. The scientific community is not kind in their peer reviews. Even the slightest whiff of uncertainty, and they'll eat you alive."

Lana chewed her lip. "Sorry, professor. I'll adjust. One sec."

Her fingers tapped relentlessly on the keyboard. The clacking ratcheted up in ferocity and frustrated huffs began punctuating the keystrokes.

"Tightened up the tolerances. Scanning. Still nothing."

Cedric sighed dramatically. He eased up on the throttle, then moved to stand over her shoulder.

"Your triangulation appears to be acceptable. I might have done..." he said, then placed a hand on her shoulder and reached over with the other. A perfectly manicured fingernail tapped on the keys. "That. Now your scans should deliver more nuanced results."

Lana blushed, and that hand resting on her shoulder gave it a condescending pat.

"You did your best," Cedric said.

I watched the exchange with a puckered mouth and narrowed eyes. I hated backhanded compliments. If you want to insult someone, just do it and be done with it. Rolling up an insult in a cute little jumper and sticking a 'you did your best' bow in its hair is too much work. Me and Cedric differed in that opinion. The truly unfortunate part, though, was that Lana was oblivious. I watched the effect his words had on her and cringed. She honestly thought he was complimenting her.

"I'm so glad I could help, professor," she gushed.

In any other circumstances, I thought ruefully, *she'd be a client inside of a week. Guaran-frickin-teed.*

Cedric returned to the boat's controls. He slid the throttle forward, and we picked up speed.

"Isle Royale has a dock," he said without turning. "We can drop you off, then circle back. How long do you think you need to do whatever it is you're going to do?"

It was a good question. One that I had no way to answer.

"Maybe ten minutes. Maybe an hour. It all depends on..."

Her, I thought.

"... how it goes," I said aloud.

"Well, however it goes, you'll need to be there for about two hours."

"Two?" I gasped. "C'mon. You aren't serious."

Cedric's shoulder lifted a fraction of an inch. "There's an old allegory about beggars and choosers. You should read it sometime."

"That assumes he can read," Lana added.

"I don't like you," I said.

"Right back at'cha."

Her animosity didn't bother me. It was clear what was behind it. Lana had obviously expected to have Cedric all to herself for a day on the lake. I was the proverbial third wheel.

"Fine. Two hours is fine. Just. You know. If you can make it less, that'd be swell."

Lana scowled. Cedric ignored me. Maybe a half hour later, a small mound on the horizon marred the endless expanse of water. Once I'd noticed it, I watched it grow and take shape. Unprompted, Cedric started to lecture his captive audience about the collection of rocks called Isle Royale. If Jay had given me the CliffsNotes, Cedric was determined to give me the entire tome. In 1783, the Treaty of Paris established the boundary between the United States and Canada. Despite being closer to the latter, rumors of rich copper deposits made Benjamin Franklin squiggle the country's proposed border above the island so it fit inside the United States. Despite being closer to Minnesota than Michigan, Minnesota wasn't a state yet, so Michigan got to claim the island as its own.

"Wow," I muttered, doing my best with that single syllable to express how not interested I was. Despite his apparent smarts, Cedric apparently didn't know what sarcasm was. He continued to lecture, shifting effortlessly from a history lesson to a biology one. Isle Royale was uninhabited. It was designated as an International Biosphere Reserve in 1980. It was home to only nineteen mammal species. From there, he segued to geology. It wasn't an island. It was a archipelago. The islands resulted from a geologic syncline, or folds in layers of rock caused by an ice-age glacial advance about twelve-thousand years ago. The bedrock held numerous minerals, including prehnite, datolite, quartz, calcite, and pumpellyite.

"Wow," I said again.

"Shut up," Lana snapped. "You have no idea how lucky you are. People travel from all over the world to hear the professor speak."

"Whatever you say, Mary Ann."

She added a little confusion to the mix of animosity and disdain in her glare.

"Mary Ann? From *Gilligan's Island*?" I said. When she continued to stare, I laughed. "Seriously? Huh. And you call yourself educated."

"Ignore him, Miss Delridge. He's referring to a ridiculous television show that originated in the early 1960s. It followed the supposedly comedic antics of seven castaways. One was a professor. Another was a woman named Mary Ann."

"Who was totally into the professor," I said sagely, then smiled at Lana's blush.

By the time the boat reached the island's dock, I'm not sure who was happier: me or Lana Delridge.

Chapter 7

There was only one good thing about my situation: I had made it to the Rock of Ages Lighthouse. Everything else basically sucked. I was stranded and fully at the whim of some stuffy academic and an ill-tempered grad student. I was freezing. Gordon Lightfoot had sung about the gales of November. My immediate concern was the stiff breeze of October. The wind cut through my jeans, and my biker jacket had style, but no insulation. Within minutes, my ears hurt, my fingers ached, and my teeth chattered when I tried to curse.

Also, I might have made a bit of a strategic blunder. Shocking, I know. I'd been in such a rush to get off the phone with Jay that we hadn't really gotten the lay of the land. Yes, we learned that Isle Royale was an archipelago, and yes, we learned its lighthouse served as a warning about a siren's territory. The dots hadn't connected for me, though, until that moment. That archipelago had hundreds of little islands poking up from the water. Rock of Ages, the one I was standing on, had the lighthouse and the best name. Cool, but there was no way of knowing if it was where the siren nested. The big island had all the hiking trails and camping sites. Seemed like it would be a bit busy for a solitary killer. The other four-hundred or so little islands, though? Any one of them might be where I needed to go.

"Shit," I muttered, my chattering teeth making it come out as *shit-t-t-t*.

I don't know what I'd been expecting. My job usually came with an address for a place that didn't cover hundreds of square miles.

"Welp, August. You really outdid yourself this time."

I looked across the Rock of Ages. From the dock, you could see the big island stretching off into the distance. I craned my neck and looked up to the top of the lighthouse. It had to be over a hundred feet tall and likely offered a hell of a view.

"And it's got to be warmer inside, too," I reasoned. "Okay, then. Into the spooky lighthouse, I go."

The lighthouse's double doors were metal and painted the same dark blue as the lighthouse's base. A decorative portico framed the door and offered some small shelter from the wind. It amused me to see the brass numbers of an address on its front. The thought of a mailman being at the only building on the rocks and wondering if he'd found the right mail slot tickled my odd sense of humor, and I laughed. Then I remembered why I was there, and the laughter died. When I tugged experimentally, the door moved on hinges desperately in need of oil. I turned my shoulders to fit through the opening and stepped inside.

Unsurprisingly, the room was roughly circular. I knew from Cedric's lecture that the lighthouse wasn't manned. Someone automated it decades ago. Even so, I hadn't expected being unmanned to mean it would be a shithole. Bare concrete walls started at a bare concrete floor and ended at a bare concrete ceiling. Together, they contained a cluttered and cruddy space. Some time back, a few well-intentioned folks must have planned on fixing things up. They'd moved in metal tables and five-gallon pails. Saw horses and gallons of paint. Even a toaster oven that likely hadn't toasted anything for years. After careful consideration of the leprous-looking walls, water stains, pervasive mold, and many cracks, they'd obviously thrown up their hands, quit, and left their crap behind. The room offered nothing but a decent risk of tetanus, a set of iron stairs climbing up the far wall, and a concrete stairway plunging into darkness. Annoyed, I considered my options. I was cold and more than a little scared. Exploring the pitch black depths beneath the lighthouse wasn't going to alleviate either of those. The only way to go was up.

The wrought iron treads were rough under my boots. After ten or twelve steps, the curved stairs opened to the next floor. This one was nearly as bad as the first. The remodeling crew had made a bit more progress. Studs framed a few interior walls. That was it, though. As below, the work looked abandoned more than unfinished. Rubble sat in random piles with the occasional hammer or tape measure in the mix. I looked around in the anemic light, decided there was nothing of interest, and continued up.

The third level was a marked improvement. First, my feet stood on a proper floor. Hand planed wooden boards stained a rich honey gold filled the circular space. The windows had been cleaned recently enough to let the afternoon's waning light through. I peeked out of one and whistled at the view. The top was definitely going to give me a good vantage point.

How many stories is this thing, anyway? I wondered. *I hate stairs.*

Since there was only one way to find out, I continued my ascent.

The fourth and fifth floors, each progressively smaller, must've been bedrooms. There were two metal bedframes per floor, springs laid bare. Whatever removed the mattresses from the rooms had not done so gently. Scraps of fabric and stuffing were everywhere. It was my first hint that things weren't right, but I was never the best at noticing the obvious. I stepped over deep gouges in the floorboards and continued up.

The sixth floor was barely big enough for the square wooden table it held. I imagined the lighthouse keeper playing solitaire on its top and shook my head in wonder. The thought of living in the stacked collection of rooms and keeping the lantern lit hour after hour, day after day, threatened madness. If that wasn't enough to send my brain spinning, finally noticing the room's sole occupant was.

The siren squatted in a nest of shredded mattresses. Those creepy orbs that served as her eyes regarded me. A tense moment passed as we studied one another. I had no idea what she was thinking. For my part, I was thinking something really unhelpful.

Oh. There she is, my stupid brain observed.

Yeah, like I said: not helpful.

I saw her jaw loosen and chest expand with an indrawn breath. When she exhaled, it came out as a long and haunting series of notes. If I'd still been human, I'd have been screwed. Fortunately, I wasn't. While the siren sang, a Maine Coon cat squirmed out from beneath a leather jacket, arched its back, and simply didn't give a shit.

The cat was an impulsive gamble. I'd hoped that something so supremely self-absorbed might be immune to the murder bird's charms, and I'd been right. I'd also hoped that if things did get rough, the cat might do okay. I'd read once that cats killed billions of birds each year. Maybe not ones as big as the siren, but still. Dare to dream.

"Clever shifter," the siren said in a creaky voice.

I gave myself a good shake and sat. My tail curled around my paws, and my eyes regarded the thing across from me. Despite my outward calm, a small storm of panic was brewing inside. I wasn't great at planning ahead, and had only thought about how to find the siren's nest. What I'd do when I did? That remained a bit fuzzy. Now, my lack of planning was biting me in my furry little behind. As I considered the rows of pointed teeth peeking through her parted lips, I decided that was better than actually getting bitten in my furry little behind. How to keep all the biting metaphorical rather than literal, though? I didn't have a flipping clue.

"Cat got your tongue?" the siren asked tartly. "Shift. C'mon, shifter. Shift. I won't do anything," she said in a tone she probably imagined was coy. "Pinky swear. I'm just curious. You came here. Shift so you can tell me why."

My ears folded back and my eyes narrowed as I considered what I had to do.

Knock, knock, I thought. *Death? You home?*

A moment later, human me sat buck naked on the floor of a siren's bedroom. I drew my knees up and wrapped my arms around them. Partly for modesty, but more because it was cold up there. Although, to be honest, I held myself tight, arms pulled against my shins and knees pressed into my chest, to hold myself back. The second—the literal second—that I'd become human again, the urge to throw myself into her embrace blotted out damned near everything else. Keeping that suicidal impulse in check took a lot of effort, a fact the siren noted.

"You want?" she asked with a playful shimmy of her shoulders that sent her pendulous and veined breasts swaying.

My breath came out in a pained sigh. She sighed as well, but in disgust.

"Of course you do," she intoned. Her wings stretched, shook irritably, and folded in against her back. "Why are you here?" she asked again.

Habit made my hand reach for a pocket inside my jacket. When my fingers brushed the bare skin of my chest, I remembered that the shiny black Schott Perfecto—my pride and joy—was underneath me, not on me. Pulling my card out of my ass might've had a certain humor to it, but nothing about that moment was funny. Especially the part where my bare ass was on my favorite jacket, and the jacket was on a dingy, dirty floor.

"I'm August Shade," I proclaimed into the awkward silence. "Post-relationship personal effects repossession specialist."

Hanelle cocked her head to the side, a slight crease between her black eyes.

"I get people's favorite whatever back after a breakup," I explained. "You have something of my client's, and I'd like you to return it."

Not gonna lie. I was feeling pretty damned proud of myself in that moment. I hadn't thrown myself at her, nor had I shit myself. Both were significant wins in my book. Most importantly, though, my voice managed to sound calm. One might even say blasé. I was cool as a cucumber, right up until she laughed at me.

The siren's song had filled me to bursting with unslakable desire. Her laugh? Ouch. Over the years, plenty of people, human and otherwise, had done their best to make me feel like shit. Some even did a pretty good job. In that moment, I realized they were all amateurs. Minor league. Hell, they were pee-wees. The siren's laugh sized me up and discarded me. Scraped me off her metaphorical boot. The way she laughed at me, I doubted she'd have even registered I'd been stuck in her boot treads.

Needless to say, it pissed me off. I was cold and naked and miserable, my insides torn between an unnatural desire and a very natural fear. All I wanted was Ollie's karaoke machine. Things didn't have to get mean, but she just had to go there. I considered saying something snarky. I considered giving her the finger. Neither felt truly suited to the moment. Only a master of disdain, a true pro, could hope to stand against the siren's spite. And so...

A breath later, the Maine Coon was back. My ears flicked. My tail swished. Then I rocked back, lifted a rear leg, folded forward, and licked my own asshole. It was a move I knew I'd regret later, but extraordinary circumstances called for extraordinary measures. Nothing—and I mean nothing in the whole damned world— makes you realize how completely worthless you are like having a cat stare you straight in the eyes... and then choose its own butthole over you.

I'd heard the siren's song. I'd heard her haughty and heartless laugh. That really should have been enough. I didn't need to hear her scream. The only silver lining in that particular cloud was that it gave me warning, and that split second saved my life.

There was no explaining how something so ill-formed and ungainly could move so fast. One second, the damned fiend was glaring at me from across the room. The next, gouges appeared in the floor where my cat butt had been. That butt, and the rest of me, had skittered to the side and was high-tailing it for the stairs. A whoosh of air ruffled my fur when her wings beat, and a loud slam followed the wooden table being tossed aside.

I scurried down the curving stairway to the level below. Sharp claws grated on the metal steps and angry fists pounded the walls as the siren followed. My much smaller size gave me the advantage in the close quarters, and the siren fell farther behind. I'd made it to the third story, then the second, and was feeling pretty damned cocky about my odds of survival... right up until I realized there was nowhere to go. I was on an island. I didn't have a boat. I didn't have a shift capable of swimming any significant distance. The only bird in my repertoire was a worthless turkey. If I tried to fly away, the siren would snatch me from the sky easy as a hawk plucking a chickadee up for a snack.

My furry paws skidded on the ground floor's dirty concrete. I could hear the siren, still a couple of floors above me, but raging her way down fast. Fleeing was off the table. That left hiding or fighting. With only a scant few seconds to decide, I opted for the former. Sure, I could shift into a wolverine, a gorilla, a goddamned elephant. All were badass in their own ways. Hanelle, though, was a murder machine. Decision made, I whipped my head around in search of a place to squeeze into. Unfortunately, the only option would've been to flip a five-gallon pail over, curl up underneath it, and hope the siren was as dumb as I felt.

The jig was up. In a handful of seconds, I'd be the Dearly Departed Post-Relationship Personal Effects Repossession Specialist, August Shade.

And then I remembered the other stairs. The ones that went down.

Choosing is easy when you're out of choices, I thought, then I ran.

Condensation slicked the concrete. The usually nimble cat slipped and slid its way toward a multitude of compound fractures, and then there was a floor. I paused to give myself a moment to think and look around.

Fun fact: cats can see in the dark.

Not so fun fact: they can't see in total darkness. There has to be a little light. Next to nothing by human eye standards, but still something.

As I hunched in the lighthouse bowels, my predicament became abundantly clear. You can't hide if you can't see anything to hide under. I cautiously extended a furry paw, fervently hoping my sensitive whiskers and delicate nose would prevent me from stepping on a rat trap or falling down a pit. What I sensed was cold and damp. Must and mildew and... other things.

Shifting is a funny thing. When I become something else, it can be disorienting. Not because being something else is hard. No, it's because retaining some semblance of myself in that foreign body is tough. Our human brains are wired for human eyeballs, human ears, human noses, and human tastebuds. As you might imagine, they work wonderfully together. When all those human expectations of how things should look, sound, smell, and taste get signals from an animal's senses... Welp. It's weird. Really weird. So when my kitty nose sniffed, what it smelled confused me. I knew I'd gone to a remote place. No one had manned the Rock of Ages lighthouse in years, and it wasn't exactly a tourist destination. Which meant that smelling all the people made no sense. None at all.

The other impression I had in that perfectly black chamber was a distinct lack of space. Not that the room itself wasn't sizeable. I had no way of knowing, but felt pretty confident that it filled a good chunk of the lighthouse's base. That meant a big room. I could hear the lake's ceaseless movement telegraphed through the bedrock and walls. It should have made my surroundings feel hollow, even cavernous. Instead, whatever was around me muted and dampened that relentless pounding. The only bright spot I could find was that maybe, just maybe, there'd be a place to hide.

My whiskers twitched, and a paw blindly quested. Sure enough, I encountered something. It wasn't stone or concrete. It gave way when I pressed, like a curtain. Encouraged, I rubbed my head against it and slid sideways in search of a part. Instead, a small, hard, and round thing bumped my ear. A careful exploration up a few inches revealed another, then a third.

Buttons? I realized. *A shirt?*

I didn't have time to wonder. The siren had been stomping her taloned feet around the room above. Now, her steps were descending the stairs.

"Shifter," she crooned. "You shouldn't be down there. No, no. This is for what you leave behind."

I knew better than to ask what she meant. Never mind that all I could say were variations of the word 'meow.' Even the slightest noise would give me up. I forced the damned cat to keep its trap shut and waited.

Talons scraped on concrete as the siren descended. That was creepy as hell, but she decided to dial it up a notch by dragging a few claws along the wall., too.

"Come out, shifter. Come out. I will not hurt you. Maybe I'll sing for you. You would like that, wouldn't you? Of course, you would."

Her footsteps came closer, and along with them, a distinct odor. When I'd been human, I hadn't noticed more than a mildewy funk coming from the siren. The cat, unfortunately, had a much better nose, and something awful filled its nostrils. Her scent crawled up my nostrils like unwashed rats. My little sliver of humanness resisted its effect. The cat? The damned thing sneezed.

"Ah," her creaky voice whispered.

I tensed, sure that her long, razor-tipped fingers were going to wrap themselves around the Maine Coon's neck. Instead, I heard the soft scrape of glass against metal, then smelled something oily and fishy. There was a quick scratch across a rough surface, and sulfur tinged the air. That last bit was honestly a relief. For the briefest of moments, it overpowered the siren's B.O. A burst of light followed and set my eyes blinking. I peered through my hiding spot's seam. The siren was in full view, lit with the wavery orange of an oil lamp's flame. She placed the clear glass back on its base and turned a brass key to adjust the flame's height. Satisfied, she settled into a crouch. Knees that bent the wrong way made it easy. Her palms rested on the bare floor, pendulous breasts framed by her arms. Her pose called to mind Egypt's Sphinx, albeit one from a feverish nightmare. Black eyes pierced my completely worthless hiding spot. Worthless or not, though, I had zero intention of leaving it.

"See, scaredy cat? Nothing to be afraid of. You were rude earlier, but that's okay. We all have our moments, don't we? Now, come out from under there. Talk to me. I promise I'll behave. Well," she amended with what she probably thought was a seductive shimmy of her shoulders, "I'll try. Come out, August Shade."

Something in that last request caught me. Until that moment, the only vibes I'd gotten from the siren were the bad kind. When she said my name, though, I could've sworn it sounded... sad? Lonely? Even pleading?

Let's hope I have a few of those nine lives left, I thought. The Maine Coon pushed its way free of the shirt and looked around. Cat eyes see funny, but still well enough to leave me shocked by what they saw. The room was full of stuff, in spots almost to its low ceiling. It wasn't like the upper floors, where people had tried a little sprucing up. This was something else entirely. A chaotic dumping ground. A hoarder's fever dream. After a quick inspection, I pointed a wary stare at the siren. She responded by relaxing further into her repose. It was as non-threatening as I'd seen her look. To be clear, she still looked threatening, just in a 'maybe later' sort of way. With a mental, *fuck it,* I shifted. The big, fluffy cat was gone. In its place, a naked guy rose up from his hands and knees.

"It's cold in here," she observed with a downward glance.

My middle finger twitched, but I kept it in check.

"Guess I've got some options," I remarked with a half-wave at the many shirts and trousers strewn around the space like a tornado-ravaged department store. "Mind if I grab some pants?"

The look that crossed her face was harder to fathom than the lake's mighty depths.

"Sure," she said in a way that didn't feel like she'd meant it.

Well, too bad. I'm sick of being naked all the time.

I cast about, my supposed indecision buying me time to understand what I was seeing. I updated my earlier thought that I was in a basement and replaced the word 'basement' with 'cellar.' Why that seemed like an important distinction, I couldn't say. Shockingly, it also wasn't as deep as the lighthouse structure went. Opposite where I'd come in, another dark hole plunged through the floor. If I had to guess, those stairs likely descended to the first circle of hell.

I'd been right about hiding behind a shirt. It draped a chair's seat like a cast-off skin. The fellow it had belonged to must have been big. There was enough fabric to span the chair's arms and still hang down to the floor. Its owner had either been into historical reenactments or the shirt was really old. Linen that might've been white had faded to a dingy gray. It was collarless and had wide sleeves that called to mind a pirate costume. The chair it covered looked old as well. Its wood was weathered. The leather pad tacked to its seat was dry and cracked. Despite its obvious age, it had been nice in its day. Hand-carved with loving detail. The posts framing the back resembled fish standing on their tails. Stylized waves served as a lower cross rail. The one across its middle showed an oar ship with a square sail and a dragon head at its prow. The top rail had a stylized sun at its center and billowy clouds extending to either side. I wasn't an antiquer by any stretch, but even my ignorant ass could tell it would fetch a crazy good price at an auction. Beside it, a stack of wooden crates with paper labels flaking into dust. Their faded labels proclaimed they'd once held rum.

"Rumrunner," the siren said dismissively. "Fancied himself a viking pirate, the fool."

That was telling. I knew that during Prohibition, Canadians had smuggled booze into the States. I also knew that Prohibition was a long time ago, like 1920s long time ago, which meant that the siren looked pretty good for a lady her age. If she'd known the guy with the pirate shirt and fancy chair, she was at least a hundred years old. I wouldn't have pegged her for a day over ninety-seven. Those thoughts crossed my mind as I gauged the length of the shirt and decided to rock a nightgown look. The siren make a low noise, far back in her throat, as I pulled it on, but she stayed seated. After concealing my nakedness–well, all except my skinny calves and bare feet–I tilted my head toward the rest of the cellar's contents and raised an eyebrow.

"Go on. Look," she said. "It's not like I'm doing anything with it."

Permission granted, I stepped carefully around the room and inspected its contents. As a thrift store aficionado, I fancied myself an expert on old and odd clothes, but the room's contents left me stunned. The eclectic mix of clothing didn't span decades. It spanned centuries.

I saw a *Limp Bizkit* tee-shirt. A pair of oiled leather overalls. A pocketed fisherman's vest, not unlike what Ollie favored. A black and white striped long-sleeved shirt full of hand-stitched repairs. Hats that ran the gamut from leather tricorns to baseball caps with modern team logos. The cellar was a mishmash of time capsules. A steamer trunk. An iPod the size of a book. A hand-forged iron harpoon. A flashy graphite fishing rod with a gleaming reel. Antique pocket watches and cheap digital Casios with long dead batteries and even an honest-to-god Rolex. Bills and coins, American and Canadian and other currencies I didn't recognize, covered everything like expensive confetti. A story formed in my mind, one stuck on an endless loop stretching over long years. Someone on a boat heard the siren's song. If they survived to reach her nest, they offered up whatever they had, desperate for her affection. The cellar told of their fate.

"Yeah, dating sucks," I decided.

The siren's black eyes widened, then narrowed.

"It does," she agreed.

I discerned a shift in the room's mood, subtle but real. No more did I feel like a mouse cornered by the cat. Or the cat cornered by the murder bird, or whatever. That's not to say that I didn't have significant doubts about my odds of surviving. Those odds just seemed a little more in my favor. Before, they'd been maybe ten to one in favor of me being ripped to shreds.

"You want to tell me about it?" I asked.

Not that I really cared. It was more that I was in my element. If Oliver Corbyn was to be believed, he'd actually dated this mashup of bird and lady bits. I hadn't gotten any details from him. Maybe I'd have a chance to learn more from her. If nothing else, her telling would take some time. Time I could use to imagine an escape.

Instead of a simple yes or no, the siren answered me with a question.

"Do you like karaoke?"

"Usually, no. That spot in Knife River isn't bad, though."

"Yes, it is," she snapped.

The vehemence in her voice was sharper than her talons. Awkwardness hung in the air, then she spoke.

"I love karaoke," she confessed.

A rough laugh came out before I could stop it.

"I'll bet you do," I said honestly. "Those pipes of yours? Yeah, you'd crush it every time."

The siren's cheeks reddened.

"Aren't you sweet," she said. "I'm not welcome, though. Everyone else is. Doesn't matter what they are, and it definitely doesn't matter if they can sing. But me? No. Never."

I fidgeted, weighing candor against my desire to live. As was too often the case, candor won out.

"Can you blame them? You're terrifying. I mean, come on. Luring a bunch of suckers to their untimely deaths? The lucky ones drown. The unlucky ones?" I remarked with a gesture at the piles of left-behinds. "Seriously. You think they're going to get all excited when you show up? Hell, one song from you ruined my night."

The siren stretched a wing and turned her head to nibble at its feathers.

"I'd say you've been pretty lucky," she commented between bites. "So far."

"You have no idea," I replied. "Anyway, sorry that nobody wants you to sing."

Preening done, she ruffled her wings and settled back into her crouch.

"That's not the point," she remarked irritably. "It isn't only about me singing. It's about them singing to me. No one ever sings to me. Well, almost never. There was one time. One time only."

I sized up the mishmash of ugly and felt a surprising tug at my heartstrings. Not the unnatural desire for the siren. That suicidal attraction to the edge of the cliff was still there. This was a tug of a different sort, though. That telltale tug when someone has sunk their hook into me.

Despite my best efforts to simply not give a damn, every so often a client slipped past my defenses. It wasn't sympathy for a scary as hell monster. The world was full of those and, like everyone else, they dated and got dumped. Take old Canute, the heartbroken troll who'd helped me save the world. Or even Dagmara, a demon whose entire purpose was to punish lazy and careless field hands. Sure, I could get a bit misty when some sap moped into my office and lamented their unloveableness. This wasn't that. The tug only happened when someone–or something–perpetually got the short end of the stick. That resonated with me because I could relate.

"And they broke your heart," I whispered. "That guy that sang to you. You fell in love with him, didn't you?"

A single tear formed, then spilled over and ran down her cheek. When it reached the thick edge of her jaw, it hung sadly for a moment before falling to the floor.

"You said you're here for something," she said gruffly after wiping at that traitorous tear. "I can't imagine what that would be. As you noted, few survive my song. My song," she repeated with a harsh laugh. "Anyway, if you can find it, take it and begone."

I looked around the space, but the karaoke machine wasn't to be seen. That sucked. It meant Ollie's damned toy was either further up the tower, which meant climbing stairs again, or down in the sub-cellar, which meant descending to an even scarier place than I already was.

"Great, thanks. That's great. I'll just get the thing and go," I repeated dubiously. When she didn't protest, I continued.

"So, speaking of karaoke, I need the karaoke machine and those CDs you took the other night, and I'm out of here."

Eyelids snicked over those freaky black orbs once, then twice.

"Oliver's karaoke machine? You're here for Ollie. He... hired you to steal from me?"

"I don't steal shit," I protested, trying not to squirm under the sudden threat I felt swelling around me. "I return property to its rightful owner."

"We should all do what we're good at," the siren said in a quiet voice. "Me? I'm good at ripping flesh from bones."

CHAPTER 8

Niagara Tug
June 4th, 1904
Compass failed after detecting magnetic anomalies. Ran aground on Knife Island near
Knife River, MN.
All survived.

’D SPENT MOST OF my childhood trapped in a research hospital. For years, my existence fell neatly into two categories: being tortured, and waiting to be tortured again. When I wasn't being poked, prodded, or pumped full of strange drugs, I stared at the white ceiling of my white room and listened to the clock's second hand tick menacingly. The only respite was an orderly with the audacity to treat a science experiment with some modicum of decency. Not often, because being nice to the lab rat was a definite no-no. He tried, though. In little ways, he tried. Perhaps one of his most daring acts of kindness was the movie night.

I had been ten, or maybe twelve. After a particularly grueling day, night had found me curled up on my bed's thin mattress, heaving sob after sob. The door's deadbolt clacked, and every muscle in my body had flinched. I'd expected some late night jabs from the psycho doctor who'd taken me into his care. Instead, the orderly had slipped in, pushing a tall metal cart with a TV strapped on top. One wheel had squeaked as he positioned it at the foot of my bed. I knew what TVs and VCRs were. One recurring experiment was being forced to watch long recordings of random images while the doctor observed and made notes. I'd never seen an actual movie, though. My eyes had flicked nervously from the orderly to the screen as he loaded a tape. Then he pressed play, and treated me to what instantly became my favorite flick of all time: *Mad Max: Beyond Thunderdome.*

I share this because I really liked that movie. No, I loved it. Its post-apocalyptic theme fit my mood perfectly. Of course, the world was full of horrible people. Of course, they lived to torment and bully and abuse others. At ten, or however old I'd been, I'd already spent half of my life in captivity. For all I knew, that TV had simply shown what was beyond the hospital's walls.

So, yeah. The movie touched something deep in me. More, it convinced me that there were heroes. People who fought back. Max Rockatansky, believed to be some sort of chosen one by this weird tribe of kids that survived a plane crash, ended up a prisoner in a horrible town. When people had arguments, they were settled inside the Thunderdome: a big, metal cage that two men entered, but only one would leave. When I saw Max in that cage, trapped in a duel to the death with a giant brute, a kernel of defiance took root in my young soul. Like Max, I'd been dragged to a horrible place. Like Max, I was being forced to endure horrible things. If Max Rockatansky could survive, if he could win his way free from that awful place, maybe I could, too.

So, yeah. I loved *Mad Max: Beyond Thunderdome.* Let's be clear, though. I loved it metaphorically.

Reenacting that Thunderdome scene with a siren in a lighthouse cellar? Way too literal.

Her wings pumped and her legs thrust, the combined effect launching her toward me at what seemed an impossible speed. I tried to dive to the side. Instead, I tripped and crashed into a pile. The siren's claws slashed the air where my head had been a split-second before. I grabbed a candelabra and swung its not insubstantial weight like a club. It caught the siren on her shoulder, but did nothing more than piss her off. A taloned foot lifted and slammed down where my leg would have been had I not twisted aside in the knick of time. I scrabbled around a pile of crap and dove past the attacking fiend. My human ears heard the first note of her song... and a Maine Coon hit the ground with a complete disregard for its allure. All the cat cared about was getting gone and doing so as quickly as possible.

Cats are notoriously nimble little fuckers, but the siren was putting my borrowed form's agility to the test. Her hands, with their wicked claws, grabbed and grasped. I zigged and zagged. Her taloned feet stomped and kicked. I leaped, twisted, and ducked. She screeched and screamed. I raowed and hissed. It was a stalemate until a clear path to the stairs appeared. When I bolted toward freedom, a wooden crate sailed over me and shattered against the bottom step. The loud slam and shower of splintered wood didn't just scare me. It scared me human again.

The shift caused me to stumble. I stepped on a shard from the busted crate and yelped, then yelped again when her hand caught my wrist. Before she could clutch tight enough to hold me, that same wrist narrowed, and a hound dog's paw slipped from her grasp. I scampered up the curving stairs to the lighthouse's main floor. Another shift, and my human shoulder slammed into the steel door leading to the outside world. It opened with a loud screech, and I blinked hard against the sudden light. My feet carried me over the threshold. My watering eyes scanned the rocky terrain in search of a place to hide... And my stupid human ears heard a song.

The voice stretched up from the cellar and wrapped around me like a lasso. That wasn't quite right, though. A lasso would imply something was holding me back. As her song suffused me, I simply stopped all efforts to flee, flabbergasted by the thought that I had considered leaving in the first place.

Yeah, okay, sure. You really have to leave, though, a tiny voice said in protest.

"Yeah, no," I scoffed.

No, yeah. You do, the voice insisted.

I didn't like that voice. Not one bit. As I pondered its ridiculous suggestion, that insane proposition of leaving, I realized I didn't like anything at all that wasn't the siren's song. Her transcendental voice was the only thing in all of creation worth liking. It was an indisputable fact. The song told me so.

August... that voice growled.

My forehead crinkled, annoyed, and then a very irate wolverine whipped in a tight circle, teeth bared at the danger it knew was close.

I'll never know how I'd been able to shift in that moment. I had, though, and thank whatever god was listening. The shift had been a reflex, a desperate act of self-preservation. Say what you want about gorillas and elephants. If you want to survive a scrap, go with a wolverine every time. I'd survived being tossed through a window by shifting into one. I'd won a fight with a Gorgon. Now, I happily added 'resisted a siren's song' to the list of the furry fighter's attributes. Yeah, the Maine Coon had been immune, too. But that was a cat. Badass in its own little 'who gives a damn' kind of way. The wolverine, though? Fifty pounds of teeth and claws. A pelt that could practically stop bullets. And let's not overlook a disposition that was far beyond 'who gives a damn' and solidly in the 'you want a piece of me, asshole?' category. Wolverines don't like anyone. Full stop. That lady could sing until her lungs burst. At best, I'd use her as a chew toy. At worst, they'd be lucky to find a feather or two.

As if summoned by my thoughts, the siren's head appeared in the doorway. Her torso followed, wings tucked tight as she stepped over the threshold. One taloned hand pressed against the jamb and the other reached long fingers toward me. She vibrated with the effort of holding in a terrible rage. A tense shiver working its way down her body, then she settled into her customary crouch.

"Such a strange creature, you are. Can you shift into a fish?" she asked between disturbing nibbles at one wing's feathers. "It's the only way you're getting off this island."

My spark of human awareness teetered on the edge of a dark pit. Leaving the island meant leaving her. I stared into that abyss, and the wolverine gave voice to a low growl. When something snapped deep inside, it left me stunned. Either I'd truly broken free of her charm or she'd simply decided to let me go. Probably an important distinction, but one I wasn't in the mood to contemplate. I didn't like her anymore. Even better, I didn't have to like her. That was a solid check in the win column, and that was all I needed to know.

There was a pull, a twisting, a stretch. Then I put my hands on my naked knees, gasped for breath, and tried to ignore my pounding headache.

"I'm leaving on a boat, and I'm taking Ollie's karaoke machine with me," I grunted. "Even if I could turn into a fish—which I can't—I still couldn't carry that."

"Or a tune," the siren remarked.

Unexpectedly, I laughed. Even more surprising, she laughed in response.

"Yeah, I guess," I said. "So there's only two ways this goes, lady. Give me the damned karaoke thing, or kill me. Just stop with all the love me, don't love me bullshit. It's exhausting."

We stared at one another for a long moment. Her eyes, inscrutably black. Mine bloodshot and tired. Finally, my patience gave out with a hoarse curse.

"For fuck's sake, it's a stupid speaker and some stupid CDs."

I saw her draw breath. I readied to shift, but what came out of her mouth wasn't a song. It was a long, sad exhalation. Without warning, she turned and went back inside. I heard her scraping footsteps fade. A few minutes later, they grew louder, then she stepped through the door. One hand held a binder of CDs. The other, the handle of Oliver's karaoke machine.

"Take it," she said as she set my client's personal effects on the ground. "Take it all, and be gone."

I took a tentative step. When she didn't react, I took another more boldly. My hand wrapped around the machine's handle and I tested its weight. Still, the siren looked at me.

"So, that's it, then?" I asked.

A nod.

"And you're just... You're really going to let me go?"

Another nod.

"Thank god," I said with a heavy exhale. "Welp, pleasure doing business with you. Okay, that was a lie, but bygones and whatever, right? Hey. Now that we're back to a strictly professional relationship, maybe I could get my clothes, too?"

The siren's thin lips twitched up. She stepped aside and gestured into the lighthouse's interior.

"I suggest that you hurry, shifter. You're trying my patience."

"Right back at'cha," I replied, and headed back inside.

My clothes were where I'd left them, which was a relief. Having Cedric and Lana arrive to find me naked would've been a level of humiliation I wasn't in the mood for. After dressing, I hurried back outside. The siren watched me roll Ollie's machine down to the dock. Watched me take a seat on one of the pilings. Watched me wave her off with a shooing gesture. The distance made it hard to tell, but I'm pretty sure she frowned at that. Even so, she went back inside her lighthouse, and I was finally alone.

Time passed. Gulls cried forlornly from above, and the waves murmured endlessly below. In between, a cold and tired shifter tried not to think at all.

"Why are you still here?" a voice said.

She scared the bejeezus out of me. Once I'd gotten my heart out of my throat, I cursed the universe. Something as scary as her had no business being sneaky as shit, too.

"Oh, hey," I said guardedly.

"Oh, hey, yourself," she replied. "Why are you still here?"

I gestured toward the wide lake and explained that my ride home was still an hour or so away.

She cocked her head, the gesture more birdlike than not, then turned her back and walked her strange walk away. Every muscle in my body tensed while I waited, wondering what in the hell she was going to do next. Fortunately, I didn't have to wait in terror for long. The siren had gone into her lighthouse, and was now on her way back. This time, though, she was holding something: the end of a blaze orange extension cord.

"I was thinking we could pass the time," she said quietly after reaching the dock. "I don't often have company."

While I watched, she uncoiled the karaoke machine's power cord and plugged it in. Next, she unzipped the binder full of CDs and flipped through a few sleeves.

"I'm Hanelle," she said awkwardly, eyes on the silver discs in their plastic pockets.

"August," I replied.

"I know. Maybe. I thought perhaps we could. You know," she finished with a tentative gesture at the karaoke machine.

"Un-flippin-believable," I exhaled. When she flinched, I added more gently, "I mean, yes. Sure. Why not? Let's sing some karaoke."

I'd had a strange life full of strange moments. If that life ended up being a long one, too, I had no doubt that singing karaoke with a siren on the shores of an uninhabited island in the middle of Lake Superior would stand out as one of the strangest.

After flipping through Ollie's collection of CDs, Hanelle settled on Natalie Merchant. Her solo stuff, not The 10,000 Maniacs. While not a fan, I appreciated Hanelle picking my favorite decade for music. The song she sang was *These Are Days*, and it was...

It was...

It was epic. Breathtaking. Legendary.

Should I have been surprised? Probably not. I knew the siren could sing. Her usual song, though, didn't really qualify as music. Hearing her belt out that nineties classic about loving life and all its glory shook me to the core. When she finished, I half-jokingly asked if she was worried about any innocents over in Wisconsin she might have seduced. In response, Hanelle rolled her eyes and dismissed my ignorance.

"How do you know who Natalie Merchant is, anyway?" I asked.

The siren absently scratched a talon on the dock's boards.

"I have a radio," she explained. "Sometimes, I can get batteries. The signal isn't great out here, but once in awhile, I get to listen to music."

How she'd picked up that radio in the first place and how she refilled her supply of batteries were things I decided not to wonder about. Even if I had wanted to know, I lost my chance to ask more questions when she dropped the CDs in my lap.

"Your turn."

A bashfulness sent waves of red up my neck and over my cheeks. For a moment, I wondered at my reluctance. I'd sung, not once, but twice, to a bar full of veritable strangers. Now, alone on a deserted island, I was suddenly embarrassed.

Yeah, but it's not deserted.

"Nah. You don't want to hear me sing," I muttered.

"You're not wrong," she agreed, "but there is no one else here, so I guess you'll have to do. Sing something, August. This is the only chance I'll likely have to do karaoke. Sing something. Please."

I flipped through the binder. Ollie's selection was eclectic. I'd give him that. Classic Motown to modern hip hop. Old bluegrass to new country. Where rock was concerned, that book of CDs had everything from Air Supply to ZZ Top, including one number that instantly felt right. As I slipped the CD from its plastic sleeve, Hanelle craned her neck.

"What did you pick?" she asked.

"Just wait," I replied.

I had to hold the disc close to my chest to keep it from her prying eyes. Fortunately, it was only her eyes that were trying to pry. Those razor-tipped fingers twitched but stayed at her sides. I popped the lid on the karaoke machine, dropped in the CD, futzed with the buttons until I found the track I wanted, then finally met her eyes. Music played, a chord progression as iconic as any in the history of classic rock. As Deep Purple's *Smoke on the Water* poured from the speaker, my head bobbed in time. Hanelle's brow furrowed as she listened. After a couple of bars, her chin dipped in time to the music. Seeing her enjoy the song I'd picked unfettered something inside of me. I found my feet, spread them wide, and started a full-on head bang, something I hadn't done in years. Hanelle leaped to her feet and mimicked my movement, tentatively at first, then harder and harder. Her stringy hair whipped around her face and her wings flapped to the beat. I held up a hand, pinky and forefinger raised in a classic devil horns, and smiled a mad smile when she did the same.

I was maybe three head bangs in when the song erupted from my throat like a wild beast set free. My words traveled through the mic, down its snaking cord, and into the rolling karaoke machine's amplified speaker. Some magic happened in that contraption, and what came out was awesome. Gulls screamed in surprise and wheeled into the air. Even the rolling waves seemed to break against the rocks in time. For five minutes and forty-one seconds–because a song that good can't be short–we rocked the hell out of that rocky island. When I reached the second round of the refrain, Hanelle lent her otherworldly voice to mine in perfect harmony. During the instrumental break in the middle, we capered and danced, pumped our fists and banged our heads. I finished the final verse, then we sang the final chorus and emptied our lungs as we belted out the words. We danced up and down the isle's dock and along its shoreline until long after the song itself had ended.

I collapsed to the ground, a smile as big as the surrounding lake on my face. Hanelle had launched into the air with powerful thrusts of her wings on the last couple of bars, then spiraled down in exhausted circles until finally landing beside me.

"I have never heard that song before," she admitted between gasps. "That was amazing."

"You've never heard Deep Purple? You gotta get out more."

And just like that, the mood changed. The joy spilled out and washed over the cold boards of the dock. Wings that had quivered with energy sagged.

"Would that I could," she lamented, gazing across the water. Somewhere out there, a fisherman who'd snagged her heart sang with friends every week, but no longer sang to her.

I cursed my stupid mouth and the stupider brain behind it. She was a siren. There was no way she'd be wanted anywhere, ever. She was terrifying. Hideous. A woman who'd lured countless souls to their deaths. Best case, she would live out her days—however many her kind had—in solitude. Worst case, the Quorum would set their sights on her and hunt her down. They tended to frown on paranormal creatures that couldn't curb their nature and not kill people. However things worked out, one thing was certain: Hanelle's life would never be happy.

"Well, shit. I just. Huh," I muttered.

We sat in silence; me staring at my boots and her staring at the water.

"I think your ride is here," she finally said.

I looked up. Sure enough, there was a speck on the horizon. It grew incrementally larger as I watched.

"I'd best go," she decided wistfully. "This was fun, August. I had fun. For the first time in I don't know how long, I actually had fun."

And with that, she was gone.

CHAPTER 9

The Hesper
May 3rd, 1905
Driven off course by a northeaster.
All hands survived.

T HE BOAT BOUNCED OVER the swells and sent plumes of fine spray into the air. Cedric gripped the wheel with both hands, haughty and aloof as ever. Lana Delridge sat beside him, shoulders hunched. The wind snagged strands of her hair and snapped them around her head. Neither Cedric nor Lana looked at me, nor did they look at each other. The pervasive mood was one of vexation. I found it to be delightful.

"Guess you didn't find what you were looking for," I said. "That's too bad. I did," I added with a pat on the karaoke machine, "but don't let that bug you. We can't all be good at our jobs."

Cedric's knuckles whitened and the creases in Lana's frowning face deepened, but neither took the bait. The boat backed away from the dock, and I craned my neck for a parting glimpse of Hanelle. All I saw was the afternoon sun reflecting off the lighthouse's glass. If there was a siren behind a window, she was invisible. I set the tip of a finger to my eyebrow regardless and gave a small salute. The boat swung around, and we were off.

The silence was killing me. Not that it was actually silent. The motor hummed. Water sloshed. The ever-present gulls cried their hungry cries. That all faded into the background, though. The silence was of the no-one-is-saying-a-damned-word variety. Not that I'm one for idle chitchat. There was nothing else to pass the time, though, and I had time a plenty to kill. Knife River was easily two hours away. I endured the silence for maybe ten minutes, then asked if the boat had a radio.

"No," Cedric replied curtly.

"Really? That sucks. I thought these things came with radios. A little music would be nice. Oh, wait."

I leaned over, twisted my neck to and fro, and then *ah-ha'd*. There was an outlet concealed beneath the bench. I flipped open its watertight cover. A moment later, the karaoke machine's lights blinked, and I began flipping through the book of CDs.

"What do you guys like? Wait, don't answer because I really don't care."

I opted for *Black Water* by the Doobie Brothers, then cranked the volume up. Karaoke versions of songs have the vocals dialed way down, but the music was still good. After a few bars, I realized I was half-humming, half-mumbling the lyrics. On a whim, I freed the mic from its clip on the speaker's side and started to sing.

"Seriously?" Lana spat, finally deigning to acknowledge me. "Seriously?"

In response, I met her eyes and sang about that old black water that kept on rollin' and the Mississippi moon that kept shining on me. The woman glowered, possibly out of aversion to The Doobie Brothers, but more likely out of aversion to me. I chuckled, the noise coming through the speaker in a loud *huhhuhhuh*. Cedric nudged the throttle, and we picked up speed. The next swell lifted our boat out of the water. When we came down with a jolt, I rocked in my seat and the karaoke machine clunked hard against the deck. The CD skipped, then The Doobie Brothers resumed their timeless classic. Unfortunately, there was something else. For a moment, I thought it was an echo of my earlier chuckle. A rhythmic *uhuhuh* pervaded the song's music. It wasn't in time with the tempo, though, and honestly made the whole thing sound like shit.

"Hey, you broke it," I complained.

"Good," Lana spat back.

I fiddled with the equalizer knobs, but it was fruitless. That annoying *uhuhuh* was still there. Resigning myself to a long and boring trip, I hit stop. The music shut off, but the noise continued.

"Please turn that cursed machine off," Cedric said through a clenched jaw.

He was easy to ignore. Figuring out what was wrong with Oliver's prized possession took precedence over anything the stodgy prude might've wanted. Some of my jobs were a little rougher than others, and sometimes my client's favorite whatever got dinged up in the process. Just because shit happened didn't mean I was okay with it, though. If Ollie's karaoke machine was busted, I was going to feel terrible.

I leaned over the karaoke machine and grimaced. Rather than turning it off, I cranked up the volume. When I did so, the sound changed and became more nuanced.

uhclickuhuhuhclickclickuhuhuhuhclickbeepuh

"Yep. You broke it," I complained. "Nice work, Skipper."

I extended a finger toward the power button, but before I could press it, Lana snapped at me to stop.

"Listen," she said, voice taut.

"Why?"

"Shush! Just shut up and listen."

I did, but couldn't for the life of me figure out why. It was an annoying noise. I'm no virtuoso, but had to believe that my rendition of the Doobie Brothers had been preferable to the buzzing, clicking, and beeping. Opinions are like assholes, though, and Lana clearly had her own. Opinion, that is. Well, asshole, too, but that's beside the point.

I kept my mouth shut and studied Lana's face. She was concentrating and waving her fingers absently in the air. The movement was hypnotic, like she was conducting an orchestra only she could hear.

"Fibonacci," Lana whispered. "It's a Fibonacci sequence. It repeats after seven intervals. The clicks split the numbers, the beeps signal the reset of the progression."

Cedric frowned, which annoyed me. Not that he was frowning. I enjoyed that in my yeah-I'm-petty-so-sue-me sort of way. It was more how even the creases in his brow looked distinguished and professional. He slowed the boat and turned with interest to his acolyte.

"What are you suggesting?" he asked.

Lana had retrieved her industrial laptop and powered it up. Her fingers moved in a flurry. The annoying sounds from the speaker grew louder without me touching the volume, peaked, then started to fade.

"Stop the boat!" Lana yelled. "Turn around. Go back."

"Miss Delridge," Cedric intoned. "I understand your frustration. Today's excursion did not bear the fruit of discovery as we'd hoped. Chasing fantasies, though, is no way for..."

"Please stop the boat!" she pleaded. "A busted speaker doesn't buzz out Fibonacci sequences. Something is causing it."

A strange reluctance crossed Cedric's face, but he obliged. The sudden deceleration made me sway to the side. I kept a protective hand on Oliver's machine and the other on the gunwale. Cedric cranked the boat's wheel and sent us in a tight arc. We were most of the way through a one-eighty when the speaker sparked to life anew with its unusually sequenced sounds.

"We need that," Lana said, jabbing a finger at Ollie's personal effects.

"Get your own," I shot back. "This one's taken."

I never would have expected Lana Delridge, a grumpy grad student, to be capable of violence. Regrettably, my life was full of unpleasant surprises. The boat rocked as she launched herself at me, hands heading for my throat. I lurched off my bench and damned near went over the boat's opposite side. We both found our feet and crouched. Her for another attack, me preparing to go-go-gorilla. Throwing her all the way to Michigan's upper peninsula was tempting, indeed. Fortunately—for her and for anyone in Michigan that might've been hit when she descended from the clouds—Cedric barked out a commanding, "Enough!"

"We need that machine," she said. "This is more important than whatever that jerk thinks he needs it for."

"It's not mine," I shot back. "I can't give you something that isn't mine. Look. When we get to shore, I'll give it to Ollie. Then you can tell him you need his shit more than he does. Until then, point this damned boat toward Knife River."

Cedric held a placating hand out to Lana and offered me a conciliatory nod.

"His recommendation is acceptable. Miss Delridge, please," he implored. "Enough of this nonsense. Yes, this has been an interesting development, one which we will explore. Not today, though. We'll speak with the owner of that ridiculous device and return to this spot tomorrow. Alone. I'm, ah, quite sure Mister Shade won't be a concern of ours for much longer."

"What he said," I grumbled as I grasped the karaoke machine's handle and wheeled it back to my side.

Lana returned to her seat, crossed her arms and legs, and watched me with naked hatred. For his part, Cedric nodded like a satisfied principal at an elementary school. With a last recriminating look at me, he pulled out his smartphone. After a few taps on its screen, he returned it to his pocket and pointed us toward shore. After far too much time, during which none of us uttered a single syllable, we arrived at Knife River's marina.

"Thanks for the ride," I said. "See you never."

And with that clever remark, I lifted Oliver's CD book and karaoke machine and set off for the bar. I glanced over my shoulder and saw Lana arguing fiercely with the professor. The smug twit brushed her aside, pulled out his phone, and made a call. Returning my attention to the walk ahead, I put them from my mind. It had seemed like the right thing to do at the time.

Chapter 10

The Madeira

November 28th, 1905

Battered by the worst storm on record. Broke up on the cliffs at Gold Rock, north of Split Rock

Lighthouse.

All but one survived.

N OT THAT LONG BEFORE, I'd asked Oliver if he was famous. His response had been that, in a town as small as Knife River, everyone took turns.

Welp, my turn had come.

It was the night after I'd survived my trip to Isle Royale, and The Thirsty Gull was fit to burst. If the town's Fire Marshall was there, he had obviously clocked out for the day. Elbows bumped and shoulders rubbed as the crowd milled about. Poor Tom was at his wit's end, even with the help of a second bartender.

"Just slow down!" he begged. "Stop drinking so fast, all of you! It's Wilson that has the eight arms, not me!"

The more he implored, the more folks laughed at his misfortune and kept the orders coming. They tapped one keg and seemed intent on emptying the rest. The mood was celebratory, and the reason was yours truly. Apparently, people had been genuinely worried. About me and my safety, sure, but more that karaoke might've seen its end. When I reunited Oliver with his magical musical machine and binder full of plastic discs, it had done more than bring an unexpected tear to his eye. It had resulted in a collective sigh of relief from damn near every person, human or otherwise, in the whole town. Now, the skin on my back stung from repeated slaps, and my blood alcohol level floated somewhere in the stratosphere.

"Listen'ta Tommy," I slurred. "I gotta shlow down."

It didn't matter how loudly I said it, or how emphatically, or even how well I enunciated the words. My adoring fans met each protestation with another shot, another pint, another thank-you for saving their favorite pastime from the evil clutches of that karaoke machine-snatching devil.

"Hanelle's no'so bad," I protested.

My humility made them love me all the more. I don't much enjoy the limelight, but it was nice to feel appreciated. More often than not, people weren't exactly thrilled about meeting me. Came with the territory, sure, but I hadn't realized how much it had gotten under my skin until I had an entire town singing my praises. And speaking of singing...

Ollie fired up his prized machine–which thankfully still worked–and kicked off the night with his customary rendition of Billy Joel's *Piano Man*. Applause, whistles, and cheers drown out the final notes. With the mic's help, the KJ overcame the racket and called out my name.

"August Shade? Get your shifty ass up here."

I winked at someone, or maybe everyone, and set out for the stage. The press of bodies kept me upright, and the alcohol kept me from feeling embarrassed by that fact. The stairs presented a challenge, but I persevered with Oliver's help. After that, the mic stand did a decent job of holding me up. I swayed from side to side, a goofy grin splattered across my face, and loudly asked what I was singing.

"You tell me!" Oliver hollered back with a laugh. "That's how karaoke works."

"Something good!" I yelled, and the crowd went wild.

The monitor's screen lit up with the words to Queen's *We Are the Champions*. Ollie lifted an eyebrow. In response, I told my fingers to curl into a fist while leaving my thumb sticking straight up. When my digits all agreed to the plan, I whooped in delight. We'll never know if I'd actually carried that particular tune, though. Even with an amplified speaker, the myriad of voices singing along were louder than my own. I finished the song with my arms above my head, Rocky-style. My bleary eyes swept the crowd, and face after happy face looked back. They clapped and whistled and cheered. Well, the humans did. More than a few PNs filled the bar as well, but they weren't clapping. Instead, they set their fists up alongside their mouths, then splayed their fingers as they pushed their hands forward. Over and over, the PNs made the same gesture.

"That'some coolass shit," I decided. "Some coolass shit, indeed."

I bowed deep and belly flopped off the stage. I'd only seen crowd surfing on TV. The actual experience put what I'd seen to shame. I bobbed across everyone's hands all the way to the bar. Things kinda went sideways at that point, and I ended up on the floor. The drinks had replaced my bones with rubber, though, and I was back on my feet in an instant.

"Beer me!" I cried out, and Tom Hanks happily obliged.

Time had passed. I wasn't sure how much. All I knew was that people were still singing, and that Tom had switched me to water. I didn't want to drink water. Fortunately, the straw in my glass didn't want me to drink it, either. Every time I tried, I only succeeded in stabbing myself in my eye, a nostril and once, my ear.

"Straw's broke," I complained to the lady next to me.

"You're an idiot," she replied.

"You started it."

"No, I did not."

"Did too."

"No, August. I did not."

Everyone knows my name, I thought proudly. *I'm famous.*

I smiled at the woman who knew my name, but she didn't return the friendly gesture. Instead, I got an epic frown. That made me sad. People weren't supposed to frown at famous folks, and I said as much.

"Oh, sure," she spat. "You're famous. You and the professor get all the glory, and for what? For being assholes. For being thieving little jerks."

The professor? I wondered, then I blurted out, "Lana Delridge! You're Lana Delridge! You don't like me at all."

"At least you got that right."

I scrunched my face and squinted my eyes. It was definitely the grad student from the boat, the one that wanted Ollie's karaoke machine.

"You get your own ka'roky machinery?" I asked. "For the boat and stuff?"

Sure, I could be an asshole. In that moment, though, I honestly hadn't been trying to be one. I was just curious. My good intentions and a buck-fifty could've bought me a pop. I asked my question, and every buckle inside of her tightened. Despite the din, I could practically hear her teeth grinding.

"I did," she started. "I drove down to Duluth after we got rid of you, found an electronics store, and bought the same make and model as his," she continued while hooking a thumb toward the stage. "The exact same. Then, to make sure I could replicate the phenomenon, I found a place that sold karaoke discs. Not easy, but I did it. And not just any disc. I found The Doobie Brothers. I hate The Doobie Brothers, but I still bought the damned karaoke CD. With my own money, too. Just like I used my money to pay for that stupid boat and two—not one, like I wanted, but two—hotel rooms for me and the professor. I didn't sleep last night. Not a wink. While normal people were sleeping, I was rewriting my program. Do you have any idea how hard it is to rewrite code to cross-reference spectrometer and multibeam echosounder feedback with a Fibonacci sequence?"

Her voice had been rising with every word. I leaned back like a gale was blowing in my face and dumbly shook my head.

"It's hard," she proclaimed. "So yeah. Up all night, and then we went back out yesterday. I was exhausted, but I was at the dock early, checking and rechecking my program. We returned to where the speaker had picked up whatever it had picked up, and we found something. I found something!"

When she finished her tirade, that line between almost yelling and actually yelling had definitively been crossed.

"Uh, that'sh great," I said, doing my best to follow along. It was tough because she was talking a lot.

Lana continued, but it didn't feel like her words were for me.

"When we got back, we had dinner. A nice dinner. A celebration. He told me we'd made a major discovery, that we were going to be famous. And he... He..."

The woman squeezed her eyes shut and shook her head angrily. Then she took a long, deep breath.

"And he kissed me goodnight."

"Awwww," I murmured happily. "That'sh nice."

The grad student glared at her pint glass. In a voice gone brittle, she said that it had been nice, and that she'd been a fool.

"For kissing a guy?" I asked. "That'sh no'stupid. Lots'a girls kiss lots'a guys."

"Not for that, you idiot. For letting myself get played."

I didn't follow and tried to say as much. It came out a bit jumbled thanks to all the booze in my blood, but she understood enough to know I was hoping she'd explain.

"He left. He left! In the middle of the night, he took it all. The karaoke machine. My laptop. My program. The multibeam echo sounder. He took everything and left. I woke up this morning, ready to analyze what I'd picked up on my scans, and it was all gone."

The crowd's jubilance pressed against her bubble of despondent rage, but couldn't penetrate it. Inside that bubble, a broken-hearted woman sat next to a shapeshifter who knew a thing or two about broken hearts.

"Here," I said.

My hand tried to find the inside of my jacket, but slipped down the front instead.

"Uh, here," I said again, and again tried to get my hand to my inside pocket. "Shit. Where'd it go?"

"Where did what go?" Lana said with complete and total disinterest.

"M'pockets. Pocket. One pocket. Just one. Where'd it go?"

I looked down, trying to see what had changed with my jacket. Something was obviously different, but damned if I could tell what. I stared at the woman beside me, as helpless as a newborn in the woods. Her eye twitched. With forced patience, she asked which pocket I was having difficulty locating.

"Th'inside one," I said with a pout. "It's on the inside, but I can't get there."

"And what are you looking for in that inside pocket, August?" she inquired in a patronizing tone.

"M'cards."

Her hands grabbed my lapels. One hand reached inside and freed my wallet.

"Are they in here?" she asked.

"Nope."

The wallet went back, and her hand reached into the opposite pocket.

"These?" she asked, brandishing a small collection of white paper rectangles.

"Yep. You get one. It's your prize. Winner, winner, business card dinner," I quipped with a lopsided smile.

"Gee, thanks," she said after sliding one free and shoving the rest back where she found them.

"Y'gotta read it," I explained. "That's how they work, ya know."

Lana did not look amused, but she flourished the card and made a big production out of reading it.

"August Shade," she started.

"Yellow!" I responded with a wave.

"Post-relationship personal effects repossession specialist," Lana continued.

My head bobbed emphatically.

"Some pets. No kids. Satisfaction not guaranteed, but at least you'll have your favorite whatever back. What is this? Some kind of joke?"

I was offended, but didn't need to come to my own defense. The guy behind me did.

"Not at all," he said, ruffling my hair. "August, here, he got my immersion blender back."

"He got my favorite LP," a nearby woman added.

"And my lawnmower," a third patron tossed in. "Even made sure to get the mulch plug and the leftover oil I had for it."

One after another, people within earshot chimed in. A Crockpot. A map with stamps on every city visited in the continental U.S. A limited edition VHS of John Carpenter's *The Thing*.

"He got Wilson back," Tom said, putting an eight-tentacled lake monster on top of the pile of things I'd repo'd. "Well, he got him back to the lake. That's okay, though. I still get to see him a lot."

Lana stared at the burly bartender with wide, uncomprehending eyes.

"I have no idea what you're talking about," she said with a shake of her head.

Tom leaned in and said in a louder voice, "He gets stuff back for people after messy breakups. Like my fish, Wilson, and Ollie's karaoke machine. No job too small, no job too big. August Shade is a legend. An absolute legend."

Lana looked at me anew. I was about to add that, yes, I was a legend, and that meant I was legendary. I didn't get the chance, though. Oliver called out my name again, and hands started pulling me back toward the stage.

"Legenbardy!" I cried out, but to whom, I had no idea. If I'd intended Lana Delridge to hear it, the effort had been wasted. The woman was gone.

Chapter 11

The Gunilda

August 11th, 1911

The yacht struck rocks because of the owner's own navigational error.

All passengers survived.

THE NEXT MORNING'S BRUTAL hangover was expected. Going to the diner for my remedy of bitter coffee, dry eggs, burnt bacon, and soggy toast was expected. Lana Delridge showing up and asking for my help? Unexpected.

"So, how does this work?" she said without preamble as she took the booth bench opposite mine and set my card between us.

A forkful of eggs hovered near my chin while I considered the woman. I decided that, despite the hangover, I still looked better, then shoved the fork into my mouth.

"How'd you find me?" I mumbled through my full mouth.

"A lady from the bar—I guess you repo'd her Belgian waffle maker—said you liked breakfast after a bender."

I *hmph'd.* The diner was the only place to eat for miles. I wasn't about to give Lana a blue ribbon for figuring out I ate there. We stared at one another until I let my eyes drop to my card.

"So, no word from Cedric, huh?" I asked.

Lana clenched her teeth and curled her hands into fists. I gave a low whistle. Some people were flat-out assholes. The grad student hadn't been very nice to me, but I still felt bad for her. She'd expected her research trip with Cedric Mulberry to become a Fantasy

Island adventure. They would have loads of time together, just the two of them. They'd make some big scientific discovery and fall in love and live happily ever after. I'd been an unexpected and annoying distraction. Couldn't blame her for being a little salty. Cedric, though? Hating him was easy. His pompous condescension. His demeaning comments. And now, knowing that he'd stolen Lana's work? Yeah, the guy was quickly rising to the top of my least favorite smart people list.

"Just tell me how this works," she said.

"Easy. You tell me what you need back, who has it, and where they are. I go and get it."

She glowered, so I explained it again more slowly, then added, "This might come as a surprise to a highly intelligent individual like yourself, but not everything has to be complicated."

Her glower deepened. She tersely replied that she'd already told me who had her things and what she needed back.

"Uh huh," I nodded. "Say, do you have a pen? You seem like the kind of person that always has a pen."

Lana slid one from a pocket. I used it to jot notes on my mostly clean napkin.

"Laptop. Karaoke machine. The other thing? The multi-whatever?"

"Multibeam echosounder."

"Yeah, that. Anything else?"

"My dignity?"

I crooked a smile. "That costs extra. Now, if you were him, where would you go?"

The woman gave it some thought, then said, "Back to Yale."

"The school?"

Lana rolled her eyes. "Yes, the school."

I shook my head and took a bite of toast. Bigger than I might've normally done, but I wanted my mouth to be extra full when I talked again.

"Sorry. Too far."

"He's not there yet," she protested. "He's driving. You could catch up."

"Uh huh. Sure. I'll just drive really fast and see if I can pass his car on the highway. Great plan."

Cedric's victim swore under her breath. The waitress dropped in and asked if Lana wanted a menu. When she looked at me, I told her she probably didn't.

"Coffee's fine, thanks," she said, then turned to me. "I need that laptop. All my data, all my findings are on that thing. I didn't back it up because I was worried someone might hack the cloud drive. Having it with me felt safer."

A laugh soaked in cynicism followed.

"Whoops. So, yeah. I need that laptop. The MBE, too, but only because it's university property that's in my name."

I studied the young woman across from me. She was holding it together, but the hairline cracks in her facade were plain to see. Cedric Mulberry the Third had really done a number on her.

So help her, that do-gooder bit of my brain said.

My schedule was pretty open. I had exactly nothing to do until the next week's karaoke night.

Except go home, I reminded myself. *This wasn't supposed to be a long trip.*

Yeah, but sticking it to Stuffy McTweedy would be worth it. And... Jay.

"You think he'd retrace your steps? Same hotels?" I asked, forcing my thoughts to the problem at hand.

Lana sipped her coffee, scowled, and pushed the mug aside.

"Yeah, probably. He'll have to pay his own way, though. I canceled my credit card."

I glanced at my watch, then looked at the weather outside. It wasn't bad. Chilly, sure, but it was October. At least there weren't many clouds, so probably no rain or snow. The guy only had a day's head start. Cedric struck me as a prude who drove the speed limit. If I didn't, and if he really was going to stay at the same hotels, it wouldn't be hard to find him.

"How big is a multibong echopounder?" I asked.

"A multibeam echosounder. MBE. It's toaster-sized."

That helped. Motorcycle sidecars weren't great for hauling big stuff, which I knew Wilson the not-fish could attest to.

"What kind of car does he drive? What hotels did you stay at?"

She gave me the details, and I added more notes to my napkin. Satisfied I had what I needed, I asked the waitress for the check. When she dropped it on the table, I slid it over to the jilted grad student.

"One hundred bucks plus expenses," I decided.

Lana slid the check back. "A hundred bucks is fine, but you're buying your own crappy breakfast."

"Deal," I agreed after dropping some cash on the table. "See you in a day or two."

It hadn't taken much time to hit the road. No need to pack a change of clothes when the ones you're wearing are just fine. Sure, I had a long couple of stretches in store, but it still qualified as a there-and-back trip. Comfort was all that mattered. Hygiene, as was usually the case, could take a number and get in line.

The miles slid under my bike's tires with a monotonous hum. Somewhere around an hour and a half into the drive, nature called, so I pulled off at a roadside gas station. The diner's food was still heavy in my stomach, but I helped myself to a breakfast hotdog, regardless. They're awesome. Exactly like regular hotdogs, but you eat them for breakfast. I don't have a lot of rules in my life, and I'm prone to bending the few that I have. One that I never break, though, is passing up a gas station hotdog.

As I took a bite of the meat tube in its soggy white bun, my mind reflexively turned to Jay. If my vegetarian friend had been there, I'd have gotten more than a hotdog. He would have added a substantial dose of judgment on the side. Just thinking about it made me smile, and I decided I was past due for a check in. The gas station had a payphone, so I tucked my pop in the crook of my elbow and dropped in a few coins.

"August!" Jay exclaimed. "You heading back? Wait. Minong, Wisconsin? What's in Minong, Wisconsin?"

The fact that he'd started all of our recent conversations by pointing out exactly where I was made me squirm. After spending the past couple of decades trying to stay off the radar, it was terrifying to realize that my whereabouts could be pinpointed so easily.

"Uh, nothing," I said between chews. "Just pulled off the road to pee."

"And eat, apparently," my friend chuckled. "Please tell me it isn't a hotdog."

"It isn't a hotdog."

"Liar. So? What's up? Are you okay? I wish you'd get a phone. I wanted to call you. There's been a lot of chatter in some strange corners of the internet, August."

I shrugged. "Isn't that what the internet is supposed to be? A lot of strange chatter and cat videos?"

"Sure, but this isn't the regular chat boards. Something big is brewing. The back channel chatter from people tied into the CDC is off the charts."

"The CDC?" I asked around another bite.

"Centers for Disease Control?" Jay replied. "Literally the worst of the worst of the government, August."

I scoffed, but it was a forced reaction. I knew about the CDC. I knew more than I'd ever wanted to about the CDC. Jay didn't need to know that, though. No one did.

"Sure, laugh all you want," he said. "Just remember who was right about the Department of Agriculture. Someone tipped off the CDC about something. All the messages are coded, though. Their cybersecurity sucks, but they're at least smart enough to use cryptic words and phrases. I'm still trying to piece it together."

"Huh," I managed.

"Yeah. Huh, indeed. And there's more. I've been jumping into more PN circles online. I mean, now that I'm, uh, warlocking. I know I'm not one of you. Not really. Still, you have to admit that I'm not your average everyday human."

There was a challenge in his tone, so I replied with a conciliatory, "Of course you're not. You're an artist."

Jay snorted. "Which means a lot, coming from you. Anyway, I've picked up on some excitement from pockets of PNs. It's almost like there's a cult or something out there. Real hush hush. Just a bit here and there, but paranormals of all sorts are talking about the time finally arriving. That phrase, used over and over. The time is finally arriving."

"So, let me get this straight. You're worried because you've been eavesdropping on a bunch of PNs and they're excited about an appointment."

The phone pointed out that I needed to add some coins, so I slipped in a few more. The distraction made me miss what Jay had said. Something about being careful, keeping my head down.

"Yeah, yeah," I agreed. "I always do."

"Except when you don't," my friend said. "I'll keep digging. See what I can turn up."

"Shouldn't you be painting or gluing things together or... stuff?" I asked.

Jay chuckled. "I used to have time for that. Now? Too much to learn and practice. Magic isn't easy, August."

"Well, sure. I mean, yeah. That's great. Just don't forget to paint or glue or sculpt or whatever, okay? I expect to see some art when I get back."

My friend's expression of relief rushed through the receiver.

"You're heading home? Good. It's too quiet around here without your constant complaining."

I promised that yes, I'd be home soon. We traded a couple of extra jabs, then I hung the receiver in its cradle. Jay's comments about the CDC had rattled me, but I pushed that worry aside. Jay was a conspiracy theory nut, and the CDC was fertile ground for any seeds his imagination wanted to plant. Whatever he'd stumbled across, odds were infinitesimal that it had anything to do with me.

Infinitesimal isn't zero, a worried little corner of my brain pointed out.

There wasn't much to say to that. Every day since I'd broken free of the research hospital had been a roll of the dice, a spin of the roulette wheel. There was nothing to be done, other than to track down a skeevy college professor with morals as sticky as his fingers, and hope my past stayed firmly behind me.

—ele—

Cedric was cowering in his hotel room's corner, half-hidden behind an overstuffed armchair.

"Pleasure doing business with you," I remarked after shifting back.

With a smug nonchalance, I redressed, then hefted Lana's industrial laptop in one hand and a multibeam whatsit in the other. After balancing them on top of the karaoke machine, I rolled the precariously balanced stack toward the door.

"Oh, and Lana wanted me to let you know that she's already got a letter written for the U.S National Academy of Sciences. It details all of her work with references and citations, and includes a list of colleagues that will vouch for the veracity of the letter's contents. It also describes your ongoing efforts to sabotage her, and your theft of her personal and intellectual property. Any attempt to contact her or engage in a smear campaign, and she'll send it to the Academy and every major news outlet in the country. You'll be finished. Clear?"

The professor made some strange noises that might have been protestations or just plain old blubbering. It was hard to tell. I'd scared the bejeezus out of him when I'd shifted into a gorilla. All that condescending arrogance had gone right out the window when he'd pissed himself and tried to hide behind the armchair.

"Clear?" I asked again.

"Yes, damn you! Yes. But you tell that no good..."

I never got to hear the rest because I started to shift again, just enough to add a decidedly simian cast to my features. With a squeal, he crawled further behind the chair.

"Thought so," I said, and left.

A few seconds later, I was in the room next to his. When it comes to hiding, I know a thing or two. Cedric might go looking for me. Check other hotels or motels. It didn't matter how many degrees he had. He'd never look next door.

I heard him leave about a half hour later, and I heard him return later that night. The force with which he slammed his door brought a smile to my face. He'd gone looking and had returned empty-handed. The hotel's thin walls made it easy to follow his footsteps back and forth across his room. They also made it easy to hear his side of a conversation when he called someone. Well, if we're being honest, pressing a glass against the wall and smooshing my ear against it helped, too. What? There was nothing on cable and I was bored. Sue me.

"The location may be compromised, but there's nothing to worry about," I heard the professor say. "No... No, damn it. I only got to about half of the files, but it would take her forever to recreate... Well, if you insist, it's because I was copying them. There. I said it. I was copying her files. There's some good work in there. I can repurpose them, publish it. Nothing incriminating, obviously. Her work on inorganic compounds is stunning. I'll be able to add three new elements to the periodic table. Well, of course, that's what is important! Not all of us have been banished from the field. Oh, spare me. At least you get funding. Yes. Yes. No! I said not to worry. What? Don't you threaten me, unless you don't want to know what I found out..."

Bored, I opted to skip the end of Cedric's conversation. He was in hot water with someone, and my give-a-damn was busted. I set the glass on my bedside table, contentedly stretched out on the bed, flipped on the TV, and settled in for the night.

The next day, I loaded up my sidecar. Many miles and a few gas station hotdogs later, I rolled into Knife River. Lana was waiting anxiously in her rented room. When I returned her repossessed items, she almost hugged me. Almost, which made the moment awkward as hell. I accepted a handful of twenties in lieu of that hug, then wished her great success with whatever she planned to do.

I thought that'd be the end of it. I should have known better.

CHAPTER 12

SS Henry B. Smith

November 9th, 1913

Went down during the Freshwater Fury, one of the worst storms recorded on the Great Lakes.
All hands lost.

I've ALWAYS FELT BAD for materialistic people. When I think of how much of their lives they waste packing, my heart breaks. That's time that could have been much better spent doing much more important things. Eating hotdogs, for example. Drinking beer. Or—and this is crazy, I know—actually getting to where you wanted to go.

I shoved what less evolved folks would likely describe as dirty laundry into my duffel bag and slung its strap over my shoulder. After one last look to make sure I hadn't forgotten anything, I opened the door, and Lana Delridge almost knocked on my nose.

"No refunds," I said.

"I don't want a refund," she replied testily. "I want credit. I want accolades. I want prestige and the respect of my peers. I want my work to be on the five o'clock news."

"Maybe start with buttoning your shirt right" I suggested as I stepped past her. While she fumed and got her denim shirt buttons sorted, I added, "I'm sure everything will work out great. Have fun being famous."

My duffel went in the Guzzi's sidecar, and the helmet I'd hung on the handlebar went onto my head. I'd just buckled the chinstrap when the grad student positioned herself in front of my bike.

"I need help," she said through a clenched jaw. "I can't get any of those things on my own. I need to rewrite my program. I need to go back out there, take more readings, confirm what I found. I need to replicate my methodology and collect careful notes. I need witnesses, too. No one will believe me when I publish this. I'll need independent witnesses to corroborate."

"Uh huh. Like I said, good luck with that."

My boot heel stomped down while I squeezed the clutch and twisted the throttle. The Guzzi complained like it always did, and my twisting of the throttle made those complaints even louder. Whatever Lana was saying was lost in the engine's throaty coughs. At least, it was until she screamed at me to stop.

I let up on the throttle, and the engine settled into a malcontent mumble.

"Thank you," she said, while waving away the oily cloud from the bike's exhaust. "Now, please. Please, August. I need this, and I don't have anyone else to ask. Just a few more days. That's all I need. And a boat. Please."

That knee-jerk reaction to not give a damn was still there, but it was a perfunctory twitch of the metaphorical knee. Lana stood in front of me, arms squeezed across her chest and chin lowered in defiance. She radiated anger and indignation and determination. All of that was there, but it was a veneer. Cedric hadn't just taken her favorite whatever when he'd left in the night. He'd taken a defining part of her. This wasn't some clay teapot she'd made in a community ed art class. Her work had consumed her. She'd poured everything into her research, and then had made the simple mistake of trusting, of loving someone she thought would help her. The woman didn't need the torn and bloody halves of a broken heart taped back together. She needed to reclaim her identity. Her soul.

I chewed the inside of my cheek while wrestling with indecision. Beneath the brains and bravado, Lana Delridge was practically a kid. She couldn't have been more than mid or maybe late-twenties. The thought of some smug asshole nearly three times her age doing such a shitty thing to her irked me. So, yeah. There was some sense of noble purpose at play when I felt my resistance softening. The other reason wasn't altruistic at all.

I was packed up, sitting on my idling bike, ready as I'd ever be to head back to Minneapolis. Ready to grab a drink at Betty's bar. Ready to eat a hotdog at Uncle Sid's. Ready to recline in the old beanbag in Jay's art studio. When I thought those thoughts, though... When I actually made them specific images in my mind, only two of the three were genuine. I missed Betty. I missed my favorite hotdog spot. But Jay? Every time I thought about the guy, I saw his face on that late summer night. The night when he'd wanted to kill a woman and shove some other lady's ghost into that new body.

"Oh, what the hell?" I decided. "A few more days won't hurt. Hop on."

"Where are we going?" she asked.

"To see a guy about a boat."

It took a bit to find Oliver Corbyn, but only because I'm an idiot. I'd figured the guy lived in a house or apartment like a normal person. I should have known he lived on his boat.

There's something almost magical about a fishing boat on Lake Superior. The very picture of serenity and relaxation when the weather is kind. A stark reminder of our insignificance when it's not. Viewed against the sprawling expanse of water, Oliver's boat was a speck. A blue and rust colored mote. Small waves lapped the chipped paint on its sides, hungry for what they felt was their due. One look at the vast lake, and you knew it was only a matter of time before those waves had their feast. The boat hardly seemed fit to resist their appetite. Its builders had clearly intended it to be squat and sturdy. To me, with all of Lake Superior in the background, it looked like a tin can balanced on the edge of a rippled mirror.

The fore held a three-sided cabin with a hail-dented roof and windows streaked with grime. The aft had a mounted chair and fishing pole. Between the rod and cabin, a sparse deck with a hammock suspended between the gunwales. The *Lucky Bobber,* true to its namesake, bobbed in the water, and Oliver Corbyn bobbed with her. When Lana and I walked down the dock, he gave a surprised wave from the deck. Ollie's bucket hat shaded his face, and a worn bathrobe covered his lanky frame. His bare feet were crossed, and a mug of coffee rested on his belly.

"August Shade?" he called out. "To what do I owe the pleasure, and who's your friend?"

"Ollie, Lana. Lana, Ollie," I said by way of introductions. "Permission to come aboard?"

The fisherman laughed his hearty laugh. "Granted. Want some coffee? I still have half a pot."

We awkwardly climbed onto Oliver's house while he stowed his hammock and fetched extra mugs. After the three of us had settled as much as one can on a rocking boat, I gave Oliver the CliffsNotes of the grad student's plight.

"So Lana here needs a boat to search for something weird in the middle of the lake," I finished.

Oliver rubbed his chin in thought. "Where exactly?"

"East of Isle Royale, where the Rock of Ages lighthouse is," Lana said. "I have the exact coordinates of where I want to start, and we'll need to make a big circle. Maybe a quarter-mile radius."

At the mention of the lighthouse, Oliver went very still.

"I'm not overly keen on heading that way," he said in a flat tone. "August here knows why. Honestly, I'm surprised you'd be willing to make the trip," he added with a pointed look at me.

"It's not exactly on my list of favorite things to do," I admitted, but didn't add that risking another encounter with his ex was preferable to facing my necromancer buddy back home.

Lana looked worriedly from the fisherman to me and back.

"I can pay," she said. "Not a lot. Not now, anyway. But once I publish this research, the money should come pouring in. Talk shows. Conference keynote speaker offers. A book deal. There will be plenty of money then."

"You're doing this for the money?" he asked me.

"Nope. I'm doing this because Cedric Mulberry the Third is a Grade-A asshole."

Oliver tapped his chin in thought. "And you'd risk seeing... her... again?"

"I've seen worse," I lied.

The fisherman stood and peered across the wide lake. After a long moment, he turned back and extended a hand.

"Captain Oliver Corbyn, at your service. If you'll allow me a bit of time to get dressed, we can be on our way. What are we looking for, anyway?"

Lana gripped the extended hand, eyes glistening.

"Thanks," she said, voice heavy with emotion, "and you wouldn't believe me if I told you."

It didn't take long for us to be off. Oliver ran a tight ship, so he had plenty of fuel and–more importantly–plenty of beer in the boat's small fridge. The three of us toasted the morning's adventure, then he took the wheel and sent us chugging out of the marina. Once we'd cleared the docks and the no wake zone, he opened up the *Bobber* and showed us what she was capable of. It wasn't that impressive. The boat was many things, but fast wasn't one of them. None of us were concerned, though. Lana said she'd use the time to work on her program rewrite, and Oliver had said I could help myself to the beer, the fool.

The weather was calm, and the sun took the edge off the cool breeze our passage stirred up. Gulls made their lazy circles high above, and a hungry pelican swooped and dove to scoop up his breakfast. The whole vibe was a remarkable departure from my last boat ride. I'd taken the mounted seat by the fishing pole. It was comfy enough, and I told myself to enjoy the whole experience. At least I had that option. The grad student? Not so much. Her fingers were tapping at the keyboard at a frenetic pace, and she was chewing her lip so intensely that I doubted she'd be hungry come lunchtime.

The impulse to distract her was strong, mainly because I'm a juvenile little jerk at heart, but also because people that worked so hard made me nervous. I resisted the impulse by chatting with Oliver instead. Over the span of an hour or so, I learned some interesting tidbits. His father hailed from England, but his mother was Serbian. He'd won the *Bobber* in a poker game. His favorite fish was the Northern Pike.

"They're meaner than spit and don't take no shit," he'd said with a laugh. "Can't help but respect a fish like that."

For my part, I shared that I'd been repo'ing stuff for the broken-hearted for well over a decade, and made the sailor laugh with some of my more outlandish adventures. He asked about me being a shifter. I shared some tidbits, then apologized for being the only shifter I knew. Questions about my life before becoming a paranormal post-relationship personal effects repossession specialist were gently brushed aside. Oliver accepted my diversions with his usual good nature, but I could tell he was genuinely curious. As we chatted, the sky rolled by above and the water flowed by below. Between those two unfathomable things, our idle conversation passed the time.

There were three specific moments where the easy banter faltered. The first was when he asked what I did for fun when I wasn't playing taxi for lake monsters. I'd started talking about hanging out with Jay. When he inquired about my friend back in the Cities, I faltered. What was there to say? That my best and only friend had learned how to control the elements and drag dead people back to the land of the living? I made some banal comments about him being an artist, about him having a few strange hobbies, and about how I'd always been jealous of his dreadlocks. My words dried up after that. Thankfully, Ollie took the hint.

The second moment was when he jokingly asked if I'd ever had to repo something for myself. Without thinking, I'd replied that once I had to get my soul back from a siren. That shut us both up for a bit.

The third moment was when Lana screamed.

"Stop! Stop here!" she yelled.

Oliver throttled back. The *Bobber* rocked forward, then settled into a glide.

"Please tell me you don't want to drop anchor. Mine won't come anywhere close to the bottom out here."

"Nope," she said. "No anchor. We're going to, um, troll? Is that the right word?"

Ollie grinned. "If what you mean is, we're going to go real slow, then yes. We'll troll."

"Good. This is almost exactly where we were with... him. Can you keep us close to these coordinates while I get set up?"

"Can a burbot snap a fifty-pound line with a toss of its scaly locks?"

Lana looked at me with blank eyes.

"How in the hell should I know?" I said.

"Yes," Ollie said with a roll of his eyes at the landlubbers he'd foolishly let aboard. "Yes, it can."

He looked at an old-fashioned sextant, jotted a few notes in a worn notepad, studied the sky, jotted more notes, then set a hand on the wheel and the other on the throttle. While we bobbed gently, Lana powered up the multibeam echosounder she'd mounted on the prow. When she was finished, she settled into the co-captain chair and set the laptop case on the dashboard. Oliver might've been piloting the ship, but it was Lana Delridge who was suddenly the old boat's nerve center.

"Now what?" Ollie asked.

"Now?" she asked in return. "Now..."

The woman inhaled sharply, then rolled her head on her neck and stretched her jaw.

"Okay okay okay," she exhaled sharply. After a quiet moment, she followed with, "North-northwest, please."

For the next hour or so, we crissed and crossed. We swung around in slow arcs. We trolled. The view was breathtaking, but Lana never looked up from her screen. Her fingers danced across the keyboard, stopped, and then resumed their frenetic tapping. The only words she spoke were to give Oliver directions.

At first, I was curious. Then I was bored. Then I was curious again. My interest ebbed and flowed like the icy water that stretched in every direction. Every so often, I'd stretch my neck and peer over her shoulder at the laptop's screen. It was fruitless, though. To my untrained eye, her computer code looked like gibberish.

"What are you doing?" I asked for the tenth time.

Like the previous nine times, she ignored me. I mumbled something unkind, stood up to fetch another beer from the fridge, and the storm struck.

The speed and ferocity of its onslaught left us speechless. One minute, we were chugging along under a blue October sky. The next, clouds had blocked out the sun, a mighty gust rattled the cabin's windows, and the lake's surface went from gentle swells to angry whitecaps. As the wind ratcheted up, waves grew in height and breadth until each swatted us like a giant paddle. Lana yelped and swore and fought desperately to secure her laptop. I skidded back and forth across the wet deck, my boots proving beyond a doubt they were the wrong footwear for a day on the lake. Ollie gripped the boat's wheel and did his best to point our prow toward the waves. It was a futile effort due to their inexplicable assault from all sides. The *Lucky Bobber* groaned in distress as the sudden squall threatened to tear her apart.

"Take the wheel!" Ollie yelled.

"No way!" I yelled back.

"Damn it, August. I need you to steer the damned boat!"

Reluctantly, I set my hands on the big wheel.

"What do I do?" I asked.

"Try to keep us from capsizing," Oliver replied with a nihilistic shrug. "I'll do the rest."

Before I could ask what that meant, he'd danced nimbly down the deck toward the boat's stern. Right when it looked like he'd go ass over teakettle into the water, he grabbed the back of the mounted seat and swung himself into it. A second later, Oliver had pulled restraints across his shoulders and waist and snapped metal buckles into place.

"Steady!" he cried out, or at least, I think he did. The wailing of the wind and slamming of the waves drowned out everything except my own terrified screams.

I turned my attention back to the churning water and strained my not-meant-for-physical-labor muscles. I kept the wheel from spinning, but barely. Rain pelted the cabin's metal roof hard enough to convince me BBs were falling from the sky. I braced my feet and hunched my shoulders and wondered why I was doing all the work while Oliver was floating above the boat.

"Wait, what?" I asked, blinking in vain.

I'd hoped to clear what had to be a hallucination from my eyes. No matter how much I blinked, though, the image remained. Lana flopped and rocked in her chair as another wave broadsided us. She braced one arm on the dash. The other held her laptop tight to her chest. Despite being bucked like she was riding a bull, her gaze stayed locked on something beyond the window's glass.

"Is that Oliver?" she yelled.

It sure looked like Oliver Corbyn. Or more like the ghost of Oliver Corbyn. It had his hair and his face, but both were luminescent shades of white and gray. Gone were the bucket hat with its quirky fishing lures, the fisherman's vest, the quick-dry trousers. In fact, all of his clothes were gone, leaving the rest of his pearly body on full display. I wrenched my head around and stared out the cabin's open back. Sure enough, Oliver Corbyn was still strapped to the chair on the boat's rear deck.

"Do me a favor," I called out. "Run back there and see if Ollie died, would ya?"

"Died?" she gasped, stupefied.

"Yup," I grunted as a particularly punishing wave knocked the boat sideways. "Because he's still back there, and that's gotta be a ghost."

I waved a hand at the apparition, slowly rising toward the storm like a lost balloon, then frantically gripped the wheel again as it threatened to spin. Lana turned her stricken look from me to the spectral Oliver Corbyn and back.

"What do I do if he is dead?" she asked. "What do I do if he's not?"

I shrugged, but doubted that she noticed. My whole body was lurching and bunching in its efforts to keep us pointed at the waves. When I didn't answer, Lana cursed. She shoved the laptop into an elastic net under the dash, then careened through the cabin and to the deck beyond. Meanwhile, I watched the specter, still visible but fading. I risked a glance behind me and saw that Lana had reached the fisherman's body. She gripped his shoulder with a hand and shook vigorously, but Ollie didn't respond.

"Great," I growled. "Just great. *Lucky Bobber*, my wave-spanked ass."

If I died on that damned boat, I swore I was going to haunt the nearest karaoke bar and hum *The Wreck of the Edmund Fitzgerald* over and over until they shut the place down.

"I think he's breathing," Lana gasped as she lunged into the cabin and collapsed into her chair.

"He's what?" I asked. "So, if he's not dead..."

We both peered through the window and craned our necks. Ghost Ollie was still there, but barely. A powerful gust rattled the window's rain-streaked pane, and he was gone.

"Just frickin' great," I growled again.

Another wave did its best to send us to the bottom of Lake Superior, and Lana screamed as the boat lurched.

"What are we going to do?" she asked.

"Die, I suppose," I replied.

It did seem like the only probable outcome. Lightning arced from the heavens to the water. Waves like liquid mountains rose around us. The hard rain had turned to hail the size of golf balls. Against the cabin's thin roof, it sounded like that old troll, Canute, was beating it with an aluminum bat. The freak storm was going to pound us to bits, and then we'd die. Sometimes, things aren't that complicated.

I'd never been the religious sort, but still tossed out a prayer, just in case. In response, there was a peal of thunder. A clap that made my ears ring, followed by the sound of boulders rolling down a mountainside. Then I felt a vibration, a tightening of the air, a tensing of the whole damned world. The thunder's last rumble stretched into a sustained, low note, like when a CD player was on the fritz and got stuck on a song's single note. That note went to the roots of my molars. The base of my spine. Every bone in my body hummed along with that strange, long note.

What followed was hard to describe. If the thunder had been played on an old reel-to-reel tape, and someone twisted a knob to reverse their direction, that might have fit. It genuinely sounded like that peal of thunder was being rewound.

"What the hell?" Lana had time to ask before a particularly nasty wave lifted us up and sent us crashing down.

My stomach squeezed into my nose and then squished into my toes, and then there was nothing. Nothing at all. The rain had stopped. The wind had stopped. Without its constant berating, the waters instantly calmed.

"What the hell?" Lana said again.

We both stared in disbelief as the storm clouds parted and frayed. In less than a minute, the sky was its earlier clear blue. Nothing marred that perfect expanse of sky. Well, nothing except the ghost of Oliver Corbyn. My eyes refused to blink, so transfixed was I with the descending shape. As before, his arms were outstretched and his legs hung languidly. As before, those arms, those feet–basically all of him–was a hazy, pearly white. From a distance, he was a white shadow. As he drifted lower and closer to the boat, features emerged.

"He sure looks happy," Lana whispered in a trembling voice. "What's that about?"

"The guy's always happy," I grunted. "It's annoying."

Like sunflowers tracking the sun, we pivoted to follow the boat's floating captain. We tracked him across the prow, then lost him when his ethereal toes drifted an inch or so above the cabin's dented roof. Lana and I stared out the cabin's back, breath frozen in our lungs. A long moment later, we caught sight of those toes again. Oliver continued his drift, slow and sure, toward the boat's stern. The closer he got, the lower he descended, until his pale feet touched the deck. They took measured steps, and the ghost of Oliver Corbyn walked into Ollie's limp body. Literally walked into. I watched ghost Ollie pass through the chair and into real Ollie's body. There was a disorienting alignment of legs, arms, and head, and then there was only one fisherman.

A fisherman whose back bucked and lungs sucked in half the air in the northern hemisphere.

"Whoo!" he called out. "Wow. That was a big one."

Ollie's arms waved and his hands slapped ineffectually at his restraints.

"A little help, here?" he requested.

Lana looked at me, face almost as white as floating Ollie's had been.

"What the hell?" she managed a third time, voice brittle.

I *hmph'd* and stomped across the boat's deck. When I reached Oliver, he turned a tired smile my way.

"What was that?" I asked as I unfastened his harness and belt. "Seriously, Ollie. What in the fucking hell was that?"

The fisherman stood, then wobbled and collapsed.

"No, no. I'm okay," he promised while waving off my attempts to help. "If you didn't drink all the beers, grab me one and give me a minute."

Dubious, I followed his instructions. After cracking the tab, Ollie sucked down half a can, then belched.

"Uff da. Better. Alright. Up and at 'em."

He found his feet and teetered up to the cabin. Lana was still where I'd left her, hand braced on the back of the co-captain's chair. Oliver gave her a polite nod as he slid past and settled into his seat. The chairs on the boat swiveled a full three-sixty, so he turned his and gestured for her to sit. I leaned against the doorjamb and popped the tab on my own beer. Only after I'd taken a healthy swig did Ollie speak.

"Can you keep a secret?" he asked.

Lana blinked, and I shrugged. It was enough to satisfy our captain.

"I'm a Zduhać."

"Gesundheit," I said.

Oliver chuckled. "You told me, August, that you don't know any other shifters. We have that in common. I know others like me exist, but I've not met one. All I have are my mother's stories of her homeland. In Serbia, Romania, Bulgaria, and even Greece, we'd pop up from time to time. To the best of my knowledge, I'm the only one here."

"Obviously," I said.

The man gave me a quizzical look.

"Here, as in America, not here as in the boat," Lana clarified, her tone dry enough to whisk the lake water from my soaked jeans.

"Obviously," I said again while willing my blush away.

"So, you're a paranormal. A PN," Lana stated.

"Obviously," Ollie said with a tired smile, "but I'd ask you to keep that to yourselves. I'd rather not have folks badgering me."

I scratched the stubble on my chin. "Because why? Because you can stop a storm in its tracks?"

"Pretty much, yeah," he agreed. "It's what my kind do. We protect our towns and villages from the weather's ravages. And I do," he added, "but on my own, and only when it really seems necessary. Arguing with Mother Nature is tough enough already. I don't need folks making a fuss to boot."

"Uh huh," Lana said. "I mean, c'mon. What's there to make a fuss about? You just, you know, leave your body and float up into the clouds and then crazy storms go poof. No need to make a big thing about it."

The fisherman nodded. "Exactly."

Lana chewed her lip for a moment.

"I don't know what I should be studying. What's down there," she said while pointing at the deck, "or what's right in front of me."

Maybe it was because of my already-fried nerves. Maybe the boat's constant bobbing had unsettled more than my stomach. Whatever it was, Lana's flippant remark flipped a switch in me.

"No goddamned way!" I blurted out.

My response was visceral. It was angry, loud, and startled Lana so badly she damn near jumped through the cabin's window.

The beer I'd almost finished clattered to the floor. My fists clenched at my sides, and every animal under my skin clamored to get out. My chest heaved with ragged breaths.

"August...?" Oliver tried.

"No. No. Just no. Don't even think it. He's not some frog for you to dissect."

I glared at Lana through a film of red. The fisherman who could stop a storm as big as the great lake stood and faced me, thinking he could calm my rage. I met his eyes, and he sat down.

"August, please..." he said, attempting to bring my boil down to a simmer. "She didn't mean anything by it."

I squeezed my fingernails into the meat of my palms, took a deep breath in through my nose, and let it slip out in a long hiss through my clenched teeth. After another few breaths, my blood pressure felt like it was approaching a safer level.

"Sorry," I muttered. "Sorry. I just... I'm sorry."

Lana worriedly asked what she'd done, but I waved it off.

"Nothing. Really. Forget about it."

Telling her that was easier than delving into my distant past, where a maniacal doctor had kept me imprisoned and poked and prodded me to the brink of death. Both Lana and Oliver still watched me warily, but the conversation resumed after a few faltering attempts.

"Paranormal biology isn't my thing, anyway," she said, then forced a laugh. "Not saying that what you did wasn't amazing, Oliver. It was."

"Cheers," he replied with a dip of his chin that set the lures on his hat brim jangling.

"It's just, I mean. I think I've found something bigger. And I'm not only talking about size."

She placed her open laptop on her lap, took a steadying breath, and turned its screen to face us.

"This is rough. Without my full program and earlier data, I had to broaden the parameters a lot, so it's fuzzy. Even so, this is definitely... something."

When she was sure she had our full attention, she tapped a key. The screen went blank, then a green dot appeared in the upper left corner. It blinked three times before suddenly zipping across the screen. There were a couple of green flecks spaced at random internals across the row. After reaching the right edge of the screen, the dot dropped one row and zipped back to the left. Again, it left bits of green in its path. Over and over, like an old dot matrix printer, the green dot went left to right, down, right to left, down. Every pass added additional bits of green to the screen. Slowly, it became more and more apparent that her laptop monitor wasn't glitchy. Those bits of green were coalescing into something else.

"Is that a picture?" I asked. "What's it of?"

Oliver leaned in to study it more closely.

"A ship?" he exclaimed. "No. It can't be. I mean, it could be. Old Gitche Gumee has plenty of wrecks. Hundreds of old bones littering the lake's bottom. As we so recently saw, storms can come up quick. Although, not usually as quick as that last one..." he said with a puzzled frown.

I frowned as well, but it was for Lana.

"So you found an old ship? All of this was for that? Talk about anticlimactic."

"Well, I guess it would depend on how old we're talking about," she said cryptically, "and where the ship came from."

Oliver clucked his tongue in thought, then glanced up through the window.

"Well, Miss Delridge, if you've found what you think you were looking for, might I suggest we be on our way? That little line over there, that's Isle Royale. I'd rather not get much closer with sunset closing in, if it's all the same to you."

I followed his look and felt a tightening in my chest. Hanelle and I had parted on as good of terms as one could hope for, but it didn't mean I wasn't still terrified of her. Or attracted to her. Like Oliver, there simply wasn't any way to see her roost on the horizon and not want to steer clear.

"I second that," I said roughly. "Let's get moving."

Lana didn't object, likely because her mind was plumbing the farthest depths of a very deep lake. Her silence was assent enough for our captain, though. Oliver spun the wheel and eased the throttle forward. Soon, Isle Royale and its fearsome inhabitant were faded memories, lost in the blood-red rays of a setting sun.

Back on shore, Ollie tiredly tied off the *Bobber*, then headed for the Gull. Lana collected her gear and trudged after him. Since they were heading to a bar, I followed. We claimed three stools, and the grad student offered to buy the first round. When Tom came to take our order, though, her shaking hands couldn't work her wallet. After watching her try—and fail—to pull some bills free, I ended up sparing her the trouble.

"Geez. What is it? What's with the jitters?" I asked her, after passing Tom a twenty.

Rather than answering my question, she lifted her laptop case to the bar. A moment later, we were confronted by that strange green image.

"Ever hear of the Baltic Sea Anomaly?" she asked.

Oliver shook his head, and I did the same.

"A Swedish diving team discovered it on a treasure hunting trip back in 2011. They only had sonar, and those aren't great at hi-res images. I mean, unless you can afford multi-receiver synthetic aperture sonar and can whip up some fast imaging algorithms. That's tough, though, because the point target reference spectrum and algorithms to decipher it are super complex."

"Yeah, I'm out," I said, and turned to go.

"Wait!" she begged as she grabbed my arm. "Sorry. I just like this stuff. Anyway, that diving team caught something on their sonar, and it sparked a lot of interest. For years, everyone from amateur cyber-sleuths in their mom's basement to large research organizations wanted to inspect what was at the bottom of the Baltic Sea, but getting permission is impossible."

"Okay…" I said, "and that has what to do with this, exactly?"

By 'this,' I meant the picture on her screen.

"What do you see?" she asked in reply.

I frowned, sensing a trap.

"A triangle."

"Isosceles," Lana corrected.

"Obviously."

She gave me a skeptical look, then moved on.

"Nature loves symmetry, but not that much. Those two sides are the same length. Exactly the same length. It can't be a natural formation."

Ollie tapped the screen with a finger.

"And it's big," he remarked. "You had me going back and forth so you could trace its edges, didn't you?" When Lana nodded, he whistled. "Damned big."

The grad student's smile was infectious. "Yep. Even stranger, that symmetry isn't just the lengths of its sides. It doesn't even really have sides, because it isn't flat. I think it's conical."

I squinted, which prompted her to explain that meant it was shaped like a dunce cap. With a respectable amount of effort, I bit back a retort.

"What about the pattern, then? Those angled lines running across it?" I asked.

Oliver's weathered and cracked fingertip brushed the screen and traced the screen's image.

"If it's a cone like you say," he said slowly, "then those could be flutes and lands?"

I squinted again, which prompted Ollie to explain the basics of a drill bit to me. Again, I bit back a retort.

"You'd said you thought you found a ship, Miss Delridge," Oliver continued. "I know ships. Tugs, trawlers, yachts, schooners, freighters, sloops. That isn't any of those things, and it certainly doesn't look seaworthy. What do you think it is?"

She took a deep breath and let it out through her nostrils. The grad student's eyes were wide and serious when she replied.

"The Lake Superior Anomaly. A regular object that is clearly a made thing, not a natural occurrence. A metallic object, but spectrometer analysis shows the metals aren't found on our periodic table."

She paused and studied our reactions. Oliver's was one of befuddlement. Mine was one of dismissal. I'd heard that tone before. Many times, in fact. Pretty much every time Jay opened his mouth.

Lana pushed past my disinterest. "An object that was never intended to travel on the surface of the lake. A drill-shaped object at the bottom of a lake..." she prompted.

"No..." Oliver said as the dots connected.

"Exactly," I added with a disdainful sniff. "No. It's not."

My arms crossed as I leaned back, and I pulled on the most skeptical expression I had. One I reserved for the rare times when Jay had really gone off the deep end.

"Not a craft that burrowed its way up from under the surface? Somewhere so deep that our science hasn't been able to penetrate it yet?" Lana challenged. "So, you're the expert here, huh?"

I was about to say that yes, I was the expert. I'd been abducted earlier that fall by two thugs from the Department of Agriculture. I had seen how slowly they'd moved in a refrigerated room. I had watched one's nose pull away from his face after the scuffle that should have ended my life. I had seen the scaly skin beneath that fake nose. Then I'd been lectured by my best friend on Hollow Earth Theory and how a race of humanoid reptiles were trying to change the surface of the planet and humanity's DNA so they could move up, make weird hybrid babies, and take over the outside of the planet, too. So, yes, I was about to say that I was the expert. Then I realized that my supposed expertise was lining up nicely with her theories.

"Uh…" I said.

Lana crossed her arms defiantly and looked at me.

"'Uh?' That's all you've got?"

"No," I retorted with a defiant look of my own. It's confusing when you start what you assume will be an argument and end up agreeing with the person. "It's just. I mean. Jay said a race of reptilians live under the Earth's crust, down closer to the core where it's really warm. But Jay's crazy."

The words left my mouth, and I cringed. Whatever reaction I'd expected, all I got was a wide-eyed blink from Ollie and a question from Lana.

"Who's Jay?"

"No one," I blurted. "Just a guy I know. He's into the weird shit."

"Reptilians, huh?" Lana mused. "Like PNs from deep under the surface?"

This time, it was Oliver's turn to get riled.

"They are definitely not like paranormals," he snapped, shocking both me and Lana. With a quick backpedal, he added, "I mean, whatever made that thing, it probably wasn't a PN. There are a lot of odd paranormals, but none that I know of that live by the Earth's core and build big drill rigs."

"Me, neither," I offered, partly to mollify the still-smoldering embers in his eyes, but also to firmly reestablish that I was arguing with Lana.

"It's refreshing to be among such esteemed experts," the grad student sneered, but softened it with a sad smile. "Well, whoever made it, it is definitely the find of the century. I can understand Cedric wanting to get the credit. Science is cutthroat. I get that. I hate it and I don't condone it, but I get it. What I can't understand is why he'd try to destroy the evidence. Where's the upside?"

I rubbed my chin in thought.

"I know a thing or two about relationships." When Lana raised an eyebrow, I glared and pressed on. "Sometimes, when people split up, they take something they want. More often, though, they take something they know the other person wants, and they do it for no better reason than it's a shitty thing to do. The really rotten ones don't just take it. They trash it. If they can't have it, they make damn sure no one else will have it, either. Those jobs are the worst. I show up and there's nothing to repo, and I have to tell my client that their favorite whatever is gone for good. Your professor sounds like that kind of guy."

Lana's eyes glistened.

"I guess so," she whispered, then added with a steely edge, "but he failed. I found it. I found it!"

Oliver raised a glass, and Lana clinked it hard enough to send her drink sloshing over the rim.

"So?" I asked. "What now?"

The grad student sighed. "I have a lot of work to do. Document my methodology. Refine my assumptions. Improve my analytics. I'll need to spend more time on the lake, too. Ollie, you interested?"

The normally affable fisherman squirmed like a worm on one of his hooks.

"Please?" she asked.

"I'm all for advancing the sciences," he hemmed. "The light of knowledge should shine bright, as they say. It's just. You know. The weather, especially this time of the year. We're bumping up against November. Storms, the likes of which would put today's to shame, are the norm, not the exception. The *Bobber* will be going into dry dock soon, so..."

"So we'll head out again tomorrow," Lana decided.

Oliver fixed me with an appraising stare.

"And you, Mister Shade? Would you be up for another adventure?"

Another adventure was the last thing I wanted. I wanted peace and quiet and a well-stocked beer fridge.

And I don't want to be anywhere near some weird reptilian drill ship, I silently added.

I readied myself to explain all of that. I took a breath. I held it. And then...

"Fuck it. Why not?"

The relief in Lana's eyes was palpable, and the ends of Oliver's grin nearly reached his bucket hat.

"That's settled, then," the fisherman declared. "Once more into the fray, as they say!"

We toasted and drank, then drank some more. Finally, thankfully, Tom suggested that I call it a night. My bike's shocks squeaked as I straddled it. For a long moment, I looked at the bar where I'd sung karaoke. Where I'd met the friend of a lake monster, a KJ that cleared storms from the sky like people brush away cobwebs, and a siren who should've ripped my still-beating heart from my ribcage. Where I fell in with a jilted grad student who was chasing sunken mysteries with probes and karaoke machines. When I'd left home, I'd wanted to get away and clear my head. What I'd learned instead was that the world was crazy no matter where you were.

With that philosophical thought in my not-sober-but-hopefully-not-too-drunk-to-drive mind, I reached a hand down to my belt loop to free my keys. I squeezed the carabiner, pulled them free of the belt loop they'd been clipped to, and slid the bike's key into the ignition. Then someone yanked a dark bag over my head and strong arms pulled me backward. There was a sharp pain in the side of my neck, and I was falling into waters even darker than those of the nearby lake.

Chapter 13

SS Benjamin Noble
April 27th, 1914
Helmed by the youngest captain on the lakes. Disappeared in a severe storm off Knife Island.
All hands lost.

NOT TO BRAG, BUT I'm a bit of an expert on losing consciousness. I've been blackout drunk enough, hit on the head hard enough, and pumped full of tranquilizers enough to know a thing or two. One might assume that clawing your way back from those various depths wouldn't be too different. Spoiler alert: they are.

Waking up after a bender sucks. Your insides feel pureed. Your mouth tastes like a cat crapped in it. You can't help but believe an angry imp is attacking your brain with a plastic sword-shaped olive spear. Coming-to after a run-of-the-mill concussion just hurts. Pretty much what you'd expect after some blunt force trauma to the old brain bucket. Regaining consciousness after being tranquilized is disorienting as hell. Compared to the others, it's more like post-bender than post-concussion. What sets it apart is the tilt-a-whirl sensation. Someone brewed up a batch of chemicals, and those chemicals detach your nerves from any sensory input. It takes a bit for all those receptors to fire again and leaves your poor brain confused as hell.

So yeah. I've had enough alcohol, head trauma, and nefarious pharmaceuticals to know a thing or two. What I knew in that moment—that exact moment when I became aware again—was that something else entirely had happened to me. Whatever my abductors had shot me up with wasn't your average old tranquilizer. Sure, I had that tilt-a-whirl sensation. The whole world seemed to wobble around me. There should have been a returning of the rest of my nerves, though. Painful tingling in my fingers and toes. A telltale ache where the needle had gone in. None of that was there. Or, to be more specific, there simply wasn't anything there. My eyes worked. My ears worked, or at least, I think they did. A bitter taste filled my mouth, so it seemed pretty certain that my tongue was working. My nose smelled something like burnt sand. Beyond that, though? I might as well have been a head in a bell jar because I was getting zero input from anything below my chin.

"The hell did you guys do to me?" I asked rhetorically, seeing as how I was alone. Then, because rhetorical questions should never be asked just once, I said, "What in the actual hell did you do?"

I blinked my eyelids to combat their sticky dryness, but more to convince myself I had some measure of control over the damned things. They worked fine, as did my mouth. To beat down the mounting panic, I reminded myself of those facts. It made the growing realization that I couldn't feel, much less move, anything else a smidge more bearable.

"Hello?" I called out. "Where am I?"

All I heard was the quiet hiss of air through a vent. I rolled my eyes around and, sure enough, saw a grated duct high up a wall. Never in a million years would I have thought an air duct would fill me with such elation. If there was a vent, that meant there was air. If there was air, it meant things were supposed to breathe. If I was someplace where things breathed, that ruled out being dead and stuck in some boring afterlife. So, yeah. I was probably alive and not in purgatory. The room was still pretty boring, though.

The wall with the duct was somewhere in the gray-beige family with no distinguishing features or details to catch my roving eyes. Process of elimination convinced me it wasn't wood or glass. Beyond that, I couldn't be certain. Maybe sheetrock. Maybe concrete. Maybe metal. It was really anyone's guess. I looked straight ahead. Doing so convinced me I was lying on my back. An illuminated square on another expanse of gray-beige glowed above me. In my experience, lights were usually in ceilings. Since the light was directly in front of me and maybe six or seven feet away, it seemed reasonable to conclude I was on my back.

"Nice work, Sherlock," I grumbled. "Any other stunning deductions you can come up with?"

Unfortunately, there weren't. The grand sum of my observations amounted to: I was alive, I was lying on my back in a really boring room, and I quite possibly no longer had a body.

"What did you do with my body, you assholes?" I called out.

Again, it was rhetorical. There was no one to answer. At least, that's what I thought until someone did. The man's voice had aged, but was immediately recognizable.

"August, please," he said, each syllable clipped to a tidy edge. "You, of all people, should know. We can't have you shifting, so we've induced a chemical paralysis. Autonomous bodily functions will continue, but..."

"... voluntary movement has been neutralized," I whispered, and then succumbed to the nightmare. Back and back I fell through the years into a dark past that I wished wasn't my own.

"We can't have you shifting, so we've induced a chemical paralysis. Autonomous bodily functions will continue, but voluntary movement has been neutralized. Do you understand what that means?"

I didn't. I couldn't. The terror was all-consuming. I screamed and wailed, my young voice at once shrill and hoarse. I had no concept of how long I'd been screaming. All I knew was that I'd been taken. My parents had opened the front door, and a stranger's firm hand had squeezed my wrist so hard it hurt. He had pulled, and I'd been too small to resist. Feet tripping over each other, I'd lurched along as the stranger yanked and dragged. I'd wrenched my neck as far as I could to plead with my parents, but they were motionless. Mom had her face buried in my dad's chest, and his arms had been wrapped protectively around her. There'd been another forceful yank, then those hands shifted from my wrists to my upper arms. Something sharp had stabbed my neck, then I'd been lifted and heaved into a white van. My last glimpse of light, of my life, was abruptly cut off as a sliding door slammed. The darkness inside the van paled in comparison to the pit of nothingness I slid into. How long I floated unconscious in those terrifying depths, I couldn't say. When I woke, there was only the terror of knowing I had been taken. Home was gone. My parents were gone. I was in a room full of strange machines with glowing screens and glaring lights that hurt my eyes, and I couldn't feel my body. All I could do was scream and wail, and so I did, right up until a hand slapped me hard across the face.

"Enough," the man said.

The hand belonged to the man that had taken me. Tall, thin, and pale. A pinched face with close-set eyes barely separated by a narrow nose, and a mouth that only seemed able to frown. HIs clothes reminded me of my schoolteachers. A white collared shirt and dark pants separated by a shiny black belt. Despite his clothes, I knew he wasn't a teacher. Teachers didn't come to my house or make my mom cry. Teachers didn't grab me, not ever, and they'd never throw me into a van. Teachers wouldn't stab my neck and make me sick. And so I screamed and cried.

"This won't do," the man said.

I saw his hands move to a clear plastic bag beside me. A moment later, I felt something. Maybe in my arm? I couldn't be sure. An icy warmth spread. Maybe to my chest? I couldn't know. Whatever it was, it smothered my cries. Breathing became hard. Crying? Impossible. I labored to pull air in and push it out again.

"Better. Now, let's begin your orientation, shall we? We will start with introductions. I am Doctor Emmett Tuttle. You are August Shade. You are in my care, August. Do you understand?"

I didn't. I didn't understand any of it.

"Speak, August," Doctor Tuttle instructed. "The drugs have not rendered you speechless. That is simply your own fear. Do not be afraid. Speak."

"Why?" I managed. "Why? Why, why, why?"

The doctor's response was swift and cruel. A hand struck me again, but the words that followed were worse.

"Because! Because, because, because!" he screamed. After visibly regaining control of himself, he spoke. "If you speak without directly answering my question, I will hurt you. If you speak without being asked a question, I will hurt you. And so, I ask again: do you understand?"

I forced a breath, then managed a lie.

"Yes," I replied, voice hitching a few extra syllables to the word.

"Excellent," he said, then scratched a pen across a clipboard. "Excellent. We are off to such a good start, August, and we are going to do great things."

⁓

It was him. Doctor Tuttle. Doctor Emmett fucking Tuttle. Somehow, someway, I'd ended right back where I'd started, with the psycho who'd taken me from my family those long years ago.

Not really a taking, though, was it? I thought bitterly.

I don't remember my parents well, and I only ever knew them as a little kid. What I do remember is that neither one expected to have a shifter for a son, and–as subsequent events proved–neither had wanted to have a shifter son. For my first few years of life, I'd been human. As human of a kid as one could be. I even had a dog. A big hound dog named Rufus. We'd been playing in the backyard, and that play had gotten rambunctious. I chased him and he chased me, and then everything changed. Literally.

I'd fallen and cut my palm. Rufus had slipped and scraped his side. Terrified that he'd been badly hurt, I'd pressed my hands against the blood on his coat. Then it was me running on four legs. Me being chased by my dad. Back and forth across the yard, we went, and it had been a glorious game. When I tired, I shifted back, and my dad dropped to his knees. I learned shortly after that Rufus was dead.

The next shift, maybe six months later, was our big Maine Coon, affectionately named Catzilla. He'd done what cats do: knocked something off a counter. A big glass vase. When it shattered, I had startled and fallen backward, and a large shard sliced my hand. Catzilla scared himself, too. When he jumped down, he cut his paw and yowled something fierce. I'd grabbed the cat, grabbed his paw with my own bloody hand, and then I was the cat. Again, my dad had chased me. When he finally caught me, I shifted back... and learned our cat was dead.

So yeah, it was a lot for a couple of human parents to handle. Their young son wasn't just shifting into a dog or a cat. Their son was shifting into the exact dog and the exact cat that had died... because of their son.

It took a few years and a lot of introspection, but eventually I realized I hadn't been taken. My parents gave me away. There was a spell where I tried to be furious with them, but every time, I failed. Were my mom and dad truly monsters, or were they victims? Did they regret what they'd done? Had they tried to find me? Should I have tried to find them? Long after I'd gained my freedom, the questions would still bubble up. When they did, I'd crack a beer and drown them. Well, those and all the other memories that came with them, because most of those involved torture.

The doctor didn't want me to become any old animal. He wanted me to become animals that fit his specific goals. It was just my rotten luck his goals were mostly research into infectious diseases. The cat was a serendipitous subject for fecal toxoplasma. A gorilla to test simian foamy virus. An elephant for cowpox. A bull for trypanosoma. A turkey for bird flu. A wolverine for trichinella. A coyote to simulate urban vectors for all a wide variety of horrible things. The dog was a convenient subject for testing everything from weed killer to muscular dystrophy treatments. And the octopus? The damned doctor wanted to study the medicinal properties of its venom between tests to better understand its complex neurology. Ironically, he never added a guinea pig.

Each new animal gave Tuttle a ready subject to study all manner of maladies and supposed treatments. That alone should have killed me a dozen times over, but I'd been surprisingly resilient. With each subsequent test, Tuttle would push the envelope a little further. It didn't matter that my existence was horrendous. There was only his pursuit of 'great things.'

Being a pin cushion for an endless array of syringes was bad. Being infected with some of the planet's worst diseases was worse. Forced to endure all manners of treatments and experimental cures? Horrible. What really sucked, though, was how each beast became part of my repertoire.

I couldn't become anything I wanted. That would have been too easy. For me to shift, there had to be an emotional bond first, followed by an exchange of blood. Then, and only then, could I add that new beast to my repertoire. The truly dreadful part, though? Nature favored balance. Every single living organism is unique. Two identical animals tipped the universe in ways it didn't want to be tipped, so my curse ensured there would be only one.

Tuttle sussed out pretty quickly that a simple blood swap wasn't enough. That emotional bond was the key, and his solution was elegant in its cruelty. I would be introduced to an animal. Tuttle would let me feed it and even play with the safer ones. My loneliness was so complete, so crushing, that I would revel in each new opportunity to have a companion. Then, once Tuttle was sure I'd developed that crucial bond, the glass wall would go up. I could see my companion, but couldn't touch them or talk to them. All I could do was watch as Tuttle would starve and torture them. Whatever bond had planted its seeds, seeing the animals in pain and distress solidified it.

Try as I might, there was no way to harden my heart against their suffering. Instead, I learned I could mask. After the coyote, my young heart had been broken. It reminded me so much of my old dog. Being forced to watch its suffering nearly broke me. When the doctor came again, some strange reflex kicked in. I figured that if the doctor thought I'd gone, I wouldn't be forced to endure another shift. An orderly checked on me. When Tuttle came again, I became the orderly. It had been a pathetic attempt at deceit. A child's attempt at a devious ploy. All it earned me was a new battery of experiments by Emmett Tuttle.

That doctor and his endless torments had been my entire world for thirteen years. I'd been afforded an education, but not for my benefit. It was to satisfy his perverse desire to determine if shifters learned in the same manner as humans. He allowed some creature comforts, but only to compare if my reaction to them was similar to humans. Any semblance of humanity Tuttle had shown was to serve his own ends, never mine. When I'd finally managed my escape, I swore that I would never, ever end up in his clutches again.

"Welp, I guess that plan is good and truly shot," I muttered.

"Still prone to your incessant mumblings, I see," Tuttle remarked.

"And you're still prone to being a deranged asshole," I shot back with what little bravado I could muster. Sadly, bravado doesn't come easily when you're scared shitless and can't move.

Tuttle shook his head in an imitation of sadness. I knew he was faking it because I knew he was incapable of human emotion. He stepped out of my field of vision, then I heard a door open, followed by heavy footsteps. The next thing I saw put that fear of Doctor Tuttle to shame. Instead of the good doctor's face, something else appeared. Something truly terrifying. Well, to me, at least. Jay would have been filled with righteous vindication.

The face was vaguely humanoid on a human-sized head. Two eyes. Two holes that served as ears. Two slits that were likely a nose. A thin line that might've been two lips pressed together had it been born with lips. Its scalp was hairless, the face was smooth, and every inch was covered in green-gray scales. It was a strange face, and also strangely recognizable.

"Schnozz," I guessed.

"Kchenthan, actually. Nice to see you again, Mister Shade," the reptilian operative from the Department of Agriculture said. Free from having to pass as human, his native accent stretched all the esses.

"Kind of sssurprised to sssee you, Schnozz. Figured the Quorum had ssorted you out,"

I said honestly.

Schnozz laughed, or at least offered its reptilian equivalent. Out of costume, he didn't seem inclined to keep up the rest of the human masquerade. The laugh was a series of truncated hisses. Definitely not human.

"Oh, they rattled their swords. More than that? Never," he cryptically replied.

Even if I'd wanted to probe that further, Tuttle leaned into frame and cut me off.

"Quite so. Now, you two have had your little reunion. The objective of this moment, Mister Shade, was to impress upon you the seriousness of your situation. Before, I was operating within the boundaries of American law. With my new benefactors, such constraints no longer apply. You will be tractable, or you will suffer in ways you simply cannot imagine. Well, you'll suffer regardless, but there is always a matter of degree, isn't there?"

My mind was whirling, its belts threatening to slip their wheels. For the briefest moment, I saw the world through Jay's eyes. Suffice it to say, I didn't enjoy the view.

"What does the Department of Agriculture have to do with this?" I asked, more to buy time than anything else.

"With Tuttle?" Schnozz asked. "Nothing. We also control the Department of Health and Human Services and the Centers for Disease Control. Those agencies are quite interested in his work."

"So you've infiltrated the entire government? Sounds exhausting."

"It is exhilarating," the upright reptile replied fervently. "To be so close to achieving our goals? Exhilarating."

I had no idea what he was talking about and didn't much care. I was more focused on my left foot, specifically the slight itch I felt on its sole. Whatever drug they'd pumped me full of seemed to be weakening. If I could just get a little more time, maybe–just maybe–I'd be able to shift.

"Speaking of close, where are we, anyway? Still close to Minnesota, or am I, you know, there? And please tell me that, wherever we are, you brought my jacket."

Since I had zero clue as to how long I'd been out, it was a fair question. For all I knew, they'd shipped me back to that place I'd escaped decades ago. Hell, I might've been on the moon or another solar system. Reality had bent far enough to make anything possible.

"Plum Island?" Tuttle asked. "Oh, no. That facility was shuttered after your escape. Those weak-stomached liberals in Congress made sure of that. However, every cloud has a silver lining. Isn't that the saying? After years of scraping by, my esteemed colleague, here, offered a new base of operations."

"You're terrible at answering questions," I growled while half-listening to Tuttle's words. The itch in my foot was spreading and was demanding more of my attention.

"Indeed," Tuttle said with a frown. "Technically, we're in Michigan, but at these depths, no one cares where one state ends and the next begins. Oh, and yes. If you must know, we have your jacket."

My right hip itched, and I could feel the pressure of a restraining strap across my left thigh.

"Phew," I exhaled with heartfelt relief. "I love that jacket. Wait. Back up the boat. Depths? Are you saying we're in the lake? Are we at the bottom of the goddamned lake?"

Schnozz's laugh sounded like an asthmatic iguana. Tuttle's was worse.

"The very bottom," the doctor said between nefarious chortles. "No escaping this time, August. Oh, we are going to do great things. Great things, indeed."

<h1 style="text-align:center">CHAPTER 14</h1>

C.F. Curtis

November 18th, 1914

Lost amid heavy snow and high winds, along with two schooner barges in tow.
All hands lost.

I'D NEVER HAVE IMAGINED that I'd feel bad for boxes. What is there to feel bad about? You fill them up with whatever, stack them atop one another, slide the old dolly underneath, and wheel them to wherever. I'd done it myself more than a few times. Not once had I considered what the boxes might've thought about the whole thing.

When the surface I was lying on tilted forward, the straps held me in place. In a few places, I could almost feel them. Almost. After tilting me upright, Schnozz slipped behind me. I had no way of knowing if he was pushing me or just operating some controls. A soft whirring made me think it was the latter, but I also heard grunting. It really didn't matter. I was no better than stuff stacked on a dolly. How that dolly worked was the least of my concerns.

Unbidden, thoughts of Clarissa Steyer came to mind.

If she could've seen my future, would she have seen this? I thought sourly. *Me being carted off to my inevitable doom like some schlub's packed-up apartment?*

It was a depressing thought. To be fair, I was in a depressing place. The hallway's walls were that same nothing color and completely bare. At least the old research hospital on Plum Island had some decor. True, most of it was of photos of Doctor Tuttle accepting awards, oil paintings of Doctor Tuttle trying to appear regal, and the occasional motivational poster because his sadism knew no bounds. Still, it was something to look at. This hallway was unrelenting in its sameness. Maybe reptilians were brilliant and had technology that put humanity's to shame. That brilliance stopped at interior decorating. When I finally saw something other than flat gray-beige, my eyes drank it in like a desert sucks down a drop of rain.

My first thought was that someone had hung an Escher print. It had a strange geometry that I struggled to decipher. As we drew closer, I decided it was more like hieroglyphics. Maybe even words, albeit in a language completely foreign to me. Only when we were almost at the odd markings did I realize two additional details. One, they were beside a door. Since there was no frame to speak of, nor a knob, it would've been easy to miss. The other detail was the small sticky note stuck beneath it. The words 'Weather Control' written in black marker filled the pale yellow square in crisp, clear English.

My table-turned-dolly glided to a stop, and Schnozz stepped up beside me. There was a soft whoosh, and the door slid open to release a whiff of that burnt sand smell. My head still wouldn't turn, so I forced my eyes to roll as far to the side as I could. The view was blurry, but I could make out a room full of monitors. Most had a hunched-over person peering at the screen. Standing behind them were more reptilians.

"Report," Schnozz commanded.

"No clue, boss," a lizardy guy replied. "That storm should've lasted another seven minutes. More than enough time to sink one little boat. We're running scenarios on what went wrong."

"Perhaps what went wrong is that humans did the work. Perhaps they need to be reminded of what the consequences are for failure."

There was a hissing from the reptilian and a terrified whimper from the humans. A scaly hand reached out, grabbed one human's shoulders, and dragged him to his feet. Another walking lizard stepped up and pointed an inside-out umbrella at the guy.

Seriously. Picture grabbing a cane umbrella, one with a hooked handle, and stepping into a stiff gale. The wind grabs it and–SNAP!–pulls it all the way inside out. That's what it resembled, and it definitely didn't look threatening. In my post-tranq state, I almost expected it to be the start of some bizarre musical number, like *Singing in the Rain, Reptile Style* with a scaly Gene Kelly.

There was a soft hum, and I quickly learned how wrong my assumption had been. The poor guy sailed across the room and hit the far wall with a sickening thud. When he slid to the floor, his head left a bloody smear. Fortunately, the door shut, and we were on our way before I had to witness any more.

The journey continued. We passed other reptilians. None paid us any mind. We also passed a few humans. All stepped aside and dipped their heads in deference. Besides that, the trip was unbearable in its sameness. Long stretches of unadorned corridor. The monotonous hum of my dolly's wheels. The hissing inhales and exhales from my reptilian chauffeur. Occasionally, there were intersecting passageways, but we took few turns.

"This is the worst ride ever," I complained. "I want a refund."

"You have no idea how bad this ride is going to get," Schnozz replied with another hissing chuckle, "and there are no refunds."

More strange graphics appeared on the wall. Again, someone had stuck a helpful translation beneath it.

"GMO DNA," I read. "I hate you guys. I really, really hate you guys."

"The feeling is mutual," Schnozz replied. "Not to worry, though. Everything is progressing nicely. Once the humans are properly subjugated, we'll take care of you paranormals. Thanks in advance for the help, by the way. Much appreciated."

Our journey reached its end at a door marked 'Virology and Biological Weapons.' It slid open and revealed a larger space than where I'd started. The room I'd woken up in was the size of a small bedroom with a low ceiling. This had to have been three times that big, maybe more. My reptilian chauffeur wheeled me inside. Our destination was a large circle of light in the room's center. Upon arrival, he pivoted me in a one-eighty, then tilted the table back to its flat position. During our trek from the door to the room's center, I'd gotten a good look around. What I saw was unsettling.

A row of enclosures filled the back wall. Their plexiglass fronts displayed each cage's resident. One had what appeared to be a human inside. I realized my error when I caught the shine in her eyes and saw two impossibly long incisors. Another fellow paced the space restlessly, his movement more wolf-prowl than walking. A third was sitting on a small platform a few feet above the floor. Below that platform, the cell was full of water. Whether it was a mermaid or selkie or some other PN, I didn't know. All I knew was the misery in her eyes. The other cells held a coblyn, an elf, and a squat ogre in grease-stained coveralls. A patch on his chest said 'Knife River Boat Works.' Another patch opposite the first said 'Arnold.' The ogre's creased and warty face turned toward mine, and it hit me. He was the Arnold that had been having trouble with his wife. The one the townsfolk thought had up and left. The woman in the water-filled cage must've been the hairdresser who'd vanished. The guy I was sure was a werewolf? The cook from the local diner. No siren had snatched those poor PNs away. Something—someone—else entirely had taken them.

Seeing those paranormals was bad. Seeing what was in the other glass-walled enclosures? Much worse.

One thing might've been a cross between a lion and a bearded dragon, but someone forgot to keep the number of limbs at four. Another looked like an anaconda with two heads. A third had fans rippling on either side of its gaping mouth and fleshy growths wiggling below its chin. Each monstrosity paced—or slithered—its enclosure, looking restless and hungry.

Reptilians were humanoid, so it wasn't hard to imagine them having human-like things in their lives. Restaurants. Amusement parks. Shopping malls full of heat lamps and oversized sunning rocks. Probably even zoos. What I saw struck me as just that: what reptilians might have in their zoos. An image of Schnozz grabbing Missus Lizard and their little newts for a trip to see their inner-Earth fauna rocked my brain. I decided right then and there that I would never, ever go to a reptilian zoo.

"Mister Shade, meet your new repertoire," Schnozz said with a wave at the bizarre monsters.

My eyes rolled in horror.

"Them? You're going to make me shift into them?"

"Of course," Doctor Tuttle chortled. "I've advanced my research, August. Human maladies were all well and good, but we've much more to do if we're going to help Kchenthan and the rest thrive on the surface. You're economical, August. Having you as a polymorphous test subject saves a tremendous amount of effort."

Great, I thought, choosing surliness over fear. *Just flipping great.*

"And the... the others?" I asked over a hitch in my throat.

"Ah, the others," Tuttle said, eyes gone wide and rapturous. "They are my compensation for my work. They are mine."

That itching in my foot had spread. More importantly, wherever there was an itch, I felt other sensations, too. The press of a restraining strap. Rough fabric against my skin. When the fingers on my left hand tingled, it took every ounce of willpower I had to not wiggle them. Whatever they'd drugged me with was obviously wearing off. So far, neither

Tuttle nor Schnozz had noticed. If I was going to have a chance at getting out of there, it was going to be a slim one, and there wouldn't be any do-overs.

"Sounds exciting," I said in a bid for more time. "I bet you'll tell me all about it, Scooby Doo villain-style."

"If you insist," Tuttle said as he wheeled a cart toward my table. I couldn't see its contents, but I could see the syringe he lifted. After flicking it with his finger, he pressed the plunger and sent a small squirt of orange liquid into the air. "It started with my bene-factors' desire to improve their resistance to viruses and bacteria that exist on the surface. They have disease where they come from, but those afflictions are very different from what exists up here. In order for their goal of human-reptile hybridization to succeed, they needed to develop immunity to our common contagions."

"Right. Cool. Cool cool cool," I said. "And these little lizard-human hybrids. How does that work, anyway? Do baby lizards crawl out of human ladies, or do little human guys break out of lizard eggs?"

Tuttle chuckled. "Someone's passed sixth grade biology. Well done, August. You've made me so proud."

I chafed at his dig, but bit my tongue. The game was to gain time, not win the best zinger award. My skin was practically crawling as the itching spread. Remaining motionless was becoming more challenging by the second, but I knew I couldn't actually move. Not yet.

"So? Which is it?"

"Female reptilians are rare, so human women will be the carriers," Tuttle explained. "We're adapting their reproductive apparatus."

"Wow. Who said romance is dead?" I quipped. "So when the little hybrid babies are born or hatched or whatever, what are they going to look like? Are they getting Schnozz's flawless skin or your receding hairline?"

Tuttle impulsively put a hand to his shiny pate, and his eye twitched.

"The offspring will look more like humans," he replied.

"They'll get better looking, though," Schnozz added. "It'll take a generation or two, but we'll get it right."

My eyes rolled to look at Tuttle in time to catch his reaction. It was swiftly hidden, but had been there just the same. For the tiniest of moments, I saw the disgust.

Trouble in paradise, I realized. *I can use that.*

"But they'll be getting human intelligence, right? I mean, I hope so. You lizards are obviously dumb as the rocks you sun on."

Tuttle's eyes twinkled, so I looked to my other side and saw Schnozz scowl.

"I mean, you've got to be dumb, right?" I continued. "Otherwise, you wouldn't need him, would you?"

Schnozz's odd eyes flicked up to look at Tuttle.

"We don't need him," the reptilian snapped with extra emphasis on 'need.'

Tuttle's response was immediate.

"Is that so? You can boost your own immunity? Acclimate yourself to the surface? Make your lizard cows fertile? You can do all those things yourself, can you?" he asked mockingly. "No. That's why you found me. Me! Remember that, my esteemed colleague."

The bickering escalated from there. Schnozz gestured at the space around them and bragged about their technological prowess. Tuttle waved his big syringe and said that his research was light years beyond theirs. Schnozz said hatchlings down below did harder science than his. Tuttle said he could count the hatchlings down below on one hand because reptilian healthcare was worse than West Virginia's.

My eyes rolled back and forth, tracking insults and retorts like they were the ball in a ping-pong match. Meanwhile, the itching spread. Both hands tingled, and I could feel the strap across my chest. Another minute, maybe two, and I could try to shift. It would either work, or that forgotten syringe would quickly be remembered, and I'd be screwed.

My window of opportunity opened when Schnozz stomped around my table and shoved a finger into Tuttle's sternum. Affronted, Tuttle shoved his finger into Schnozz's chest. The reptile responded with a shove. Tuttle stumbled a few steps, then charged and shoved back. A full-on scuffle ensued, and the menagerie in the glass-walled cages started to whoop and cheer and hiss and clamor.

No time like the present, I decided.

I closed my eyes, took a deep breath, and felt an immediate tightening of my restraints. For a moment, I was worried they'd used the gorilla-proof ones, then rivets popped, and I was free. Naked, but free. The shreds of my clothes slid from the table, and my size twenty-seven feet hit the floor. I raised my fists, intent on thumping my chest, but the room tilted, and I staggered to the side.

"He's not supposed to shift!" I heard Schnozz cry. "You said he wouldn't be able to shift!"

Tuttle might have responded had he not been running for the door. I saw his white lab coat slip from view as he sprinted for the hallway beyond. After regaining my balance, I tried a menacing step toward the walking lizard. Tried, and failed. Whatever they'd pumped me up with was apparently still doing its best to keep me down. Instead of a deliberate step forward, I took two cross-steps to the side. My burly arm reached out, and my palm found the front of a cage. The scaly nightmare with as many limbs as teeth scraped and bit ferociously. Despite there being easily three inches of solid glass between its mouth and my fingers, I still yanked my hand back in fear. Too late, I realized sudden moves were a no-no. There was a moment where a gorilla pirouetted on one foot like a big, hairy ballerina. The next, I was flat on the floor.

"Gwwerrah," I cursed. "Gurph. Mmmrgh. Chzurk."

While I was busy cursing in gorilla-ese, Schnozz tried to multitask. In one hand, he held what must have been a walkie talkie. The irate reptile hissed and spit. The words were meaningless to me, but they sounded angry. His other hand rummaged through Tuttle's rolling cart of medical instruments. He picked up and discarded a scalpel, a bone saw, and some wicked-looking forceps. He upended a box of gauze and threw a spare plasma bag across the room at me. It wasn't until I'd leveraged myself up to all fours that he found what he'd been seeking: a syringe full of orange liquid.

With a few last words into his walkie talkie, Schnozz slapped it onto his belt and settled his gangly frame into a crouch.

"You have been nothing but difficult the entire time I've known you," he remarked. "A trait that I've found to be quite consistent across all you paranormals. You're unpredictable. Undisciplined. You don't follow any rules, not even the basic rules of physics. A minute ago, you weighed less than two hundred pounds. Now you're what? Eight hundred? No respect for the law of conservation of mass. I've seen vampires cross a room in the blink of an eye. Might as well just give your Albert Einstein and his Theory of Relativity the finger. Can you even begin to comprehend how much energy moving that fast should take? A small star's worth. That's how much."

While he talked, he made a slow circuit. Why, I couldn't imagine. Usually, when you're trying to keep someone in captivity, you don't want them to reach the nearest door. In Schnozz' case, he was practically rolling out the 'escape this way' red carpet for me. Step by careful step, he circled to his left.

"And all the magic. Magic!" he spat. "It makes no sense. None at all. Wiping you all out will be a boon to the universe."

I'd been watching him warily. More specifically, I'd been watching the syringe he was holding like a dagger. In better circumstances, I'd thump my chest a time or two, gallop over, and flatten him into a scaly pancake. I still hadn't sorted out my internal wiring, though. If I tried to thump my chest in my current condition, I was likely to knock myself unconscious. Might as well just tilt my head and show him where to jab that big needle. Instead, I bided my time. Schnozz could tell I wasn't exactly in top form. His circuitous route was moving him closer to striking distance. One drop of that orange elixir would mean game over for August, the badass gorilla. Then there were the things in the cages beside me. The PNs were screaming for me to get up, beat his ass, save myself, send help. The beasts from far beneath the Earth's crust were writhing and lashing and chomping in agitation like a shiver of sharks that had scented fresh blood. Combined, the cacophony was more than distracting to the poor gorilla and made rational thought a bit tricky. Experimentally, I attempted another menacing step. Like before, it was more drunk-after-last-call than anything else.

"Guurhawh," I cursed.

Schnozz smiled, his lipless mouth curling up in delight. The reason for his gratification became clear a moment later. The door whisked open and no less than five reptilians squeezed through the opening, including one as familiar as Schnozz.

Tranq? Seriously? I complained. *I really thought those guys were sorted out.*

True to his nickname, Tranq had the same rifle I remembered from our encounter at the Minnesota State Fair. While the other lizards with him fanned out, he set its stock against his shoulder, closed one of his yellow eyes, and twitched a scaly finger. There was a pop, then a *plink* as the steel-tipped dart bounced off the far wall.

Psych, I thought triumphantly.

Tranq had aimed at a damned big gorilla's center-of-mass. Lucky for me, that spot was a few feet above the pissed off wolverine that had taken the gorilla's place. My claws scrabbled madly on the smooth floor as I charged the reptilian and his buddies. While I was accelerating–maybe not in the straightest line, but still–Tranq tried to load another red tailed dart into his rifle and his pals sprang into action. Two of them dove to tackle an angry little wolverine and bounced off of an elephant's sides. My trunk raised up to trumpet a challenge, and my meter-long tusks waved back and forth in search of something, anything, to gore. One caught Tranq on the side of the head and sent him sprawling. I trumpeted again, and the strangest thing happened. The other lizards dropped to their knees and pressed their palms against the sides of their heads.

Huh, I thought, then trumpeted again.

I heard their anguished groans. One was in so much pain that it fell to its side and curled up into a ball. I filed the strange event into my elephant's massive memory banks but didn't have time to contemplate it. The handful of reptilians had quickly become the least of my concerns. More pressing was the gang of humans rushing through the door. By my count, there were at least ten. A mix of men and women wearing everything from security uniforms to lab coats to pajamas. A strange sense of pride warmed my heart. I was apparently quite important and merited all hands on deck.

The mob surrounded me. The ones dressed like security guards held billy clubs. The others flexed the fingers of their empty hands with a mix of menace and trepidation. You could practically see the thought bubbles above their heads wondering what in the hell they'd signed up for. I took a couple of heavy, woozy steps and swung my tusks from side to side. The drug was still messing with me, and there was the added bonus of shifting too many times too quickly. It always left me feeling addled. Fortunately, I was also jacked up an adrenalin and spoiling for a good scrap. I guess being abducted, dragged to the bottom of a great lake, imprisoned in a bizarre drill ship from deep underground, and confronted by the boogeyman of your tortured past will do that. I gave voice to a final trumpet to keep the reptilians squirming, then went back to my best shift for a clobbering. The gorilla spread its feet and fists, bared its teeth, and tried to not wobble. One of the braver humans took a step forward and raised his club. Then the melee began.

Here's the thing about fighting. When it's you against one other guy–or lizard, or whatever–you want to be coordinated. When you throw a punch, you have one target to hit. A brawl is a different story. If you're up against three, four–or in this case, ten or so–other guys, it's actually easier. You can just swing and your odds of hitting someone you don't like go way up. Like, a thousand percent. At least, I think so. I'm not great at math. I was good at swinging my massive arms like King Kong at a rave, though. The sound of my fists meeting flesh, the screams of people getting slugged by a gorilla, and the moans that lingered after they'd gone down filled the lab. Even so, I was taking my fair share of punishment. Clubs rained down from all sides, and fists and feet hit like hail. Yeah, I was a badass gorilla, but I was still flesh and blood. Speaking of blood, I slipped on a small pool that had spilled from a guy's nose after I'd broken it. I dropped hard and was immediately hog piled by the crowd. A club caught the side of my skull and a foot found my kidney. Someone stomped on my kneecap and someone else bent one of my fingers back. Images of Gulliver being swarmed by Lilliputians filled my brain as I fought to break free. I managed to roll onto my stomach, then heaved myself up.

The PNs were glued to the front of their cages, mouths wide and fists pumping. I galloped at the one holding Arnold. He jumped back, but the reaction was unnecessary. That glass was strong as steel. I had enough time to pound its surface ineffectually with my fists, then the mob was on me again.

More blows were exchanged. More bodies sailed across the room. I was giving more than I got, but was still getting one hell of a beating. I tried to convince the gorilla to save the captive PNs, but it was more concerned about its own hairy ass. While that tiny bit of human me screamed for it to stop, to go back, to help them, the gorilla galloped toward the door. I'd just cleared the threshold when something sharp stabbed me in the butt cheek. I whipped my head around and saw Tranq's victorious expression. Then I cleared the door and careened down the hallway.

The jarring of my four-limbed lope sent waves of pain through my body. That was worrying, but not as much as the slowly creeping numbness clawing its icy fingers over my hip. I stumbled, but forced myself back up. Doors passed with their strange reptilian signs and sticky notes with English translations. None were helpful. I didn't care about 'weaponized consumerism and infomercials' or 'CO_2 production and monitoring' or 'talk radio programming.' All I wanted was a way out.

One leg stopped working, but I kept moving while dragging it behind me. With no sense of where I was going, I turned at a branch in the hallway. Ahead was more of the same: featureless walls and occasional doors with ominous signs. 'Religious indoctrination' and 'influencer psy-ops' went by in a blur, then I took another turn. Suddenly, the signs were less nefarious and more mundane. I passed a laundry room, what had to have been a bathroom, and even a mess hall. That last one's door was open, and a bunch of surprised faces turned as I lurched past. One human had just taken a bite of a donut. The reptilian face across from him had a spoonful of what might've been crickets. My other leg was weakening, but I kept pushing myself forward. I managed another few yards, then shifted and fell to my now-human stomach.

"Come on, August," I panted. "Come on!"

I got myself up and peered down the hallway at something unusual. Something I hadn't seen before. A small, amber light winked steadily above a strange circle in the wall. I used a hand to steady myself and hopped ahead. When I reached the light, I almost collapsed with relief. There were more strange hieroglyphics and a sticky note that said in all capital letters: EMERGENCY EXIT. I slapped an orange button beside the note right as a voice far behind me yelled stop, stop him, don't let him get away. Instead of a doorway sliding open, a hole opened like an iris. With no other options, I belly flopped through the opening and used my weakening arms to drag myself in.

Cushions took my weight, and lights winked to life around me. A monitor lit up, and reptilian symbols flashed on the screen. There was another hiss. My ears popped, and G forces squished me back. I heard a rushing sound and a fading alarm. Right before I blacked out, I had one last—and not especially helpful—thought:

Welp, I know a thing or two about losing consciousness. I've been blackout drunk enough, hit on the head hard enough, and pumped full of tranquilizers enough to know a thing or...

CHAPTER 15

SS Onoko

September 15th, 1915

Developed a serious leak under its machinery while passing Knife Island.

All hands survived.

I WOKE UP. AFTER waking, I added a fourth kind of emerging from unconsciousness to my list. It was every bit as distinct from the others I'd experienced. Different from the day after a bender, or blunt force head trauma, or even a cocktail of lord knows from some shady chemist's lab. It started with feeling like a mob beat your ass six ways to Sunday and ended with a song.

For an eternity, I simply listened to the beautiful melody. Gradually, the gentle ebb and flow of its haunting stanzas and lingering refrains let more of the world in. I lay on my stomach, arms bent at awkward angles. The sound of lapping water reached my ears, and a chill breeze ran across my bare skin. After a minute or an hour, I decided I must be at sea. When I paid attention, I could feel my body's complaints. My brow furrowed, and a worried groan passed through my chattering teeth. Something was wrong. Very, very wrong. Or something had been wrong. Maybe. I couldn't remember. The song eased the darkness. Set my worries adrift and let the tides draw them away. There was only contentment.

The edges of the serenade sharpened with urgency, stern with command. No more would I be allowed to waft in hazy contentment. There was more expected of me, more needed from me. My eyes opened, but they were blind to the blinking lights of an electronic panel or the hinges of my vessel's now-open lid. They didn't see the broad expanse of black water stretching in all directions, or the blanket of stars spread across the night sky. They saw a vision. A radiant vision. One that I had to reach, no matter what.

"I'm coming," I croaked. "Please. Wait. Wait for me."

I had every intention of pushing myself with my feet and legs. If I still had those, they weren't willing to help. If I didn't, it was of no concern. The song coiled around me and pulled, and I felt my chest inch forward. Another pull, and cold water reached my elbows. Another pull, and I was free. Free, and then sinking. I tried to resist, but the weight of oblivion is heavy indeed. A single word passed my lips as liquid ice closed around my face. A single name, uttered with lust and longing and love.

"Hanelle..."

Then I was gone.

Chapter 16

SS Chester A. Congdon

November 6th, 1918

Ran aground in a thick fog near the northeast point of Isle Royale.

All hands survived.

"He's breathing. Holy hell. He's breathing."

"No, don't move him. He might have broken something."

"You already moved him."

"What did you want me to do? Leave him on his back and bail the water out of his lungs with a bucket?"

"Stop it, both of you. Just let the man be, for chrissake."

"I still can't believe he's breathing. How long do you think he was under?"

"Not long. I didn't know it was him. I had no idea it was him."

"And if it hadn't been him? What then, huh? You would've just let whoever it was die? You're a monster."

"Enough! Everyone shut up. He's alive, but we have to get him back to shore. We can point fingers later."

"Or talons."

"Careful, warlock, or I'll point one at you."

"You be careful, harpy, or I'll send you into orbit."

"Touch her, and you'll be sleeping with the fishes."

"Try and stop me, and all the water in this lake won't be able to douse the fire I start on your boat."

"Damn it, knock it off. What's wrong with you guys? He's safe. He'll be okay. Let's just get back to shore."

Chapter 17

SS Kamloops

December 7th, 1927

Last seen steaming towards Isle Royale, heavily coated in ice.

All hands lost.

Tom Hanks set another glass of whiskey gently on the bar. My wooden fingers reached for it, but like the last time, couldn't grasp it. There might as well have been flippers extending from my wrists.

"Here, let me help," Jay said.

My friend placed a supporting hand on my back while using the other to bring a rocks glass to my mouth. I swallowed, then grimaced at the burn in my throat.

"Better?" he asked.

"Sure," I said after a soft cough. "All better."

The fact that he was there bent my brain in uncomfortable ways. Tom Hanks made sense. We were at his bar, after all. Oliver made sense. He spent almost as much time at The Thirsty Gull as Tom Hanks did. Lana Delridge's presence wasn't all that surprising, either. The grad student and Ollie had been the last people I'd seen before being abducted by Tuttle and Schnozz's goons. Jay, though... I couldn't figure that one out at all. There he was, his dreads tied back with a handkerchief, a paint-stained work shirt over a thermal undershirt, his face a study in genuine concern. How he'd known to come to my rescue, how he'd known where to find me, were questions I'd have to find answers to later. When I'd come to on Ollie's boat, Jay's presence had been too much to process. Now, in the sheltering embrace of the town's watering hole, warm and dry and wearing someone's borrowed clothes, with a little whiskey in my belly…

Nope. Still too much to process.

After assuring everyone that I was all better, I sat quietly on a stool, elbows on the bar's top and sternum pressed against the rail, and let my best friend serve me whisky like a terribly irresponsible mom helping her toddler with a sippy cup.

"You'll feel better soon," he promised. "Just give it time."

Time was a funny thing. I knew some had passed, but had no concept of how much. After I'd come to and coughed up half of Lake Superior, I'd slipped in and out of consciousness. Awareness didn't kick back in until they'd heaved me off the *Bobber* and onto the dock. It had been dark then. It had been dark when they'd kicked open the bar's door, propped me up on a stool, and served my first glass of whiskey. It was still dark. Time had come and gone, but not much. I knew that, but didn't feel it. Eternities seemed to stretch between each moment.

"That's good. That's real good," Jay said encouragingly as he poured more spirits into my glass. "There's no hospital anywhere near here, so we figured whiskey was the next best thing."

"You weren't wrong," I said tiredly.

It seemed like the kind of thing I was supposed to say. My suspicion was confirmed when Jay offered a relieved smile.

"See? You're okay. You are okay, aren't you, August?"

"Peachy. Now, if you don't mind, more whiskey, please."

I'd tried again to grip the glass, but only succeeded in sliding it a few inches with my palm. Jay obliged, lifting the glass and holding it to my lips. I swallowed and coughed again. It made the side of my chest hurt, but I set that aside.

"I have questions," I started. "Let's start with why doesn't my hand work, and gradually work up to what you're doing here. I mean it, though. Go slow. Pretty sure someone hard-boiled my brain."

Jay looked at Lana. Lana looked at Oliver. Oliver looked at Tom Hanks. Tom said he didn't know what was going on. Ollie called, said it was an emergency, and told him to meet him at the bar. The bearded giant ended with a shrug and looked at Jay.

"I don't know why your hands aren't working," he said. "Maybe the same reason your legs aren't working that well. You might have been drugged."

I unbarred the door holding back dark memories and let a few slip free.

"Yup. I was drugged."

"You were in a boat. Well, not a boat, exactly. A raft?"

"A capsule," Lana supplied helpfully. "Kind of a coffin-shaped capsule."

"A capsule," he repeated. "Like an escape pod or something. Its lid must've opened automatically when it reached the surface. Then..."

He paused and clenched his jaw. For the briefest of moments, his face was almost unrecognizable. Almost, but not quite. I recognized it. The anger, the defiance, in his eyes was too much like that night with the spoon and the ghost and the hag.

"Then that siren sang to you, and you went into the water. Guess we're all supposed to be super happy, though, because she figured out it was you and rescued you."

I let that sink in. The door to my memories had already been cracked, but his words flung it open. The fight to get free from the ship below the water, the escape pod, Hanelle's irresistible voice, the freezing darkness that followed.

"Shit happens," I muttered. It seemed like the kind of thing I was supposed to say. Then, "That doesn't explain you, though." I looked at Jay. "Or any of you, really. But mostly you."

Jay's fingers worried the tip of a dreadlock, and his eyes looked everywhere but at me.

"Remember when I told you there was some weird stuff on the dark web? Chatter on some shady boards? Stuff about the CDC?"

I nodded, unsure of where he was going.

"After we talked, I kept digging. Digging into places I'd never been willing to look before. People were looking for you, August. You. Specifically you. They didn't say your name, but I figured it had to be you."

"They found me," I said without emotion.

"I'm sorry," he replied with a hitch. "I left as soon as I realized something big was up, but had no way to find you. Just the location of a couple of pay phones. Then I found your bike."

"And us," Oliver chimed in. "Miss Delridge and I were still here when your friend blew in. Literally. His wind near took the door off its hinges."

"At first, we thought maybe you'd wandered into the woods," Lana said, taking over the story. "Jay swore you'd been abducted. That you were on some very bad people's list."

"Not people," Jay muttered.

"Okay, sure," Lana amended grudgingly. "Not people, but not PNs, either, right? Who took you, August? How did you end up on the lake in that weird capsule thing?"

I turned my head from face to unexpected face. Tom and Oliver and Lana and Jay looked on in anticipation. It was hard to know where to start, so I figured maybe it was time to start at the beginning.

"Who here knows about Plum Island?"

Lana raised her hand, then seesawed it a bit with uncertainty. Tom shrugged, his wide face showing he hadn't a clue what I was talking about. Oliver said he thought it was on the east coast. Only Jay spoke, as I knew he would.

"Seriously? You know I know about Plum Island. We've talked about Plum Island. Army Chemical Corps. The Animal Disease Center. It's where the National Bio and Agro-Defense Facility was supposed to be, too, until they decided to move it to Kansas."

"Yeah..." I agreed.

"And you always changed the subject," Jay realized. "Every time I brought it up."

"Yeah..." I agreed again.

Jay helped me take another sip of whiskey, then waited impatiently while I dabbed at my lips with the back of my wrist. I noticed the shirt sleeve and raised an eyebrow.

"One of mine," Ollie supplied. "You were naked when we found you."

I looked down and sighed a world-weary sigh.

"My jacket?" I asked. When Ollie shook his head, I cursed. "Damn it. I loved that jacket. Fuck my life."

"Come on, August. Spill it," Jay demanded. "You said Plum Island. What does any of what's going on have to do with Plum Island?"

I savored the whiskey's quiet burn for another moment before licking my lips and clearing my throat.

"The Animal Disease Center was real. I was there. Sent there as a kid when my parents learned I was a shifter and couldn't handle it. Kept there for thirteen years until I broke out. Experimented on damn near every day for all of those years by a psycho named Doctor Tuttle."

Lana gasped. "Did you say Tuttle? Emmett Tuttle?"

I nodded, shocked to learn that she recognized the name.

"Cedric, I mean, Professor Mulberry talked about him. I've read some of his earlier papers. But he washed out years ago. There was some ethics scandal, and he lost his funding. He was stripped of his office and funding, had all his awards and honors taken away, and even had a bunch of papers unpublished. Blacklisted, is what I heard."

I snorted. "Ethics scandal, huh? Yeah. I guess you could call it that. Nothing that happened in that place was ethical."

"You never told me," Jay said softly. "All these years, and you never told me you'd been held at Plum Island."

"I never told anyone. How could I? All I wanted was to put it behind me. Guess that plan's a bust. Tuttle's back and he's got some new benefactors. Remember Schnozz and Tranq?"

Jay's fist pounded the bar. "The Department of Agriculture guys? The reptilians?"

"So there really are reptilians?" Lana repeated, her shock immediately echoed by the others.

For the next few minutes, Jay and I took turns recapping my misadventures with a cornflower demon, a scarecrow, and two government operatives that weren't what they appeared to be. When Jay spoke, he added more details from his wealth of otherwise worthless knowledge about cabals and shadow governments and a junk drawer's worth of other crazy stuff. When I spoke, I kept it short. I didn't want to think about all of it, so I tried to gloss over the worst bits. Especially the part about my Fetch and being shot. My glossing wasn't glossy enough though, because Oliver pierced me with his storm gray eyes.

"You really are him," he said. "I'd wondered, but never would have thought it was possible. Fergal O'Dwyer told us about you."

When I scowled in confusion, he held out his hand at about waist height.

"Little fella, about this tall. Red hair, red beard. Talks too much."

"Oh," I said. "Yeah. Him. Wait a second..."

I looked at Oliver Corbyn. Really looked at him. The simple fisherman and part-time karaoke jockey looked back. Up until a day ago, I'd pegged him as a human. Then there was that out-of-body weirdness and the storm. Definitely not human. Now, he was talking about a certain leprechaun. A leprechaun that had told him about me.

"He's in the Quorum," I stated, then set my slow wits to puzzling out the rest. "And you said, 'talked to us.' You're in the Quorum."

"Was," Oliver admitted after trying and failing to return the look I was giving him. "We had what you might call a difference of opinion on some things, so I resigned."

"What's a quorum?" Lana asked. "I mean, I know what a quorum is, but I don't think you're talking about a small Q quorum. Sounds like you're talking about a big Q quorum."

"Forget about all that," Jay snapped. "August, you were talking about a doctor and the reptilians. What happened to you? Where did they take you? How did you end up in the middle of Lake Superior last night?"

Instead of looking at Jay, I turned to Lana.

"Let's just say I got to see the inside of that thing you found down there."

Jay and Lana started asking so many questions at the same time that my head damn near exploded. I answered what I could about what I saw inside. The various rooms, the strange signs and nefarious translations. When they'd exhausted my knowledge, Lana pulled out her laptop. Within a minute, she and Jay were down the digital rabbit hole. That left me with Tom and Oliver.

"Tell me again how you escaped," Oliver said after downing his whiskey.

While Tom refilled his glass, I recounted how I'd been wheeled to the lab with the abducted PNs and strange beasts in their glass-walled cages. How Tuttle and Schnozz had argued long enough for the paralysis drug to wear off. How I'd shifted and shifted again. How I'd brawled my way free and found the escape hatch.

"So, it wasn't the siren," Tom suddenly blurted out.

I turned to look at him, but he hadn't been talking to me. His eyes were focused squarely on Oliver.

"No, it was not," he replied. "Hanelle did not take our friends, unless one or two were foolish enough to be out on the water late at night. Good luck convincing any of the others of that fact, though."

Tom reached a hand across the bar and laid it on Ollie's shoulder. "We will. We'll make them understand."

The fisherman moonlighting as a KJ moonlighting as a storm busting paranormal who also just happened to have fallen in love with a terrifying siren nodded sadly. He took a fortifying drink, then pierced me again with his gray eyes.

"Go back," he said. "You said you shifted into an elephant. You said you trumpeted, and the reptilians fell."

"Yeah. Weird, right?"

Oliver regarded me for so long I squirmed. What he did next was even more unnerving.

He straightened his back, curled his hand into a fist, and brought it up alongside his mouth. Eyes never leaving mine, he uncurled his fingers and moved his hand away from his face in one smooth motion.

"What the hell is that?" I asked with enough salt to turn Lake Michigan into the Great Midwestern Ocean.

"Let's just say this old man has a lot to think about," he said after letting his hand drop. "Would you indulge a simple fisherman and listen to his meanderings for a bit?"

I glanced over my shoulder. Jay and Lana were still engrossed in whatever was on her laptop screen. Ignoring them meant I could ignore Jay, and I was game for anything that might make that possible.

"Sure," I said. "Wait. One sec," I said, then carefully positioned my hand alongside my whiskey. Like a slow echo of Oliver's gesture, my fingers curled around the glass. Experimentally, I lifted. When the glass rose and didn't slip out of my grasp, I brought it to my lips. "Ahh. Better. Okay. Meander away."

"So much of life is about control," he began. "Hanelle can make men do the most foolish and suicidal things with her song. I can tame the angriest storm. Your friend is a warlock. He..."

"Controls the elements," Jay said, turning to face us.

The fisherman and warlock held each other's gaze for a breath, then Oliver nodded.

"Indeed. Even Miss Delridge there seeks to control things by making the inexplicable fit into some understandable framework. So much of life is seeking control. Order. Corralling the chaos that makes up the very fabric of the universe."

"You're starting to sound like my ex," I complained. When Oliver tilted his head, I shrugged. "She was an oracle, and she loved to lecture about entropy and negentropy and fate and free will."

Again, Oliver regarded me for too long of a time. His face, his entire body, had gone still. Finally, he licked his lips and said, "An oracle, was she? Interesting. Well, your ex knew a thing or two about a thing or two, as they say. Anyway, as I was saying, we all want to control things to some degree. Humans are the worst. Their society. Their laws. Their religions and their politics and their sciences. Always this obsession with knowing and defining and, yes, controlling. Personally, I think it's because their lives are so short. When death is looming practically from the moment you're born... Yes, I can understand their desire to find solace in the illusion of control."

Unbidden thoughts of Tony the Douchebag Warlock came to mind, which brought even more unbidden thoughts of my best friend. The impulse to glance over my shoulder and make sure he wasn't trying to raise the dead or anything was strong, so I channeled it into lifting my whiskey glass and draining its contents. Tom raised an eyebrow, and I tapped the glass in response. After it had been refilled, Oliver continued.

"Paranormals tend to be a bit different. Many PNs are blessed—or cursed, depending on who you ask—with long, long lives. It gives us a different perspective from our human counterparts. When you can watch the world and all its changes over centuries, you start to appreciate the patterns, the cycles, the inevitability of things. For some, this feeds a fascination for prophecies and predictions. History has shown there will inevitably be a great darkness, and history has also shown there is always a champion of the light. Rather than seeking to control, paranormals are more inclined to let the great wheel of time turn. Live according to your nature and trust that the patterns will repeat. There will be a darkness, but there will also be a hero. It must be so, because it has happened so many times before. Do you follow me so far?"

I'd had more whiskey, but was still early in the descent to inebriation. I paused to consider his words, and decided out loud that yes, I was picking up what he was laying down.

"Excellent. So, there are humans, and there are paranormals. We're sharing this planet for better or worse. Humans, endlessly trying to decipher and decode and control. PNs, a bit more inclined to let things run their course with the occasional nudge from some inevitable hero. And then there are the others."

The way he said 'others' was dark. I hadn't known Oliver Corbyn long, but he'd seemed to be a man of infinite good humor. That perception of the man changed in an instant. He was capable of hate, and that hate had a very specific focus.

"Those reptilians," he spat. "Yes, I know about them. The Northern Quorum has for a long time."

That caught everyone's attention. We all stared, astonished, until Tom Hanks spoke.

"I've never been the sharpest tool in the shed," he said humbly. "But, Ollie. All this about reptiles and quorums and that siren not being the one taking our friends and neighbors and him..." He faltered with a look at me, then doggedly continued. "Him being here. I just. I guess I just don't know what in the heck is going on."

"Ditto," Lana said.

Oliver *hmph'd*, the sound weary and sad.

"Too much is going on. Too damned much. The Northern Quorum is a group of powerful paranormals that act as a court or arbiter of sorts. They judge and punish PNs that step too far out of line. It's why me and Hanelle," he said in a voice gone raw, "made it impossible for me to stay with them. When they learned people were disappearing, those damned fools believed the rumors. They wanted to hunt her down and end her."

"I'd like to see them try," I scoffed.

"You say that, but you don't know what they're capable of."

"Not much, apparently. The Quorum had those two reptilian douchebags dead to rights, but let them go."

Oliver grimaced. "You aren't wrong, but you have to understand how we—how they—think. The Northern Quorum governs paranormals. Those lizard bastards aren't PNs. Not by a long shot. Not our jurisdiction, so to speak."

Jay looked up from Lana's laptop and uttered a harsh laugh.

"And they've weaseled their way into humanity's governments. So no help from the humans," he concluded.

"Exactly," Oliver continued. "Worse, they've been a steady flow of gas on the human fire. If Icarus flew too close to the sun, I guarantee it was those damned reptiles that made his wings. The humans, they're being manipulated. Duped. Reptilians don't want to move to the surface and coexist. They want control at a level that puts the humans to shame. They want to eliminate chance. To stomp out free will by subjugating every living thing on this entire planet."

I considered what I knew from my brief encounters with Schnozz and Tranq and Doctor Tuttle. The pieces Oliver was setting out for consideration fit uncomfortably well together.

"So, what of it?" I asked, choosing churlishness over further contemplation. "Reptilians are the pits. Now what?"

Oliver regarded me with his storm gray eyes, expression thoughtful.

"It appears a darkness is rising again," he said, "and perhaps I left the Quorum too soon. Or perhaps I've played my part and had to step aside for one better suited to the moment."

"And what moment would that be?" I asked as I drained the last of my whiskey.

"The moment when this generation's hero arises," Oliver said seriously.

I didn't get what he was implying. He pierced me with those steely eyes and forced understanding on me. Unbelievably, I realized he meant me. The bastard was talking about me. I leaned as far back as I could, my face a study in shocked incredulity. In response, Oliver Corbyn brought his fist up to the side of his mouth, then pushed it forward and opened his hand.

"The Singing Warrior," he said. "You're the prophesied one, August Shade."

"You've got to be kidding me," I sputtered. "No way. I can't even carry a tune."

Ollie's countenance was serious, but he winked all the same.

"Maybe not," he agreed, "but you can karaoke."

Chapter 18

USS Essex

October 14th, 1931

Taken from service and burned.

THE DRIVE FROM THE Thirsty Gull to my ramshackle cabin was a short one, but felt like it took ages. Oliver's loaner clothes hadn't included a jacket, and the October breeze was reminding me too much of the lake's icy waters. Maybe that's why I was shivering. Or maybe, just maybe, it was because I'd had one hell of a day. Barely twenty-four hours ago, I'd witnessed a grad student discover something bizarre at the bottom of Lake Superior. Less than twelve hours earlier, the boogeyman of my past had dragged me down to that reptilian drill rig. Less than six hours earlier, I'd fought my way free only to nearly drown in that damned lake, thanks to Hanelle being Hanelle. The fact that she'd saved me curbed my irritation, but not by much. Then there was Jay, of all people. Yeah, he'd been getting all warlocky and playing with the dead. Even so, he'd raced to my rescue the second he'd thought I'd been in danger. I wanted to be terrified of the guy, but it was hard when he kept being such a damned good friend. All things told, my recent misadventures should have been enough for one day, but no. Oliver had to reveal that he was part of the Northern Quorum, and worse, that the Quorum and a bunch of other PNs thought I was some prophesied hero. My head was spinning. Worse, every revolution left me thinking more and more about Clarissa Steyer.

Trees passed on either side, their nondescript gray taking on more nuance and texture as the rising sun stretched faint rays across the town. It reminded me of how she'd once tried to describe her future-scrying gift. She didn't just see the future. She saw multiple futures, endless possibilities. As chance and choice danced their endless dance, some of those futures became more likely and would brighten.

Except mine, I remembered grumpily. *I was born under the sign of the Thirteenth Zodiac. I don't have a future. I have all the futures. I'm special. Shyah. Right.*

Clarissa had lost her magic eyeball after that fateful night on Nicollet Island, and with it, her ability to gaze into the future. It hadn't stopped her from talking about it, though. More than a few times, she'd gone on about all the possible futures, about fate and free will, and about me being some strange exception to the rules. It hadn't been a conversation I'd wanted to have. Apparently, it also wasn't a conversation I could avoid.

Luckily, I'd been driving slowly. Any faster, and my jaw dropping off my face and landing on the road would've caused my front tire to buck, my hands to slip off the handlebars, the bike to swerve and tip. It was easy to imagine me going ass over teakettle, snapping a clavicle, and shredding the skin off half of my face. Then I'd have rolled, banging an elbow and cracking a kneecap, before finally ending in a bloody heap. None of that happened, though. When I spied Clarissa Steyer sitting in the Adirondack chair beside my rundown cabin, my jaw dropped, but I didn't lose control. My still-wooden fingers relaxed their grip on the throttle, and the bike rolled to an anticlimactic stop. For a long moment, I simply stared at the woman sitting in the headlamp's circle, my brain sputtering like the bike's idling engine.

I hadn't seen her in months. After saving the world, we'd dated for a few weeks. One morning, I woke, and she'd been gone. It had hurt then. It still hurt now.

"Hey there, August," she said with a small wave.

"Hey, Clarissa," I replied with an impulsive lift of a hand.

I considered myself to be a bit of an expert on weird. Over the course of my illustrious career as a post-relationship personal effects repossession specialist, I'd encountered things ranging from unexpected to downright bizarre. You might have thought me inured to being surprised. You would have been wrong. Seeing her there was one hell of a surprise, and it shook me to my core.

And that was before I realized she was looking at me with two eyes.

"Mind if I come in?" she asked.

I didn't know if it mattered what I wanted. According to her, she couldn't see my future. That was with the old eyeball, though. The one she'd lost. Maybe this new one was an upgrade.

"Uh," I replied. A twist of a key killed the bike's engine. I swung my leg over the saddle and made my way to the cabin's door. "After you, I guess."

The woman stood, straightened her familiar cardigan and smoothed her long skirt, then took steady steps that left me envious. Her shoulder brushed mine as she passed, and I shivered with sudden desire. That emotion lasted all of three seconds before my much more appropriate anger smothered it.

"Make yourself at home. There's a couple beers in the fridge. Bathroom's over there, and that's the bed. You know. The thing you can leave while I'm still sleeping in it."

She settled into the room's only chair and looked at her folded hands.

"I deserved that," she said softly.

"You deserve worse. You deserve an epic ass-chewing. You deserve me throwing dishes at walls and kicking over garbage cans. Lucky for you, I was drugged by walking lizards and had a few glasses of whiskey, so my reflexes aren't so great right now."

I crossed my arms to hide my trembling. She picked at a cuticle. Neither of us spoke. Finally, I closed the door and opened the fridge. When I held up a can, she nodded, so I lobbed it across the room and grabbed another for myself. Since she had taken the only chair, I dropped onto the bed, pulled my can's tab, and finished about a third of it in one pull.

"So?" I asked.

"So," she answered quietly.

"Are you going to make me drag it out of you? Fine. Why are you here, Clarissa? We'll skip past how you knew I was here and get to the heart of it. Why in the hell are you at my cabin in the middle of frickin' nowhere?"

She finally looked up, her two eyes meeting mine.

"Still too bright," she muttered. "Like a firefly in a room of lightbulbs."

So, it's not an upgrade, then, I thought. *Good.*

Rather than answer my question, Clarissa posed one of her own.

"How have you been?"

"How have I been? How have I been? Unreal..." I said, making the last word into an incredulous curse. "Just fine, thanks for asking. Keeping busy. The usual, I suppose. Let's see. Since you vanished in the middle of the night, a scarecrow scared me half to death, a coblyn thug beat the snot out of me, and sentient walking reptiles from the center of the earth chased me through the State Fair. I met my Fetch, got shot, got saved by a leprechaun, had to stop Jay from doing something truly awful, then ran away because he scared the crap out of me. Hmmm. What else? Well, over the past few weeks, I saved a lake monster and helped a bunch of folks get their shit back. Got ensorcelled by a siren, kidnapped by a mad scientist who's now working for those reptilians I mentioned a minute ago, dragged down to this weird drill ship at the bottom of the lake, and almost died escaping."

"And you sang some karaoke, I heard," she said with the start of a smile.

"Damn it, Clarissa. If you already know everything, why bother asking?"

That smile crumbled.

"I asked how you've been, not what you've been doing," she said defensively.

"Fine, Clarissa. I've been doing fine. And you? Got a new eye, huh? That's nice."

She set the tips of her fingers under the brown eye that shouldn't have been there.

"Yeah," she agreed. "I thought I was free. Shows what I know."

The deep sadness in her voice cut through my ire and exposed something akin to sympathy.

"What happened?" I asked, despite myself.

"Gumball machine," she said with a lopsided grin. "In Ely. After I... left... I took a bus north. It stopped at a gas station. There was a gumball machine with little plastic balls inside. They were supposed to have silly toys inside. Mine had this," she finished with a pointed tap on her cheekbone.

"Oh," I muttered. "Crap. Sorry?"

"S'okay," she said after a sip of her beer. "We all have our part to play, I suppose. Which brings me to why I'm here."

The night was already cool. Fall was holding on for dear life, but winter was getting impatient. I told myself that's why it suddenly felt so much colder.

"Don't do it," she said. "Whatever they think you should do, don't. Just leave. Go. Get away. As far as you can, August."

I stared at the once and now again oracle.

"What do you mean? Why? What's going to happen?"

Clarissa refused to meet my eyes. Her tightly-folded hands, the curtains, my duffel bag in the corner, even the ceiling were fair game for her gaze's restless prowling. Me? Nope.

"I... don't know," she finally admitted.

The anger I'd wrestled down surged. I lurched to my feet and jabbed a recriminating finger at where she sat.

"No. I'm not doing this again. You don't get to just show up with your cryptic bullshit and turn my life upside down. I'm not some stupid top for you to spin when you get bored. You know what?" I snapped as I snatched the beer can from her hands. "You've had enough, and so have I. Thanks for stopping by. Door's over there."

Woodenly, she stood and walked across the cabin. When she reached the door, she turned and looked at me imploringly.

"August, please. Please leave."

"You know what's down there?" I asked.

"Yes."

"You know who's down there?"

She nodded silently.

"Of course you do. Then you know I can't just leave."

The admission surprised me. Up until the moment she'd told me to get gone, I'd had every intention of doing exactly that. I wasn't even going to tell anyone. My very reasonable plan had been to pull on an extra flannel, shove the rest of my stuff in my duffel, and go. I'd fled Tuttle once before. There was zero reason not to do it again. Well, except that nothing would change. I'd still be forced to live in the cracks, to always be looking over my shoulder. Plus, I'd have the added bonus of knowing that the damned doctor wasn't just torturing the occasional unfortunate paranormal. He was actively advancing a nefarious reptilian plot to subjugate humanity and exterminate paranormals. That was epically shitty.

"It doesn't matter where I go," I said. "Tuttle will find me again. I should have stopped him before, but I ran. I'm done running. It ends here."

A single tear welled up under her fake eye and broke free to run down her cheek. She wiped it away, nodded, and told me she hoped she'd get to hear me sing karaoke someday.

"What?" I nearly shouted. "Karaoke? That's the last thing you're going to say to me? Oh, forget it. Just go."

She left. Unbelievably, she turned and left. I watched her walk away, the morning sunlight trying and failing to bring some color to her colorless clothes. Her clogs crunched on the drive's gravel and carried her to the road. A few steps later, the trees hid her from view. I filled the cabin's doorway, seething. My blood pressure was through the roof and my breath came out of my nostrils in hot puffs.

She has to come back, I thought. *Has to. She can't just show up and leave again like that.*

Apparently, Clarissa didn't get that particular memo. I stared at the trees for a solid five minutes, but the only thing I saw was their bark and branches and browning leaves. No oracles moved among their ranks.

"Fuck," I cursed.

My head turned, and I looked at my bike. After leaving the Gull, I'd had running on the brain. It had seemed like the only reasonable option. I liked being alive. Doing anything other than hightailing it out of there would be stupid. But when Clarissa had told me to leave, I'd said I couldn't.

Where in the hell did that come from? I wondered.

Maybe that was her intent the whole time. Maybe she'd only shown up because she wanted me to stay. Maybe she was up to her old game of nudging people from one possible future to another.

"I liked her horoscopes better," I decided. "At least people read those because they were looking for advice. This whole reverse psychology thing is just mean."

Unless it wasn't reverse psychology, I thought. *What if she really does want me to run? What if she really is worried about me?*

The top analogy I'd spun at her had been a good one. My head was certainly spinning. I still had both cans of beer in my hands, so I drank the one Clarissa had barely touched, finished the other, threw the cans angrily at the wall, and collapsed on to the bed.

I hate you, Clarissa Steyer, I decided, and tried to make myself believe it.

CHAPTER 19

SS Emperor

June 4th, 1947

Ran aground at Canoe Rocks on the north side of Isle Royale. The weather was fair.
Twelve hands lost.

Tom Hanks lifted his pint in a toast, and we all clinked glasses and drank. Oliver wiped the back of his hand across his mouth, then pierced us each with his storm gray eyes. First, the bartender. Next, Jay and Lana. I suppose he saved me for last because I'd come up with the plan.

"We're sure about this?" he asked.

I wasn't. Not at all. After I'd sent Clarissa packing, I'd spent the day in a fitful sleep. My eyes would close, and there'd be Tuttle and Schnozz, leering and jabbing with giant syringes while strange monsters cavorted in glass cages. My eyes would open, and the cabin's room looked like a reptilian lab. Through it all, Clarissa's plea for me to leave wound around me like a searching noose. Oblivious to my dark ruminations, Tom gave a hearty thumbs up, and Jay took Lana's hand and nodded.

Huh. That escalated quickly, I thought. *I wonder if he's shared the whole he's a necromancer thing, or if that's more of a third date topic.*

The thought made me feel guilty. Jay had shown up to help me. To rescue me. He'd done exactly what a good friend should do. Even so, I had taken the barstool farthest from his when I'd arrived at the Gull and shared my plan.

"No," I admitted, then downed the rest of my pint. "It's suicide, but there are worse ways to die."

Oliver's look was appraising.

"Maybe not the pep talk I was imagining," he admitted, "but it'll have to do. Let's go over the details again."

Step one was stating in no uncertain terms that I wasn't some goddamned hero fulfilling anyone's prophecy.

"This has nothing to do with that," I said definitively. "This is just me being sick and tired of being sick and tired. Tuttle's been a dark cloud hanging over my life for too damned long. I'm doing this for me."

"Gotcha," Oliver had replied. "Zero prophecies being fulfilled here. Roger that."

Step two was finding the capsule I'd used to escape the ship. We figured the window on that was short. It wasn't the sort of thing a sneaky bunch of lizards would want floating around for any old boat to bump into. Hanelle and Wilson were going to help with that. She'd scour the lake's surface from high above while Wilson searched from below. Once they located it, the siren would guide Oliver and Tom while the lake monster made sure it didn't drift away.

Step three was getting to the drill rig. That's where Lana and Jay came in. Jay would use his water magic to drive the capsule down, and Lana would use her MBE to guide him.

"Like a whirlpool or something?" he'd exclaimed. "Oh, August. That is so cool. I can definitely do that."

Step four was masking and hunting down Tuttle. An elephant or coyote would definitely get noticed once I was inside the ship. I was hoping that I could find someone, take them out of commission, and borrow their face long enough to find the damned doctor.

Step five? Take out the doctor.

"No, not like that," I'd clarified when everyone had gasped. "I mean, like capture him or something. Drag him back up here. Get him to the authorities."

They'd all sighed in relief. Well, everyone but Jay. He made snarky comments about the authorities being in cahoots with the reptilians. What can I say? Jay was always going to Jay.

Step six, get the hell out of that damned reptilian drill ship.

"All the hallmarks of a solid plan," Oliver had said approvingly. "A good framework with clear objectives, but not so detailed that if one bit goes wrong, the rest unravels."

"Uh, yeah," I agreed, reluctant to admit that the lack of details was because details weren't really my thing.

The only point of contention was that I was going down there alone.

"I have to do this alone. There's no way I'm risking anyone else falling into that psycho's clutches," I explained again over Jay's protests. "And besides, the capsule only holds one."

It was a hard reality to accept, but reality none the less. The pressure at those depths was mind-boggling. There was literally no way to get anyone else down there.

"Well, if you die, I'm bringing you back," Jay declared.

I think he thought it would make me feel better. It didn't.

Oliver led the way, and I followed. Jay and Lana twined their fingers and came after. Tom Hanks brought up the rear and flipped the bar door's sign to 'closed.' We stepped into the parking lot, and were faced with easily half the town. Well, most of the PNs anyway. I'd crossed the door's threshold when they all brought a closed fist to their mouths, then splayed their fingers and raised their hands up and away.

"Maybe," Oliver called out. "Maybe not. We can hope, though, can't we?"

"No, we can't," I grumbled as loudly as I could grumble. "All of you, just piss off. I'm not your damned Singing Warrior or whatever, so drop it."

I saw a ripple in the back of the crowd. An eddy of bodies stepping aside, then closing ranks again. Only when the very front row parted was I able to see who it was.

"Top o' the evening to you, Mister Shade," the leprechaun said with a quick jig and a bow.

"Fergal O'Dwyer," Oliver said. "Why am I not surprised?"

"Because the wheel is turning, as it always does," the red bearded man replied before turning back to me. His bright eyes held mine as a small hand went into a pocket of his green vest and returned with a golden coin. A thumb sent it into the air and gravity pulled it back down. Again, it sailed up, glinting in the evening's sun, then came down again.

"There's no luck I can offer this time," Fergal said as I watched his coin go up and down. "This, you'll have to do on your own. Do you understand me, lad?"

I watched the coin go up and down, up and down, my chin rising and dropping as I did.

"Good," the leprechaun said, dropping the coin in a pocket.

"You could help," Oliver complained. "You and all the Quorums. Those scaly bastards aren't just a northern problem. They're everywhere. Together, we could send them deep underground once and for all."

"No, we couldn't," Fergal proclaimed, "and you know why as well as I do."

The two set to bickering. Fergal, towing the line that prophecies had to do what prophecies do. Oliver pushing the point that prophecies were all well and good, but actually getting off your ass and doing something was a lot more effective. After a few minutes, they settled the latest round in a long fight by grudgingly agreeing to disagree.

"We'll see," Oliver said with a shrug. "Well, the least you could do is send us off with a song."

Fergal grinned. "What did you have in mind?"

"The Wreck of the Edmund Fitzgerald," the karaoke jockey decided. When I gave him a look, he explained, "It's like saying 'break a leg' before a show."

Fergal nodded, then raised his voice in command.

"It's a Gordon Lightfoot send-off, lads. Let's do it right and proper."

As one, the gathered crowd gave voice to a song about a shipwreck. Like a funeral procession, we moved toward the water, the singing voices at our backs. The final words faded away as we climbed aboard *The Lucky Bobber*. Her captain started the engine, and we were on our way.

The boat puttered along, its engines the only sound. After we'd put a mile or so behind us, Oliver gave Tom the helm and stepped to the prow. With a self-conscious look over his shoulder, he cleared his throat and sang.

"When I wake up," he started, then continued into the opening verses of *Five Hundred Miles* by The Proclaimers. Without the plucky guitar or two-part harmonies, the song took on a different timbre. Stripped to its essence, the love song reached a purity I'd have never believed possible.

"He really is good," Lana whispered, impressed.

The final words cleared his throat, and a hush fell. From some impossible distance, the refrain found its way back to us, ethereal as the wind whispering over distant waves.

"Ah," Oliver said. "There she is."

A minute, maybe two, passed before I saw the siren. At a distance, the speck might've been a gull on the horizon. I wasn't sure which impressed me more: that'd we'd been able to hear her, or that she'd been able to hear Ollie. While I pondered that largely pointless question, I kept my eyes fixed on the horizon. Her wide wings carried her closer, and the siren's ungainly form took shape. Talons scraped on the cabin's roof, and the *Bobber* rocked as it took her weight.

"Oliver," she said as she hopped down to the deck.

"Hanelle," he breathed. "We need your help."

The siren's black orbs studied our motley crew. Tom Hanks fidgeted, the unease at odds with his burliness. Lana and Jay leaned away so far they risked going over the gunwale. I wrapped my arms tightly around my chest, not out of fear, but to hold in my sudden longing. Eyes downcast, I half-listened while Oliver explained our plan. It was hard to concentrate over the nips and jabs of jealousy. Fortunately, Tom Hanks gave me a welcome distraction. He'd gone to the prow, stuck his fingers in his mouth, and let out a series of shrill whistles. The first few were excited. The next, a tad worried.

"I hope Wilson is okay," he said. "C'mon, little fella. Where are you at?"

"Wilson kinda strikes me as this puddle's apex predator," I said reassuringly. "I doubt anything down there could bother him."

Tom nodded, his bushy beard bobbing in counter-rhythm to the boat's movement.

"Yeah, he's a tough one. Maybe he can't hear me?" he wondered, then let out another ear-splitting whistle. When nothing happened, Tom gripped the rail and his knuckles whitened.

"Maybe you're right," I reasoned. "It's a big lake. He could be anywhere. Here. Let me try."

I grabbed a life preserver, twisted, and tossed it overboard. When the others noticed and started bubbling with questions, I replied with a cavalier thumbs up.

"Don't worry. Just going to call Wilson."

Before they could pepper me with any more questions, I shimmied out of my clothes and dove overboard. The second my fingers touched the cold water, I shifted, then reached out a tentacle to snag the passing life preserver. I slid my way up onto its surface and reveled in the sensation of tubing behind the comparatively immense boat. Duty called, though, so I set my strange octopus mind to the task at hand.

Wilson? Hello?

Wilson?

TOM HANKS FRIEND HELLO!

Tom's on a boat. He needs your help.

Important.

Can you find us?

In a manner I'd never be able to explain, I shared where we were. Humans were so limited in their senses. Conveying a sense of place was almost always visual. The octopus wasn't nearly so constrained. My entire body was riddled with nerves that sensed things my tiny spark of human awareness couldn't fathom. The shifting of the currents, the taste of the water, even the quality of the light all went into my understanding of where exactly I was. I packed it all into a thought and shared it with my much larger cousin.

SWIMMING SEE YOU SEE TOM.

Thanks, Wilson.

With another shift, I went from being a little cephalopod enjoying a bumpy ride above boat's wake to a cold and naked guy being dragged through the water.

"Little help, here?" I cried out.

Oliver cut the engines, then he and Tom hauled on the rope. A moment later, they'd pulled me up to the deck, and Lana tossed me a towel.

"Wilson's on his way," I said through chattering teeth. "Could someone grab my pants, please? I'm fricking freezing."

While I dressed, Tom excitedly paced the boat, his head turning this way and that. When he caught sight of a telltale ripple in the water, he let out a happy holler.

"Wilson! Hey, Wilson! Over here!"

A moment later, two thick tentacles gripped the *Bobber's* side, and two bulbous eyes looked up adoringly—at least, I think so—at Tom.

"The bird lady's going to find a tiny boat. When she does, you're going to hold it so it doesn't float away until we get there," he explained to his former pet.

Wilson curled the tip of a tentacle into his lake monster equivalent of a thumb's up.

"The bird lady?" Hanelle repeated with a sneer. "Really? The bird lady."

Wilson raised more tentacles and flapped two of them like wings. Bubbles erupted from the water around his partially submerged head.

"He thinks he's funny," Tom explained apologetically.

"He isn't," Hanelle replied, but not before the corner of her mouth had crooked up. "Hopefully, he's fast, though. I don't like waiting."

With that, she crouched, leaped, and took to the air with a mighty flapping. Wilson gave a short wave and booped Tom Hanks on the nose, then slipped under the water. I watched in awe as his silhouette moved at incredible speed out to sea, or lake, or whatever.

"Welp, now we wait," I proclaimed. "Thoughts on how to pass the time?"

"We could sing," Oliver suggested.

"Or not," I replied.

Lana worried endlessly over her laptop while Jay offered the occasional encouraging comment. Oliver and Tom took turns at the wheel. I sat, arms crossed, and tried very hard to not think about what I was about to do.

You've survived worse. You'll be fine.

That's not a very encouraging argument.

Okay. Have it your way. You're going to die.

Shut up, please.

Too soon, a speck on the horizon resolved into a bird lady. Hanelle dropped heavily to the deck and turned her black orbs to Oliver.

"That way," she said, extending a ropey arm and a clawed finger.

Tom turned the wheel, and we continued our journey. Hanelle positioned herself at the prow, and Ollie joined her. Lana and Jay huddled over her laptop in the stern. And me? I sat awkwardly in the middle, thinking of all the things that were bound to go wrong and wishing I'd listened to Clarissa.

—ele—

When we reached the capsule, the sun was a misty ball balanced on the edge of the world. I contemplated the escape pod's greenish yellow hull and doubted every single decision I'd made in my life that led to that moment. It was an escape pod. Why anyone would use it backward was beyond me, and yet, there I was.

"Operation Deep Shit is a go," I proclaimed as I readied myself to leap to the capsule. "Everyone ready?"

Lana tapped at the keyboard. "I've got a good bead on the reptilian rig, but the capsule has definitely drifted. We're the better part of a mile away."

"Jay?" I asked.

The warlock scratched his nose in thought, then suggested it would be easier if we were closer.

"I'm not sure how much it'll take to push the capsule down. I guess the shorter the distance, the better?"

"On it," Oliver declared with a turn of the wheel. "Miss Delridge, if you'd be so kind."

For the next fifteen minutes or so, *The Lucky Bobber* chugged across the swells, its course being charted by a grad student and her computer. At first, I thought we were approaching a bank of clouds piling up in the distance. It wasn't until Oliver said everyone best get ready to move that I realized those clouds were moving toward us and moving fast.

"Again, with a damned storm," he complained. "Those weathermen aren't to be trusted, and that's a fact."

"I don't think that's a natural storm," Jay said, studying the approaching clouds with a quizzical expression. "August, didn't you say you saw something down there about weather control?"

"Yeah. It was on one of the sticky notes by one of the rooms. Wait. Seriously?"

"Seriously," Jay replied, his expression going from confused wonder to genuine worry.

In the span of a heartbeat, Oliver Corbyn went from affable fisherman to captain of his vessel.

"Mister Hanks, the helm. Keep the prow pointed toward that storm. It'll be driving the waves at us. Mister Shade, to your craft, and may the wheel's turn favor your fortunes. Mister... uh. Jay. Are you ready to do what you do?"

"Aye aye, Captain," he replied with a quick salute.

"Hanelle, get to safety."

The siren crossed her arms and lowered her pointy chin. "No."

"We'll be fine, Hanelle. I'll see to that. But I'll be less distracted if I'm not worried about you. Please," he implored. "Please."

Her hand extended, and her long and taloned fingers intertwined with his.

"I'll see you soon," she promised.

After the siren had launched herself into the sky, Oliver wiped at a moist eye, cleared his throat, and turned to face Lana.

"Miss Delridge?"

"Yes?" she asked excitedly.

"Strap in, please. It's going to get a little bumpy."

Suddenly, we all had our orders. With zero ceremony, I hopped down to the waiting capsule. Belatedly, I realized I had no clue how to close the damned thing. My puzzlement became moot when it shut of its own accord.

"Be careful!" I heard Jay cry. There was more, but a pressurizing hiss made it impossible to hear.

I gave a thumbs up through the clear canopy, then saw thick tentacles wrap across it. There was a jolt, then another, as Wilson used jets of water through his spiracles to start my descent. After a third jolt, the tentacles pulled away and something else entirely took over. An escalator-like sensation replaced the jerk and tug of Wilson's descent. The evening sunlight faded as I descended into a murky gloom that incrementally darkened. Soon, the only light came from the green glow of strange symbols on the capsule's console. Still, my journey continued.

"Damn, Jay," I breathed. "How in the hell are you doing this?"

Again, my imagination foundered when I tried to comprehend the burgeoning warlock's magic. The ability to control earth, wind, fire, and water simply didn't have any correlations for me. His easy mastery sent a fresh chill down my already frozen spine.

"At least, I hope he's mastered it," I muttered, "or this is going to be a short trip."

Time passed. I spent it worrying about what was happening up above. All I could do was console myself with the knowledge that I was still moving. If something truly bad had happened, Jay's magic would have stopped.

Or the boat capsized, and they all died except Jay, and he's clinging to some bit of the hull and still doing his magic while slowly succumbing to hypothermia because he's a dedicated son of a bitch, a chipper bit of my brain offered.

Nice, August. Real nice.

You're welcome.

Suddenly, the smooth descent of Jay's magic changed. An amber light blinked on the monitor, and a low whir signaled the spinning up of what sounded like turbines. Some sort of autopilot engaged, and the capsule swerved, dipped, swerved again. There was a series of chimes, then a shudder that rattled the craft. I felt more than heard my enclosure fit itself into a tube. A few thunks, a whirring, and a hiss later, the hatch lifted. An iris of light opened, and I saw the inside of the ship.

"Operation Deep Shit," I said with a sardonic grimace. "More like Operation Dumb Shit."

There was no sense in arguing the point. I took a deep breath, let it out through clenched teeth, and headed inside.

Chapter 20

SS Scotiadoc
June 20th, 1953
Rammed by a Canadian steamer on a day of heavy fog.
One hand lost.

WHEN YOU'VE RIDDEN A strange submersible down a magic underwater escalator to the bottom of a very deep lake to infiltrate a drill ship occupied by reptilians bent on taking over the world so you can seek out the psychotic doctor who tortured you for years, it's reasonable to be a little glum. No one, and I mean no one, has ever woken up in the morning and thought to themselves, 'Yup. That seems like a great way to spend the day.' Fortunately, I'd had a life full of unpleasant experiences. It hadn't exactly inured me to the reality of my situation. It had, however, given me a certain tolerance. That, and a proclivity for searching out silver linings.

Case in point: My boots didn't squeak when I stepped into the corridor. The thermostat was probably over eighty, but at least it wasn't a hundred. I'd had a pretty good crap before heading to *The Lucky Bobber,* so there'd be no need to find a bathroom. If those little wins were the whipped cream on my sundae, what I saw next was the cherry on top. There was only one other person in sight, and he was a plain old human janitor.

Perfect, I thought. *Guess I'm buying a lottery ticket when I get back.*

If you get back, a more realistic corner of my brain corrected.

Shut up.

Just sayin'.

I shoved that voice down and studied the man. I'd wanted someone to mask so I could move unobtrusively through the ship. The man's gray coveralls covered a medium build. His sandy brown hair wasn't too dissimilar from my own. And if he was on floor cleaning duty, he likely didn't qualify as a badass by anyone's standards. A janitor was exactly the sort of disguise I needed, and I wouldn't even have to work that hard to get it.

"Hey, buddy," I said after creeping up behind him.

I cocked a fist as he turned, then let it drop to my side. In all my years as a post-relationship personal effects repossession specialist, I had never seen someone look so despondent. The name 'Kablewit' written on a chipper 'Hello! My name is…' sticker on his chest didn't help.

"Hello," he said, those two syllables telling a sad tale that started with countless wedgies and ended with being picked last for kickball.

"Hey… Kablewit," I managed, pronouncing it *cable wit*. "So. Huh. How's it going?"

A look of suspicion gave way to a resigned shrug. Whatever game the janitor thought I was playing at, he already knew it would be at his expense.

"Kablewit," he corrected, emphasizing the *ka*, *blew* and *it*. "And I'm fine," he offered. "Cleaning the floor."

I nodded with approval. "And you're doing a damn fine job, Kablewit. Damned fine."

Again, that suspicious glare, followed by a question whose tremulous hope near broke my heart.

"I am?" he asked. "Really?"

"Yup. I can see the difference," I said, studying the section of corridor he'd recently swabbed. "It looks. You know. Wet, but in a clean way."

The downtrodden man's back straightened a little.

"Thank you."

I patted him on the shoulder. "You bet. You keep it up, and you'll be cleaning all sorts of things."

That sparkle in his eyes faded, and his shoulders stooped again. Sadly, motivational speaking wasn't one of my talents.

"Okay," he agreed lifelessly.

Indecision warred within me. I needed his face and clothes. The one, I could borrow with him being none the wiser. That alone wouldn't suffice, though. I'd still stick out like a sore thumb. Every human I'd seen before had been in coveralls or lab coats or security uniforms. Jeans and a flannel weren't exactly going to blend in. Regrettably, the thought of taking poor Kablewit's coveralls was a thought I couldn't bear. I'm a jerk, not an asshole. Then there was the problem of not knowing where I was going. A good disguise wouldn't do shit if I was wandering the long corridors of the massive ship aimlessly. I needed a map. Or...

"Hey, I wasn't kidding. I just got back from a really serious trip, and I'm so glad you're here. Spared me the hassle of tracking you down. They've assigned you to clean the floor in a very important person's quarters. How does that sound? Exciting, right? Maybe even a chance for a promotion."

The janitor brightened immediately.

"Promotion?" he asked, voice gone rough with emotion. "You mean back to lead scientist on geoengineering and habitat stabilization?"

"Uh..." I hedged.

"What happened wasn't my fault. The Kilauea eruption last year was expected to be a low-level sustained emission of carbon dioxide, not a full-on volcanic event. Lydia's the one that messed around with the critical temperature-pressure metrics. Volcanology is a delicate science. Months had gone into preparing for that event. How was I supposed to know she'd changed something at the last possible minute? My team set the initial charge and—boom!—the volcano blows and pushes up to one-point-four cubic kilometers of lava out. The CO2 release is way off of our projections, and I'm on janitor detail. It wasn't my fault, though! Lydia's had it in for me since forever. She did that on purpose."

"Uh..."

"I'll do whatever I need to. Just please, please get me off of janitor detail. Have you smelled that?" he asked, pointing at his mop bucket.

I had, and it was nasty. Whatever the reptilians used to keep their floors clean, it wasn't lemony fresh.

"Right. You bet. Absolutely. All you have to do is head over to Doctor Tuttle's office, give it a quick scrub, and you'll be back in charge of all the volcanoes."

The janitor rocked back on his heels. "Doctor Tuttle?"

"Yeah. That's right. Tuttle's room. You know where that is, right?"

The disgraced volcanologist ducked his head and scratched an earlobe.

"I... Of course. We all do. No one is ever supposed to go in there."

"Uh... huh. But this is an exception, and you have to report for duty ASAP. In fact, you'd better tell me how to get there, so I know you know."

He hemmed, he hawed, and I lost my patience.

"Look, Kablewit," I began, giving voice to my annoyance.

"Steve."

"What?"

"My name is Steve. Steve Kablowski. This is part of the punishment," he said while pointing at his 'Hello, my name is' tag. "The overlords are masters of public humiliation and debasement."

The way he said it, he sounded impressed. Envious, even. I shook my head at that, then soldiered on.

"Okay, Steve. Tell you what. Point me toward Tuttle's office. I'll tell the good doctor you're on the way. Oh, and I'll make sure to mention Lydia's been messing with the, you know. Metrics. Deal?"

Steve Kablowski–aka 'Kablewit,' which was pretty funny now that I knew the circumstances–started to babble about left turns and right turns and lifts and what-nots. I had him repeat a few key bits, nodded, then swung my fist in a haymaker. The guy didn't see it coming. To my credit, I laid him out cold with that one punch.

What can I say? He set off a volcano. Some situations require being a jerk and an asshole.

Undressing an unconscious guy ain't easy, but I was highly motivated. The less time I spent in the reptilian lair, the better. With some grunts and tugs, I got the coveralls off the disgraced scientist. A moment later, my arms stuck out too far from his sleeves, the cuffs hung a few inches above my ankles, and my toes were squished into his too-small boots.

"Huh. The clothes always fit in the movies," I complained.

After a tremulous breath and stern mental admonishment to stop being such a baby, a rough facsimile of Steve's face peeked around the corridor's corner. It wasn't quite Steve, though. The details were off by a little, or in some cases, a lot. I turned and studied the janitor again, and felt my hairline recede and my nose stretch to a pointier point. My fingers scratched absently at my borrowed cheek. It wasn't ideal, but the mask would have to do. If I moved quickly, stayed unobtrusive, and got lucky, the deception would last until I got to Tuttle's.

Steve's directions firmly in mind, I moved at a steady clip. When people–human or lizard–passed, I lowered my chin and tried to exude dejection. I was apparently a pretty good actor because no one spoke to me. A few humans in lab coats laughed behind their hands. I heard one guy say, "Ka-blewit! Classic. Gossesscharess must've come up with that." Lucky for me, they were content to keep moving. If anyone had wanted to pause for some on-the-spot humiliation, I'd have been screwed. Fortunately, Steve Kablowski had reached pariah status.

Deeper and deeper, I made my way through the ship's bowels. On the upside, Lana has guessed that only a small percentage of the big ship was habitat. Engines massive enough to push the ginormous drill through the Earth's crust likely filled the rest. On the downside, it was still a long frickin' walk to Tuttle's office.

I hope Steve's directions were right, I thought sourly. *Otherwise, I'm going to ka-blow this whole thing.*

Speaking of directions, the next bit included riding a lift up a level. Not a big deal. I'd been in plenty of elevators in my day, and the one on the reptilian ship didn't seem too different. I couldn't decipher the panel's symbols, but there were more sticky note translations. It was telling that nothing more permanent had been provided to help the human crew members. The reptilians had made it very clear that this arrangement was temporary. I pressed the button Steve had mentioned and watched the door slide shut. Then scaly fingers shot into the narrowing gap.

"Out," a burly reptilian said to me. "I don't want your stink in here, Kablewit."

Panic set in. My hold on the mask trembled. If I had to wait for this jackass to finish his trip before I could take mine, my disguise would crumble and leave me exposed.

"I can't," I apologized in my best approximation of Steve's reedy voice. "Doctor Tuttle needs me to clean his quarters right away."

"Tuttle?" the creature said with a mean laugh. "Another experiment gone wrong, huh? Well, not my problem, tchreskchesser."

That last word hadn't been English, but I knew an insult when I heard one.

"Please," I begged. "I'll stand way over here. I won't even look at you."

I pressed my back into the wall, then turned a bit to hide my face. A face that was starting to itch.

The big lizard grunted and pressed the button below mine. The door slid shut, and my knees gave a bit when the compartment rose at a surprising speed. We both leaned as its trajectory curved. A reality I'd somehow not grasped until that moment hit me. The ship was a cone. Its hallways and corridors must've followed that curve. Whatever force that made 'down' feel like down couldn't have been gravity. The thought led to more. What other weird technology did these reptilians have? Why had they been fine to live far underground for so long, but now needed to be on the surface? Where were their tails? That one had been bugging me for a while. If they were walking lizards, shouldn't they still have tails? Or was it like humans evolving from monkeys and losing the tails along the way?

Or apes? Did we evolve from apes or monkeys?

"What's wrong with your face?"

The question yanked me from my musings.

"Uh," I managed though lips that were less like Steve's and more like mine, then I shifted.

When the elevator chime sounded, a gorilla draped in the tattered remnants of a janitor's coveralls heaved an unconscious and bloodied reptilian into the hallway. When the lift doors closed again, those same coveralls covered a human. My chest heaved, and my head pounded with the too-familiar headache of shifting.

"Shit," I complained as the lift resumed its journey. "Shit."

My disguise was blown. I couldn't pull Steve's face back on. Already, my memory of what he'd looked like had faded. Without being able to see him, it'd be near impossible to try to look like him. Worse, my clothes were ruined.

Oliver had said it was a solid plan. All the hallmarks, he'd said. Not so detailed that if one bit goes wrong, the rest unravels. Ollie's approval aside, I wished I'd taken the time to fill in a few more details. I'd wanted to find Tuttle and get him to the surface. I hadn't planned on doing that naked.

"Spandex," I muttered. "Why do I never buy some goddamned Spandex?"

The elevator reached my floor, stopped, and dinged. The door slid open, and I poked my head out. Despite having no idea where I was, it still felt like I was far away from everything else. Knowing that even walking lizards wanted Tuttle as far away from them as possible made my day a smidge less sucky. I peered down the corridor. What I saw lined up with Steve's directions: it led to a single door. At that distance, I couldn't read the sticky note, but I knew it had to say Tuttle.

"Gotcha," I muttered.

I kicked off the ruin of my boots and crept down the hallway, my mind running through the many ways I could subdue the doctor. He was skinny, soft, a typical intellectual. I wasn't exactly a tough guy, but figured I'd win in a fair fight. I also had zero intention of keeping it fair. If push came to literal shove, I'd go-go-gorilla, lay him out, and carry him like a sack of evil grains to the capsule.

And along the way, if you bump into anyone? What then? I asked myself.

Easy. Drop Tuttle. Beat people up. Pick him up again.

Uh huh. And if they have guns?

Leave off, already. You're getting annoying.

I'd reached the door and realized another gap in my plan. I had no idea how to open it. There wasn't a knob or handle. No button beside it. Just a few thin lines at right angles showing its shape. Palming my forehead in frustration, I tried to think back to how they'd opened before.

C'mon, I berated myself. *You saw Schnozz and Tuttle open doors. Just do what they did.*

Near as I could recall, they hadn't done anything. The doors opened on their own. Maybe everyone had a special gizmo in their pocket. Something that some sensor would recognize when they got close? I thought back to Steve and the remnants of his coveralls in the elevator.

Worth a try, I decided. After everything I'd already done, rubbing some shredded coveralls around the door wouldn't look weird at all.

I turned to go fetch the remains of Steve's coveralls from the elevator. That simple pivot left my bare ass facing Tuttle's door. When it suddenly opened, I didn't get to tackle the doctor like I'd planned, but I did get to moon him. That was a close second.

"What in the…" he sputtered, before I spun around and swung a fist at his jaw.

It should have connected. It should have laid him out like I'd done to Kablewit the volcanologist a few floors below. Instead, I punched air. Where the doctor's face had been a moment before, there was nothing. A few feet below where it should have been, something truly unexpected looked up at me. Tuttle the human doctor had become Tuttle the Komodo Dragon.

"Uh," I said unhelpfully, and then Tuttle attacked.

The Komodo Dragon was recognizable because a few years back, Jay made one out of paper mache. Hell if I could remember why. He'd found some story about the nuclear test ban treaty Kennedy had signed back in the '60s. Jay being Jay, he'd followed the glow-in-the-dark breadcrumbs to some conspiracy or other. Then, Jay still being Jay, he'd made art to protest the Illuminati or Bilderbergs or something. Thinking back on that protest du jour, I couldn't help but appreciate the artist's attention to detail. The beady eyes. The pebbled scales covering its rounded snout. The rows of razor-sharp teeth.

Yeah, like the real ones snapping at you right now, a warning voice said.

Shit. Right.

I backpedaled down the hallway, cursing every step of the way. If you've never had a ten foot long lizard attack you, do yourself a favor and keep it that way. As experiences go, it ranks pretty low on just about every list.

While the Tuttlemodo Dragon lumbered at me, I ran through my very limited options. Another shift was going to leave me disoriented as hell. Not shifting was as good as suicide. There was nowhere to run, nowhere to hide. I needed a weapon. Something–anything–that might even the odds. The corridor was a bust for that. All I could think was maybe Tuttle had something in his room I could use. Unfortunately, the dragony doctor, in all his scaly, meat-eating glory, was between me and that possibility.

All that careened through my brain in a matter of seconds as I stumbled, tripped, and staggered backward. Right as I reached the elevator and slapped frantically at the button, the dragon lunged. Time slowed down, as it tends to do when something horrible is about to happen. I saw my outstretched arm. I saw the dragon's jaws open wide and envelop my wrist. I whimpered a sad farewell to my hand because I knew it was about to be severed from the rest of me. Those jaws closed, those pointy teeth headed toward my flesh and bone... and a skinny, naked old guy's human chompers bit down on my forearm.

I'm not going to lie. The thought of a Komodo Dragon biting off my hand had been horrifying. The reality of Doctor Tuttle's sticky lips and wet tongue instead? Worse. Much, much worse.

"Yuuugh!" I yowled, as I yanked my arm back and set to wiping my wrist on the wall. "Gross. Ugh. Yuck."

The gleam of victory faded from Tuttle's eyes. Frustration replaced it, quickly followed by purest rage. He rippled–actually rippled–and his skin turned scaly. His face stretched, his arms shortened, and the start of a gray-green tail protruded from above his bony ass crack. Then the transformation reversed, and he was back to being a skinny, naked old guy, complete with flabby little moobs and a slight paunch. The only thing even remotely close to reptilian about him was the turtle-looking man-bit between his bony thighs.

"Reptile dysfunction is the worst. Amiright?" I quipped.

The impulsive jab was more of a reflex than anything else. Inside, though, I was reeling.

Tuttle had shifted. Actually shifted. How, I hadn't a clue. Or maybe I did.

"You stupid son of a bitch," I gasped while still rubbing my forearm on the wall. "You've been experimenting on yourself. With me. With my DNA."

Tuttle sneered. "That's science, Mister Shade."

"That's psychotic."

"That's semantics."

I shook my head in disbelief.

"Why?" I asked. "Why would you do that?"

"Everything has a weakness. You, though…" he spat. "You're invincible. I subjected you to the worst diseases this planet has to offer. Used treatments that the FDA would never approve. Well, not its human members, anyway. And yet, despite all of that, you survived."

"And all this time, Jay was worried about me eating hotdogs," I replied. "So, this wasn't for the reptilians. All of this has been for you?"

"I prefer to call it a win-win. They've granted me license to do things the human government would never allow. Great things."

"Oh, sure," I scoffed. "Your Komodo Dragon was super great, right up until it wasn't."

Again, that rage twisted his features and his skin rippled. This time, dark hair sprouted from his arms, and his face stretched took on a canine shape. Rather than shrinking down to a wolf's size, though, he started to get taller. His feet stretched and shoulders broadened. I took a step back, shocked to realize Tuttle was shifting into a werewolf. A flipping werewolf. I shifted as well, then staggered to the side as my big gorilla's head swam. My mitts came up as I readied for a slugfest, but let them drop when Tuttle failed yet again. The fur melted away, and he shrank back to nothing more than Emmett Tuttle once again.

"Churff. Urghaww," I said meanly, then I grabbed his head in my giant gorilla hand and bounced it off the wall.

The naked doctor crumpled to the floor, unconscious. I shifted again and slumped down beside him. Uneven waves of nausea roiled my stomach, and my temples throbbed. Despite his proclamations, I didn't feel invincible. I felt like shit. Shifting had its upsides, sure. I'd gotten out of more than a few tight spots thanks to my ability. There'd even been times when I'd shifted just for the fun of it. Always, though, there was the threat of staying shifted too long, the discomfort of going from human to animal and back, and the dark knowledge that another living creature had died for me to wear its form. Why anyone would want that was beyond me. Why they'd want to shift into paranormal creatures was even more incomprehensible. I'd met werewolves. One had thrown me through a window. They sucked.

With a salty curse, I pushed myself to my feet and stumbled toward Tuttle's quarters. Thankfully, the door had stayed open. I stepped into his room and did my best to ignore the notebooks and charts. Sure, I wanted to tear them to shreds, but also knew it would be pointless. In this digital age, his research would be secure from my wrath. Maybe I couldn't destroy what he'd created. What I could do was bring the damned monster back to the surface and dump him at the closest police station. I didn't want to do that naked, though.

The room had a wardrobe and a chest of drawers. Tuttle and I weren't quite the same height, so his pleated trousers were too long. We weren't quite the same build, so his button-down shirt was too tight. They were clothes, though, and that made them good enough. Fortunately, his shoes were a half size bigger than mine. With an extra pair of socks, they fit well enough. I grabbed a lab coat from a hook and a belt from the dresser's top drawer, then clomped down the hallway. It took a minute, but at the end of my efforts, I'd wrapped the unconscious man into the lab coat. The creative use of two shiny leather belts made it a straightjacket. After another trip to Tuttle's dresser, I'd trussed his ankles together with some dress socks. One more trip, and I'd gagged him with a pair of his own bikini briefs–yep, bikini briefs–then tied one more sock around his head to hold it in place.

All I had to do was drag him down the hall, get him in the elevator, get him out of the elevator, and drag him down another series of long hallways to the escape capsule. It stood to reason there were more escape pods. Hell if I knew where they were, though, and I was in no mood to go looking. So, yeah. I only had to schlep an unconscious guy halfway across the big drill rig. And not bump into any humans or reptilians along the way. And hope that he didn't come to and shift again.

"Great. Just freaking great," I complained. "Why is nothing ever easy?"

CHAPTER 21

SS Edmund Fitzgerald
November 10th, 1975
Caught in near hurricane-force winds and waves thirty-five feet in height.
All hands lost.

MY LUCK HELD OUT long enough for me to get to the elevator, ride it down–around?–a few floors, and step into the corridor. I'd dragged Tuttle by the ankles over the lift's threshold when the alarm went off. The low, discordant tones made me think of distant tugboats tooting their horns. Bands of red light appeared in rings that wrapped the corridor ceiling, walls, and floor. They pulsed like arteries more than flashed like lights. It gave me the unpleasant impression of being inside of an earthworm. It also let me know that something bad had happened.

"Hrrtssthetich. Intruder. Hrrtssthetich. Intruder," an automated voice intoned between blasts of the alarm.

Shit. Guess they know I'm here, I decided.

It would have been nice to pick up the pace. Unfortunately, moving quickly and dragging an unconscious guy are pretty much the textbook definition of mutually exclusive. I settled for the same plodding pace I'd maintained so far and hoped for the best. As usual, I didn't get it.

I was passing a door when it opened. The reptilian that bolted from the room clipped my shoulder and spun me around. When I completed my rotation, I looked into Tranq's alien-but-still-familiar face.

"You," he said.

"Me," I agreed, then shifted.

The effort almost made me pass out. Fortunately, elephants are pretty steady on their feet. I raised my trunk to trumpet, knowing it would bring the damned reptilian to his knees. I didn't get the chance, though. Tranq had one of those funny inside-out umbrellas in his hand. A split-second later, a wrecking ball walloped me right between the eyes. If I'd been a turkey, you'd have been able to fit what was left of me into a baster. The elephant's thick skull saved me, but just barely. A million stars exploded behind my eyes, and the pain folded my legs beneath me.

"Watch him," Tranq yelled, then his heavy footsteps pounded down the hallway.

Woozy, I blinked my elephant eyes, then blinked my human eyes. The remnants of Tuttle's clothes fell away, and I curled up into a ball beside the still-unconscious doctor.

"Don't move," a voice said.

With a ridiculous amount of effort, I looked up. Looking down at me was a guy that couldn't have been over twenty-five. Dark hair flopped over his forehead, and a failed effort at a goatee dirtied the skin around his mouth and chin. The lab coat marked him as one of the many scientists employed—or enslaved—by the reptilians. In his hands, one of those inside-out umbrella pointed at my glowering face. I didn't know how the damned clobbersticks worked, but the kid's shaking hands convinced me a misfire was more a question of when than if.

"Okay," I said. "I won't."

A lump the size of a golf ball was growing on my forehead. I poked it experimentally with a finger and decided to leave it well enough alone. It hurt plenty without me making it worse.

"Hrrtssthetich. Intruder. Hrrtssthetich. Intruder," the automated voice repeated.

"Yeah, yeah, I know," I complained dejectedly.

My misadventures had reached their inevitable end. They had me dead to rights. Tuttle would come to and my torment would begin again. A tear worked its way free and slid down my cheek. Ollie and the PNs had been wrong, and Clarissa had been right. I wasn't anyone's hero. I should have run. Like the people erupting from the room. A group of humans and a few of their overlords were pouring out through the door and hoofing it past me.

"Hrrtssthetich. Intruder. Hrrtssthetich. Intruder," the automated voice repeated.

"I know," I moaned miserably. "I'm right here."

Why they were running away from me, though, I couldn't understand. I was done. Spent. An absolute zero on the threat scale. A frustration welled up with enough force to make me want to scream, but my splitting headache made screaming an impossibility. Fortunately, other people were doing it for me.

Wait. What?

The kid with the clobberstick looked over his shoulder, then back at me.

"Don't move," he said again, with a tremor in his voice.

"Still not moving," I grumbled.

Again, he looked over his shoulder. Again, I heard screams. I'd promised not to move and didn't want to get walloped for disobeying, but the impulse to see what happening was too strong. I pushed myself up to a sitting position and leaned to see around the kid. Fortunately, he wasn't paying me any mind. His attention was on the horrible scene unfolding far down the corridor.

There were people, and there were reptilians, and there was a lot of blood. It geysered as bodies fell. More screams filled the corridor, but there was something else, too, and damned if it didn't sound like someone singing. Even stranger, it was a song I recognized. Either someone had let Axl Rose onto the rig, or there was one hell of an impersonator belting out Guns and Roses' *Sweet Child of Mine.* The singer let out a 'whoah-oh-ooh,' and I saw two reptilians slap their hands to the sides of their heads and stagger. When one fell, I finally saw what was ripping through the bodies at the end of the hall.

"Hanelle?" I gasped.

The siren screeched out another 'WHOAH-OH-OOOH!' Two more reptilians fell to the ground, and her taloned feet made short work of them. The remaining humans trying to stop the murder bird lady were failing miserably. One lady swung a billy club, but only succeeded in braining her companion when Hanelle darted to the side. A moment later, the woman's chest opened up with four long bands of messy red, and she crumpled.

The kid responsible for watching me took a few terrified steps backward and tripped on Tuttle's legs. With a surprised yelp, he fell, then scrambled to his feet.

"Come work for an advanced civilization, they said. Use your smarts to take over the world, they said," he babbled. "Great work-life balance and benefits, they said. Fuck that. Fuck all of that!"

He took off at a sprint. If Hanelle hadn't stopped to check on me, he'd have been a goner.

"August," she said. "Are you hurt?"

"Yeah, but I'll live," I managed. "You?"

She looked hurt. Blood covered her from head to taloned toe.

"No," she replied.

"How are you here?" I gasped as she hauled me to my feet.

"The warlock made an air bubble and sent me down. He wasn't sure it would work, but things are not good above. We must hurry. Do you know where 'Weather Control' is?"

I sort-of did and said as much. I looked at Tuttle, still unconscious, and clenched my fists.

"Shall I rip him to shreds?" Hanelle asked.

The dispassionate question was chilling. She might as well have asked if I'd like a refill on my tea or if I wanted to go to the post office.

"No," I decided, after giving it some serious consideration. "No. He needs to pay for what he's done. Death is too easy."

What can I say? I'm usually dumb, but not stupid. Every now and then, though, I'm stupid, too.

We headed down the hallway, each step bringing the massacre into sharper relief. There must've been twenty bodies, most of whom were dressed like scientists or maintenance staff. None looked like security. All looked very, very dead.

"Geezus, Hanelle," I breathed as I tried to find a clean path through the gore.

"What?" the siren said. "The warlock said that any humans down here were 'co-conspirators.' Doesn't that mean they're bad?"

I thought of the kid who Tranq had put in charge of watching me. I thought of Lana Delridge being used by Cedric Mulberry. I thought of Steve Kablewit.

"I don't know," I confessed. "Maybe. Maybe not. How about we try not killing everyone first, though? Maybe we do the killing as a last resort?"

"They are trying to kill us," she said disdainfully, "and if we don't find Weather Control, they will succeed."

The hallway still pulsed with its red bands of light, and an automated voice still proclaimed in regular intervals that there was an intruder. Fortunately, no one else had hastened to intervene. We hurried past long expanses of unmarked walls and the occasional door with its strange symbols and sticky note translation. All the doors were open, and all the rooms were empty, a testament to the fact that everyone close by had responded to the alarm.

"There have to be more," I muttered as I scurried along beside the siren. "Isn't there security or something? Where is everyone?"

My question was answered as the final syllable passed my lips. We reached the room marked Weather Control. The door slid open, and a woman old enough to be my grandma stepped into the hallway.

"Who in the..." she started, then she screamed and stumbled back.

I grabbed Hanelle's wrist a split-second before she would've opened up grandma's throat.

"Last resort, remember?" I screamed.

On the upside, I'd kept Hanelle from murdering another person. On the downside, I'd made us the center of everyone's attention, and that was a lot of attention. When I'd been captive, me and Schnozz had passed that same room. There had been a few humans and a couple of reptilians inside. Now? Each desk with its big monitor had three or four people squeezed around it. They were shouting and arguing and making a ruckus. Where before, there had been a couple of reptilians, now there were ten, maybe twelve. When my stupid ass had yelled to stop the siren, damn near every face in the place turned to look at us. Which was bad.

Worse, a new group had rounded the corridor's bend, and that group plainly wasn't a bunch of lizard-loving nerds. They looked serious. Tough. Ready for action.

"Oh. There's security," I pointed out unhelpfully.

The group was clearly more disciplined than the first wave Hanelle had encountered. There wasn't a mad charge. Instead, they fell into formation. Humans were in the front rows—because of course they were—and the reptilians were behind them. I didn't see any rifles or guns, but there were more than a few billy clubs and at least two of the reptilians had clobbersticks.

"Right," I realized out loud. "No guns in a submarine."

"What are you talking about?" Hanelle hissed as she crouched and flicked her black orbs from the room full of dumbstruck weather controllers to the phalanx slowing advancing on us.

"Just wondering why there aren't any guns down here. Then I realized that we're under like a million miles of water. It would suck to start poking holes. I mean, I suppose the outside wouldn't get hurt. It's a big drill, right? Crawled its way up from who knows how deep. Bullets wouldn't bother that at all. The inside, though? Where we are? All these corridors and rooms and stuff. How thick do you think the walls are? Probably thick. Maybe not, though. Some guy pops off a few rounds? That'd be bad."

The siren shook her head and set her stringy locks swaying. "Do you always babble at the most inopportune times?"

"Yeah, especially when I'm scared shitless."

"Would a plan help?" she asked.

I shrugged.

"You deal with this weather control thing, and I will deal with the security."

"Why not?" I agreed. "Because I totally know what to do about the whole weather control thing."

Hanelle scowled, clearly exasperated. "Do you know how to break things?"

"Sure..."

"Then do that, August. Go break things," she said with more than a hint of exasperation.

Her legs thrust and wings flapped, and she brazenly attacked the forces marshaled against us. That left me and a room full of shocked onlookers. Ruefully, I found myself thinking again of Ollie and his comment about plans.

I guess he'd approve of this one, I decided, then drew on the dregs of my strength, set aside my splitting headache, and shifted.

As a kid, Tuttle's imprisonment hadn't come with many perks. My room at Plum Island hadn't come with a Nintendo or a pinball machine. Years after I'd found my freedom, I learned what I had missed out on. A bar had opened up in Minneapolis with a bunch of retro arcade games. Jay took me once, and I'd refused to leave until I'd spent every dollar in my wallet. All the games were amazing, but one in particular spoke to me: a game called Rampage. The premise was simple. Start by picking a monster. You could be a giant wolf, a Godzilla-looking mofo, or King-flipping-Kong. Then all you had to do was smash shit, like buildings and cars. Of course, I'd picked the gorilla, and of course, it had been awesome. Fortuitously, it had also trained me for that exact moment.

The gorilla still had a goose egg on its forehead, but where elephant me had been woozy and human me had been half-blinded with the pain, the gorilla was just pissed about getting knocked on the noggin. I thumped my chest, let my irritation loose in a roar, and set to smashing. Humans screamed and ran, their lab coats flapping behind them. The handful of reptilians took a bit longer to decide what to do, but ultimately followed their human minions. That left me and what had to have been a gazillion dollars' worth of computers.

Well, it was probably worth a gazillion dollars before I got there. After my little tantrum, the damned reptilians would've had trouble selling it for scrap.

Exhausted, I shifted. My knuckles were split and bleeding. My shoulders and biceps ached from my efforts. My knees threatened to buckle. Despite it all, a smile split my face from ear to ear. Whatever the weather controllers had been throwing at my friends on the surface, there was no way it was working now. Feeling smugly victorious, I stepped into the hallway and turned to see how Hanelle was faring. What I saw wasn't good.

The siren was seriously outnumbered. Yes, each of her limbs ended in razor sharp talons, and yes, her rendition of *Sweet Child of Mine* was giving the reptilians in the bunch pause. Unfortunately, there was no way she could fight and sing. Every time she paused to catch her breath, a reptilian would struggle to its feet and take aim with one of their damned clobbersticks. I knew from recent experience how much those damned things hurt. Seeing Hanelle weather multiple wallops both impressed the hell out of me and made my stomach lurch. The siren was tough, I'd give her that, but it was only a matter of time before she would go down.

"Hang in there!" I hollered, readying myself for yet another scrap. "I'm coming!"

"No, Mister Shade, you are not," I heard Tuttle say, then I got walloped again.

This time, there was no thick elephant skull to protect me. I felt a rib crack, felt my shoulder dislocate, one leg went numb, and I swear my brain squeezed out through my nostrils. On a scale of one to getting hit by a speeding garbage truck, that clobberstick's punch had been a locomotive with hyper-drive. And that was just from the sonic impact of the strange weapon. When I fell to the floor, the already-large lump on my forehead broke my fall.

"Why?" I moaned in agony.

"Because," Tuttle responded, clearly not recognizing a rhetorical question when he heard one. "I'm not done with you, Mister Shade. Not even close."

A hand grabbed the ankle of the leg I could still feel, a hand that was much bigger than Tuttle's had any right to be. I had squeezed my eyes shut to hold back pained tears, but morbid curiosity made me crack one open. A gorilla, not unlike my own, but different in a myriad of small ways, was dragging me down the hallway. I tried to struggle, tried to shift, but the pain was too great.

Tuttle-gorilla picked up speed, and I added floor rash to my list of injuries. The reason for his haste became clear when, after maybe a minute or so of practically sprinting down the hallway, the gorilla stumbled and shifted back into Tuttle. The doctor fell to his hands and knees, panting heavily and muttering curses with each exhalation.

"I'll perfect it," he promised menacingly. "Until I do, though..."

He got to his feet, turned to face me, and lifted both of my ankles. Leaning back, he began dragging me. It was much slower than the gorilla's progress, but we were still moving. As if my bruises and broken bones weren't enough, I got to add the mental trauma of Tuttle's full frontal.

"Why?" I whimpered after squeezing my eyes shut too slowly to help.

Our pace had slowed considerably, but it didn't matter. We'd nearly reached our destination: another exit tube. Tuttle slammed a button, and the iris opened to reveal its capsule. Since I could barely move, I had to suffer through Tuttle pulling me up and wrestling me inside. The horror didn't stop there, though. After I was inside, he crawled on top of me. On. Top. Of. Me.

"Gwah," I gagged with a violent dry heave. "Why?"

The doctor didn't reply. He did squirm, though. We were packed in like sardines, and it took a lot of squirming to free a hand and tap the display. I distracted myself by thinking of all the industrial strength cleaners I'd need to wash the feel of his skin off of mine. There was a muted whoosh, the feel of a G or two pulling at my face, and the capsule was out and away. I didn't remember how long it had taken to reach the surface the last time, but knew that once we were there, I was screwed. Tuttle would have me in his clutches again.

The pain and despondency had mixed into a cocktail of lethargy. I didn't want to fight anymore. I didn't want to hurt anymore. I wanted it all to be over. Even so, there was that ember of defiance that even a great lake couldn't quench. I drew into myself as far as I could, past the pain and hopelessness, and found the energy for one more shift. It was bound to be suicide, but maybe not. Maybe not. I could survive a little while. I just hoped Wilson would be able to hear me, and that he could swim really, really fast.

Help! Wilson, help!

There's another capsule, a fake clamshell like you found before.

Please help. I need to get out!

Tuttle gasped in surprise when I shifted, then cursed when I latched as many of my tentacles onto his face as I could. My beak was sharp, well suited to digging into the flesh of my prey, and perfect for boring into the doctor's cheek. His curses became pained screams and his hands grabbed at my soft body.

Wilson, please.
Hurry. I can't breathe. Help!

LITTLE COUSIN SMALL ONE TOM FRIEND?
DANGER PAIN FEAR HURT?

Yes yes, danger pain fear hurt.
Can't breathe. Hurry...

I'd relinquished my multi-sucker grip on Tuttle's face and flopped away, but not before I gave him a good inky squirt. The man was furiously convulsing, his fists and feet lashing out in panicked self-defense. I was doing my best to stay away, but octopi weren't built for moving outside of the water. It didn't help that I was suffocating. With what little strength I had left, I squished myself into a crevice. If I could have shifted one last time, I'd have been able to turn into a wolverine and shred the deranged doctor. Unfortunately, I was done. Spent. Empty.

"What did you do?" Tuttle screamed, spittle flying from his lips and eyes wide in shock.

"Ruined your day, apparently," Tuttle replied.

I was oxygen deprived, so my first thought was that I was hallucinating. That pissed me off. If I was about to die, the last thing I wanted to see was two Doctor Tuttles smooshed face to face in the small escape pod.

"How did you do that?" Tuttle gasped. "How did you become me? You aren't masking. You're me. You shouldn't be able to do that. Shifters can't do that!"

The other Tuttle had little room to move, but still found me with his eyes.

"You're not wrong," he said in reply. "That pesky shifter is still here. If you look, you can just see him squished into a crack down by your feet. I'm not a shifter. I'm your Fetch.
"

I saw Tuttle's bloody face stretch in horrified disbelief, then felt a jarring thud that shook the entire capsule. I heard the ripping of metal and the rushing of water. For a moment, I reveled in the euphoric sensation of being immersed in water again, of being in my element again, but the water was fresh, not salt. I managed an agonizing breath, but it wasn't enough.

Wilson wrapped me gently in one of his tentacles and jetted away from the sinking capsule he'd ripped open. I saw a human hand and the sleeve of a white lab coat clawing frantically. I saw the face of Doctor Tuttle, blood streaming from his chewed up cheek and eyes bulging. Then I saw nothing as Wilson folded me protectively underneath him.

LITTLE ONE COME WITH WILSON
GET AWAY SWIM AWAY FLEE LIVE SURVIVE

> *Tired cannot breath tired pain*
> *Cannot survive cannot breathe*
> *Am not like you*
> *Pressure too much too deep*
> *Cannot cannot...*

HOW CAN I HELP?
HOW CAN I SAVE YOU?
YOU SAVED ME SET ME FREE
AH...
I SEE
I UNDERSTAND
I ACCEPT

What happened next was horrible. Something I would have never chosen to do, but all rational thought had fled. There was only my will to survive and my nature. That, and an understanding and acceptance. Somehow, Wilson had comprehended not just what I was, but truly what I was.

My fight with the reptilians and the doctor had left me cut and bloody. Wilson had torn open the capsule and suffered a gash of his own. Our blood mingled and within it, our bond. I felt myself stretch in every possible direction, felt the too-familiar surging of something else becoming a part of myself. The lake monster's protective embrace relaxed, and I drifted free, growing and changing as I did. A moment later, there were two lake monsters, our tentacles loosely entwined. Strength surged through me, and Wilson's faded away. Drained, he sank. I tried to gather him up, but was too uncoordinated, too confused, too heartbroken. All I could do was watch his tentacles go limp and slip from my own. Down and down and down he sank into the dark.

I learned, right then and there, that lake monsters can't cry. That doesn't mean that can't feel a crushing sadness.

For a long time, I floated in that netherworld between the lake's bottom and the sky far above. I might've stayed there forever, but a deep reverberating boom shook me from my stupor. Far below, I saw the vague outlines of the reptilian ship. Glowing cracks raced across its surface like squiggles of lava. A trillion bubbles raced upward as the hull cracked open. It felt like I'd slipped into a giant jacuzzi. One bubble in particular caught my eye. Bigger than the others, it moved in a straight line at odds with the others' crazy trajectories. My lake monster eyes were surprisingly keen, seeing a spectrum of colors in the deep water's gloom. They easily picked out the most unusual aspect of the rising bubble. It was inhabited. Jay and Hanelle were inside, her curled into a fetal position, and him with his arms outstretched and fingers splayed. Huddled around them were the captive PNs. The warlock's lips moved and his eyes stared ahead in fierce concentration. As they passed me, Jay's eyes widened for a second and Hanelle actually waved, and then they were gone. I did whatever a lake monster's equivalent of a gape was, then shot water through my spiracles and jetted after them. I broke the surface a moment after they did and saw Hanelle grasp Jay's shoulders with her feet. The siren pumped her wings and rose into the night sky, a warlock dangling beneath her. Buoyed by relief, I dipped back under the water and swam after them.

I saw the flotsam and jetsam first. A life preserver severed from its rope. A seat cushion. Some clothes floating like jellyfish from a department store. Oliver's bucket hat. Fear forced more water through my spiracles while indecision threatened to paralyze me. Did I stay near the surface and hope the boat was still there, or go deep and start looking for its wreckage among the other bones at the lake's bottom? Farther and farther I swam, my eyes peering up for any sign of *The Lucky Bobber*. When I saw her silhouette, my eight arms wriggled in relief. I broke the surface with enough momentum to make it halfway over the side. As I took in the state of the battered boat, I realized I was lucky to have found a side to go over.

Oliver, Tom, and Lana had survived the storm, but the toll it had taken on the *Bobber* was painfully apparent. From below, the ship looked rough. There were fractures along the hull and a rudder bent at what couldn't have been a good angle. It looked even worse when I climbed aboard. How it was still floating, I hadn't a clue. As I passed over the gunwale, I shifted and collapsed to the deck. Lana rushed over to frantically ask if I was okay, if I was hurt. Jay hurried to her side and repeated every single question she asked.

The rescued PNs gave voice to a thousand questions of their own. Through it all, Tom paced from one side of the broken boat to the other, asking what had happened to Wilson. Where was he? Where was his friend?

"Wilson's gone," I said.

I closed my eyes to spare me from Tom's crestfallen expression. I couldn't block out his words, though.

"Gone? He was just there," Tom stated angrily. "He put you on the boat. I saw him put you on the boat."

My fist pounded the deck with impotent rage.

"That wasn't Wilson. That was me. I'm sorry, Tom. I'm so damned sorry."

The bartender stared with palpable confusion. For the next few minutes, I explained what I was. How I was able to shift. How Tuttle had used that for his research, and—finally—how I'd used it to survive. When I finished, Jay and Lana wept openly. Oliver slipped an arm beneath Hanelle's wings and around her back to hold her close. Tom rubbed at his eyes and dropped heavily to the deck. His bearded face turned to the lake's endless and unforgiving waters.

"That Wilson," the bartender said quietly. "He was a good one, wasn't he?"

"The best," I agreed.

Tom set a heavy hand on my shoulder and squeezed.

"You saved us, and I'm glad he saved you."

His sincerity was more than I could bear. I curled in on myself and shuddered as sobs wracked my body. We'd won. The reptilian ship had been destroyed, and Tuttle's bloated corpse drifted deep below the waves. The boogeyman of my past was gone. Jay and the rest were alive. We'd survived. In that moment, it didn't matter. None of it mattered. Too many humans working on that damned drill ship had died, co-conspirators or not. And Wilson... There were too many emotions to process, so I didn't. I just let myself slip into oblivion, carried there by my sobs.

CHAPTER 22

Lsthceknenth Pchaorextha
November, 2019
REDACTED *unregistered vessel* ***REDACTED*** *explosion of unclear origin.*
REDACTED

DAMNED NEAR THE ENTIRE town was waiting at the docks when the *Bobber* limped to its berth. Stumbling with fatigue, Ollie and Tom tied it off, then let the combined hands of the waiting crowd pull them to the planks.

"It's done," Oliver said. "It's over. For now, anyway."

A raucous cheer rose up, even from those that weren't entirely sure what had been going on. More people came forward to help Lana and Jay and the rescued PNs ashore. Finally, it was my turn.

Well, at least I'm not naked, I thought. Somehow, some way, Jay had found my clothes, including my prized Schott Perfecto leather biker jacket. It didn't make up for all that had been lost, but it still helped in its way.

When the crowd got ahold of me, I wasn't pulled off the boat. They lifted me off my feet and carried me down the dock. The humans and PNs were gibbering in excitement. I'd saved them. Saved the town. Saved the whole damned world.

"Put me down!" I cried out, and finally, they did.

Fergal O'Dwyer was there. He hadn't said a word, which was remarkable. While he studied me with inscrutable intent, a gnome couple waddled between a variety of knees and past the leprechaun. When they reached me, one looked up with a proud smile.

"Singing Warrior, right? Sure, you are. I told the missus. I told her. 'That fella, there? He's the one.' Sure, I did, and sure, you are."

The other gnome, presumably the missus, nodded. "He's not lying. He told me. Didn't believe him. Not for a second. You? He was right, though. Here you are, and he was right."

"It wasn't me," I grumbled, the words edged with pain, frustration, and loss.

"Humble, too," the missus gnome added.

"Of course it was," her hubby replied.

"It wasn't me!" I said again, as loudly as my cracked rib would allow. "It was her."

I pointed, and people stepped back. The press of bodies separated until the one I was pointing at could be seen by all.

"There's your Singing Warrior," I said. "She absolutely crushed G'n'R's *Sweet Child of Mine,* too. I'd have died if it weren't for her."

"Me, too," Tom Hanks said helpfully. "And Ollie, and the smart lady, and that warlocky buddy of August's."

Arnold the ogre shoved his way forward. "Me, too, and the rest of us. It was her. She burst in, whooped all those lizards, and set us free."

A silence blanketed the previously jubilant crowd. The only sounds were the lapping of the water and the lonely cry of a gull far above. An entire town's worth of disbelieving eyeballs stared in shock at the siren. Then the gnome stepped forward—I'm honestly not sure which one—and raised a fist to the side of his mouth. It pushed that fist toward the quivering siren and let its fingers splay. Prophetic gesture complete, he bowed.

"Thank you," the gnome said somberly.

"You're welcome," Hanelle replied.

A long moment stretched, then the Nokken I'd once seen in town flipped his mane-like hair and bowed deeply. Skeet, the diner's orc cook, followed. One after another, more and more PNs repeated the gesture and offered their thanks. Even a few of the humans in the crowd got caught up in the moment until a surly nix called one a poser. Rather than igniting an argument, it elicited a laugh. That laugh became a cheer, and that cheer became a chant.

"Siren! Siren!" they screamed as they surrounded Hanelle and lifted her to their shoulders.

No one was paying any attention to me, and that was fine. I gathered up my collection of bruises and shambled toward the *bar.*

"What's going on out there?" the bartender asked breathlessly. "Tom said I had to stay inside. I told him to stuff it, but he said people might be drinking hard soon."

"Pretty sure he was talking about me," I replied. "Whiskey, double, and a pint of pilsner."

I had just enough time to take a sip of whiskey before the door burst open and the celebration began. A celebration of a victory over a rising darkness by the prophesied Singing Warrior.

The party had been in full swing for an hour, maybe more, when someone yelled for karaoke. Oliver was about to fall off his barstool, but the hardy fisherman couldn't resist. He took the stage, tipped his chin, and studied the karaoke machine thoughtfully. Rather than putting in a disc, he set the microphone aside, cleared his throat, and sang.

Queen's *We Are the Champions,* sung a capella, was an experience to be remembered. Somehow, Ollie captured the sadness of all the town had lost, and placed it alongside the victory we'd won. More than a few hands scrubbed tears from cheeks when he finished, and the applause convinced me at least some people in the crowd broke a finger or a wrist.

Jay was next. He grabbed Lana along the way. They went with Simon and Garfunkel's *Bridge Over Troubled Waters.* Throughout the entire song, they stared into one another's eyes. It was gross, but I still felt glad. My feelings about Jay were going to take a long time to sort out. I figured if he was still capable of love, though, all might not be lost. I just hoped that if things went sideways, Lana didn't hire me again.

"He's pretty good for a necromancer," a voice beside me remarked.

I turned and saw myself. The shock of seeing my Fetch sent me off the back of my barstool and onto the floor. I pulled myself up, drained what was left of my beer, and braced myself.

"So, this is it? After everything, I'm going to die in a karaoke bar?"

"What? Oh, hell no. No, no, no. You already died. I'm retired. Just doing stuff. Seeing the sights. Having experiences like this. Fun crowd."

I went cold. Colder than I'd been beneath the waves. Colder than when I'd been curled up naked on *Bobber's* deck.

"What in the actual hell are you talking about?" I asked, each syllable clipped to a brittle edge.

"They didn't tell you? Back when you tried to get to that siren? You know, after you were down in that ship? You climbed out of that capsule and drowned. The siren carried your corpse back to the boat, and your buddy there brought you back to life. I was there, too, but I guess you were too busy finally being dead to notice."

I turned a stricken look to Jay and watched him and Lana finish their song. After listening in near silence, the crowd's applause was even louder than what they'd given up for Oliver. It filled my head with a thunder that drowned out my shock at what I'd learned.

"I saw Tuttle's Fetch," I blurted out, more because I didn't know what else to say than anything else.

My own head nodded in response. "He told me. We do that, sometimes. Reveal ourselves. Especially if there's someone watching who might appreciate the show."

I tried to understand that, tried really, really hard, and then the KJ was waving to me and hands were pushing me forward.

"Enjoy your second life, August!" my Fetch called from somewhere behind me. "Try not to waste it."

The world passed in a blur. There was floor, then stairs, then the carpeted stage.

"What'll it be, hero?" Oliver asked, pressing a mic into my hand.

My mind was still blank. I'd died. I had actually died, and then Jay had shoved my departing soul back into my body. It didn't feel possible. Didn't feel real. Everyone was looking at me expectantly, and all I could think was, what are they expecting? I'm a walking dead guy.

Unbidden, a song sprang to mind and my lips gave it voice. I didn't have David Bowie's range or pipes, but it didn't matter. The crowd singing *Changes* along with me made up for my deficiencies. All the weight I'd been carrying lifted a little, and my back was a little straighter as I stepped down from the stage. I made my way through the jubilant crowd with every intention of reclaiming my stool at the bar, except it was taken.

"It doesn't matter how many futures I see," Clarissa Steyer said from her perch on my seat. "The only constant is change."

"Do you ever talk about anything else?" I asked, but with a smile.

"Shoot. Yes. No. I guess it depends on the day. It's who I am, August. A woman with one hand always reaching for the future. Or maybe it'd be more appropriate to say, one eye always looking."

Rather than responding with a quick quip or snarky remark, I checked my nature and actually thought about what I was about to say.

"I've never really considered the future," I admitted. "I lived for so long always looking back, looking to see if my past was catching up, and, welp, it did. And I beat it. I beat it," I repeated emphatically. "It cost a lot, though."

Clarissa nodded sadly. "I know. I'm sorry, August."

I shrugged it off and soldiered on.

"My point is, I don't need to look back anymore. I don't need to live in my past. For the first time in my life, I can finally think about a future, a real future, and I have no idea what it's going to be."

She sat quietly and waited. I locked my jaw and considered my next words very carefully.

"I understand why you left, Clarissa," I said. "Not completely, but maybe a little. I understand how scary it must've been for you when you lost your sight. I guess what I'm trying to say is, I forgive you and I apologize for being too dumb to really see what you were going through."

"You've always said you were dumb," she said.

"But not stupid," I finished. "Clarissa, I'd be stupid to let you slip away again."

"And I can't imagine a future without you," she replied.

I hadn't realized it, but the surrounding crowd had gone silent and was watching the exchange with rapt attention. When I leaned in and our lips met, the cheers and whistles scared the crap out of me.

"Geezus, you guys," I scolded. "Can't a guy get a little privacy?"

"In the middle of a crowded bar?" Tom replied with an encompassing gesture that sent his beer sloshing from its pint. "No. Nope. No way."

The laughter that followed was good-natured, and both Clarissa and I were caught up in it. It felt good to laugh, even though it hurt like hell.

More people sang, then the crowd went quiet. I looked up and saw Oliver and Hanelle mount the stage's steps together.

"August," my former client called out. "If you would, please."

With a confused scowl, I walked toward the small stage.

"I'd like something from my ex, and I believe this is your area of expertise. If you would be so kind, could you get my chance back? A chance at happiness with the love of my life? Think you can repo that for me?"

I looked from the fisherman to the siren, then cleared my throat and spoke.

"Hanelle, I'm a post-relationship personal effects repossession specialist. I've been employed by Mister Corbyn here. He'd like his chance back."

The mood in the room changed from fearful trepidation to nervous anticipation.

"Okay," Hanelle said.

Their kiss didn't get quite the same response that mine and Clarissa's had, but there was enough genuine emotion mixed in with the stunned disbelief to make it a happy thing. He leaned over and whispered in her ear, and for a moment, her terrifying face was made beautiful by her smile. Well, except for all the teeth, but we can't have it all.

For years, people laughed at what an odd pair Sonny Bono and Cher had made when they performed. He was maybe five and a half feet tall. She wasn't that much taller, but her platform shoes and skyscraper heels and impossibly big pile of hair always made her tower over him. He was a bundle of rags, and she was a chandelier. She had a face that could launch a thousand ships. He had a face made for radio. When they sang *I Got You, Babe,* though, all that disappeared.

Seeing Oliver and Hanelle side by side made Sonny and Cher look like identical twins in comparison. When the fisherman and siren sang that classic duet, though, it was beautiful. Astounding. By the end of the song, there wasn't a dry eye in the place.

"Seems like everyone is getting their happily ever after tonight," Clarissa remarked.

My eyes flicked to Tom Hanks.

"Not quite yet," I said, then left her side and crossed to the burly bartender.

"Come with me," I said quietly.

He frowned in confusion, but followed in my wake. A short walk later, we were at the docks.

"Shifters don't just become like something else," I said without preamble. "We become the actual thing. And even when we're in our human form, all of our shifts are right there with us. I think..." I said, then faltered. When I spoke again, my voice was rough with emotion. "I think Wilson would have wanted this."

I turned my back to Tom, slid off my jacket, kicked off my boots, and unbuckled my jeans. It wasn't easy with a shoulder that had too recently been out of its socket, but I managed.

"A little privacy?" I asked.

The bartender grunted in surprise, but turned his back. There was a splash, and August Shade was gone from the dock. In the water, a bulbous head broke the surface, and a tentacle waved happily.

"Wilson?" Tom asked in shock. "Wilson! Hey, Wilson!"

I waved again, then raised a second tentacle to catch Tom as he leaped from the dock. For the next few minutes, I sped and cavorted around the harbor while holding the bartender high above me. Folks probably heard his joyous whoops and hollers all the way across the Canadian border. When I set him gently back on the dock, he collapsed in exhausted delight. A moment later, I hauled myself up and pulled on my clothes.

"Thanks, August," he said. "Thank you for that."

He stuck his hand, and I clasped it with a firm grip.

"Dead doesn't always mean gone," I said.

I might've added more, but the bear-sized man had pulled me into a bear-sized hug. Hard to say much when your face is smooshed against the local bartender's chest. And sometimes, nothing more needs to be said anyway.

DID YOU HAVE FUN?

I HAD A HECK of a good time writing this book. If you enjoyed reading it, I hope you'll take a moment to share a rating or even a review! Ratings and reviews for authors are like tips for bartenders. We love 'em. They also help others who stumble across the book decide if they should give it a try.

Use these QR codes to easily post a review on your preferred site(s):

Amazon

Goodreads

BookBub

Humans and PNs and Reptilians! Oh My!

Thanks for reading the Misadventures of a Paranormal Post-Relationship Personal Effects Repossession Specialist!

If you've also read my Monsters in the Midwest trilogy, you might've recognized a pattern in my storytelling: There are humans, and there are paranormal creatures, and there are… other things. You know. Like aliens and reptilians and stuff.

I couldn't say why, exactly, but I really like that place where science and supernatural intersect. In my mind, there isn't a hard line between the two. It's more of a Venn diagram. I'm also a sucker for playing with magic systems, and turning the dial between soft and hard magic.

And if I've totally lost you at this point, sorry. I'll back up the bus a bit.

Most speculative fiction writers have magic systems that fall somewhere along the spectrum between soft and hard magic. Soft magic is mysterious and inexplicable. Hard magic has rules and usually a cost to the user. Here are a couple of examples: Oliver Corbyn is a zduhać. He uses soft magic. There's no explanation given for how he can do what he does. August's magic skews more toward hard magic. His ability to shift is grounded in biology. There are rules and a cost. So think of magic systems as a continuum, and magic users—from warlocks to shapeshifters—exist somewhere along that spectrum.

Now extend that concept a bit further. If soft magic is on the left side of the continuum and hard magic is on the right, our understanding of science would be just off the right side of the page. Some might even argue that science should be on the magic systems continuum. For example, ask a scientist to describe gravity. By the time she's done, you'll be convinced that gravity is magic.

So that's magic systems in a nutshell. Some authors like honing in on one part of the spectrum. I like messing around in the gray areas. In my books, there are humans with zero abilities, like Lana Delridge, and humans that can do unexpected things, like Tony and Jay. There are paranormal creatures with soft magic, like Vilde Tanck the huldra, and creatures with hard magic like coblynau and their uncanny contraption-building abilities. Throwing them all into the same world makes for a lot of interesting possibilities.

But not quite enough.

I always reach this point where I want a little more. After spending time in a world where paranormal creatures are commonplace, I want to bring the reader something different. Something that doesn't fit nicely into the rest of the world. Enter aliens, like the Gerploonkians in "Undead Cheesehead" or Schnozz and Tranq in "Scarecrow" and "Siren." Those aliens aren't supernatural or magical, but they also aren't easily described by humanity's science. Which brings us back to the Venn diagram. Odds are good that, no matter what I write down the road, there will be circles for humans, paranormal/supernatural creatures, and aliens of some sort.

Oh my, indeed!

A Bit About Scott

People say you should write what you know. That's damned good advice, so Scott writes about ordinary Midwesterners making an extraordinary mess of things. Hey, if the flannel fits...

Oh, one more thing. "Ordinary" totally includes vampires, werewolves, zombies, witches, shapeshifters, aliens and more!

Find Scott on:

www.swbauthorblog.wordpress.com

www.facebook.com/swbuthor

www.instagram.com/swbauthor

www.goodreads.com/swbauthor

www.bookbub.com/authors/scott-burtness

and in bars and bowling alleys up in the Midwest.

FREE Short Story

Get *Five Stars,* a FREE demonic horror comedy short story, when you sign up for **The Paranomedy Pint**, Scott's once-a-month email featuring a great book to read, a fun show to watch, something terrific to drink, and a little paranormal weirdness to enjoy!!

BEER-FUELED URBAN FANTASY BY SCOTT BURTNESS

THE MISADVENTURES OF A PARANORMAL
POST-RELATIONSHIP PERSONAL EFFECTS
REPOSSESSION SPECIALIST
An Oracle Walks into a Bar
A Scarecrow Wins an Award
A Siren Sings Her Heart Out

MONSTERS IN THE MIDWEST
Wisconsin Vamp
Northwoods Wolfman
Undead Cheesehead
Monsters in the Midwest: The Complete Trilogy
Bjørn Again: A Monsters in the Midwest short story

ODDS 'n' ENDS
A is for All the Monsters We Can't Stand: A Hilarious Monster-Themed Coloring Book for
Grownups
Story and poems by Scott Burtness | Illustrations by Harold Torres

EPILOGUE

THE PHONE RANG.

"August Shade. Post-relationship personal effects repossession specialist."

I held the old-fashioned receiver between my ear and shoulder while the caller rambled on about their terrible ex and their favorite whatever. I took a break from scribbling notes and held up what I'd written for Clarissa to see. The oracle squinted at my crooked handwriting, then looked into a distance only she could see. After a moment, she shrugged.

"Should be fine," she said.

"Okay," I told the caller. "I'll swing by your ex's place in the morning. You can stop by my office in the afternoon. Not during lunchtime, though. I'll be eating hotdogs."

"Another job?" I heard Jay call out from his art studio.

"Yup. Nothing special. Just someone's favorite whatever."

Jay poked his head into my office and pushed an errant dreadlock aside.

"I heard you say tomorrow afternoon. We're going to Leonard and Mona's tomorrow after I pick up Lana from the airport. It's their anniversary."

I palmed my face. "Crap. Why didn't you remind me?" I asked the oracle sitting across from me.

Clarissa shrugged and looked up from her copy of the Metro Pages.

"They're going to cancel. Leonard will forget that he has to work a double at the haunted house."

"Oh. Cool."

"Awww," Jay complained. "Well, guess it's Betty's then, huh?"

"Is tomorrow a day ending in 'Y?'" I replied.

Jay chuckled and returned to his latest art project. The obsession du jour was a hidden bunker inside Mount Rushmore in South Dakota. With Lana's help, he'd gotten architectural specs for the national monument. With mine, he'd gotten rolls of chicken wire and bags of plaster. Within a few days, he'd recreated the damned thing. Technically, the sculpture was a miniature of the monument, but it still filled half his studio space.

The subversive artist named it 'Dead Presidents.' When I asked if he planned to bring those famous four back with his necromancy, the artistic warlock-slash-necromancer refused to give me a straight answer. Clarissa insisted that things probably–that's the word she used, 'probably'–wouldn't get too weird, so I let it drop.

After the events at Knife River, things were touch and go with me and Jay for weeks. We'd fallen back into our usual routines easily enough, but both knew the other was faking it. Then Thanksgiving rolled around. It had never been a holiday we'd paid much attention to. My family had been lost to me before I'd even really known them. His were around, but had never tried too hard to include their weird conspiracy nut of a son in family affairs. It wasn't something we'd ever talked much about. Instead, we'd usually mark the holiday with a hotdog dinner–his a tofu imitation and mine the real deal–and a few extra beers. This last Thanksgiving, though, had been different.

"What are you thankful for?" he'd asked after we'd finished our holiday-inappropriate meal.

"The obvious, I guess. Tuttle's gone. Me and Clarissa are doing good. They're saying this winter won't be too snowy," I prattled off.

Jay had studied his beer can, then said, "And you're thankful you're alive, aren't you?"

The answer should have been yes. An emphatic yes. What came out was, "I think so, but I really don't know."

"I'm thankful you're alive," he'd replied. "Even if you hate me for it for the rest of time, I'm still glad I did what I did."

"I don't hate you, Jay. It's just. Dammit. I don't know. Clarissa says everyone has a lot of futures, some likely and others less so. Which one is which depends on their choices. So there's fate, and there's free will. What happened to me, what you did to me, wasn't my choice. If I'd had the chance to choose for myself, I'm not sure what I would have done."

I watched my words hit my friend and hit him hard. He'd always been a lot more sensitive than me.

"Also, not to nitpick, but I'm not super strong like Leonard and Mona," I complained, hoping my natural grumpiness would lighten the mood. "I mean, what the hell? I'm a revenant, right? Why don't I get to be a superhero, too?"

My head still spun when I thought of what those two revenants could do. Both had died. Leonard, after being pushed into a woodchipper, and Lana from cancer. That alone would've been bad enough. Unfortunately, a vampire who traded in the dark arts brought them back. When he did so, he also made them incredibly strong. Like, toss-a-crappy-car-like-a-frisbee strong. Near as I could tell, I was still just me-strong. As in, strong enough to pull the tab on a beer can, but that was about it.

"I didn't want to make it too obvious," he'd admitted. "There's layers to this stuff, August. What Dieter Saint James did, I guess I could do, too. I just. I don't want to. I don't ever want to be like him, or Tuttle, or any of them. I want to be me, and do things because they're the right thing to do."

"And you know what that is? The right thing? What someone would choose for themselves if they had the chance?"

Tears formed in my best friend's eyes. "I want to believe you would've chosen life."

"Me too, Jay. So let's leave it at that. Let's believe I would've chosen life, and that you did the right thing."

We'd clinked beer cans, drank deeply, and had let it go because that's what friends do.

I slid my notepad aside and leaned to rest my elbows on the desk. Clarissa's two eyes looked back, one at me and one at something I'd never truly understand.

"How about I call it a day?" I suggested with a wink. "We can swing by Betty's and practice for tomorrow."

She made a show of considering the suggestion, but Clarissa considered things differently than most folks.

"If you see a guy wearing a purple tie, don't let him order a vodka tonic," she finally said. "Try to get him to drink a Rum Runner instead."

"Why?" I asked, curious. "What'll happen?"

Instead of answering, my oracle girlfriend walked out of my office, waved to Jay, and headed for the door.

"C'mon, Clarissa!" I called out, hurrying to pull the light bulb's chain and pull the door shut behind me. "Clarissa! What'll happen? Clarissa? Clarissa!"

⁓ℓℓℓ⁓

AUTHOR'S NOTE

Thanks for reading! I hope you've enjoyed August Shade's misadventures. Reviews on Amazon and Goodreads are always appreciated.

I also hope you'll stay in touch. If you like paranormal comedy, sign up for my once-a-month newsletter, **The Paranomedy Pint**, *and get a* **FREE** *short story! Each month, I share a great book to read, a fun show to watch, a tasty drink to drink, and a little paranormal weirdness, too.*

If you're looking for more fun, check out my horror-comedy trilogy, **Monsters in the Midwest**. *Bowling vampires, beer-guzzling werewolves, and zombies that love to watch T.V. await!*

THE END